GEORGE'S CAFE

ΚΑΦΕΝΕΙΟ

TONY WHITEFIELD

Published by Karpasi Press.
Printed by Tenderprint.

**Also available from Amazon, Book Depository, Booktopia
and other online booksellers.**

First published in Australia 2021
This edition published 2021

Cover design, typesetting: WorkingType (www.workingtype.com.au)

ISBN: 978-0-6451008-2-2
pp292

To Katerina and Peter

CONTENTS

GLOSSARY OF TERMS

ANZAC	Australian and New Zealand Army Corps. Also used by soldiers as a place name instead of ANZAC Cove in their letters home to family.
Asia Minor	Westernmost part of Turkey, once occupied by many people from a range of countries, including Greece. In 1922-3, people of Greek heritage who were not Muslim were forcibly moved to Greece. Ancient Greeks named this land Anatolia, which means land to the east of Greece.
Ballarat	City in Victoria, Australia.
Bivouac	An improvised temporary camp, normally without tents, used by armies.
Chanak	A Turkish city on the southern coast of the Dardanelles. The city is now called Çanakkale.
Constantinople	Ancient city in Turkey, now called Istanbul (officially since 1930). However, the name Istanbul has been in use since the 10th Century.
Gallipoli	Turkish Peninsula where the Allied forces attacked Turkish forces in April 1915. The Peninsula is approximately 60 miles from the Greek island of Limnos.

Kaiki   Small fishing or trading boat.

Kastro   Old name of the largest village in Limnos, now called Myrina.

Limnos   Also spelled Lemnos. An island in the Aegean, close to the Gallipoli Peninsula (in Turkey).

Madytos   The Greek name for the Turkish village of Eceabat. It was the closest village to the Gallipoli campaign of 1915.

Mandra   (Μάντρα) Small stone holding yard or building for animals.

Meltemia   Winds from the north throughout the North Eastern Aegean, especially in warmer months.

Mezes   Μεζές — small selections of dips and side dishes served as starters.

Moudros   Second largest village on Limnos. Alternative spelling — Mudros.

Nea Koutali   Village on Limnos created for refugees from Asia Minor in 1923.

Ouzo   Base spirit made from grapes.

Pesperago   Old name for a village on Limnos — now called Paleo Pedino.

Plateia   Greek village square.

Portianou   Village on Limnos.

Pounda   Barren area of land in Limnos used during WW1 as the site for military hospitals and the Water Condenser Plant. Sometimes referred to during the war as West Moudros.

Sarpi   Name of the tent city rest camp for soldiers on Limnos during WW1. The site of the camp now

	exists between the villages of Kallithea and Nea Koutali.
Shisha pipe	A single or multi-stemmed instrument for smoking flavoured tobacco. Invented in India, it soon spread to the Persian empire. Smoke is passed through a water container before inhaling.
Therma	Name of the naturally occurring thermal water springs in Limnos. During the Turkish occupation of Limnos, a spa and baths were built (circa 1730) to accommodate tourists and locals.
Yiayia	(Γιαγιά) Greek name for grandmother.

PROLOGUE

Have you ever dreamed of striking it rich with a metal detector on your first try at searching for gold nuggets? Maybe you wished that you could stumble on a 1930 proof penny in an old shoe box of Australian coins you recently purchased for $20 at a second-hand store in a country town. Or maybe you have dreamed of casually flicking through a haphazard stack of discarded, unloved oil paintings in an opportunity shop only to stumble on that missing 'insert name here' famous artist, or in the $1 section when you find a hand painted, Royal Daulton Toby mug selling on eBay for over $500?

I never really believed those stories, but, apparently, they do happen from time to time. Then there are those people, who in the process of cleaning out an old family shed, or in my case, an attic, discover a dusty box of junk, hoping against all odds of finding something inside of extrinsic value. You know, like a container of Box Brownie negatives, rare coins, a real samurai sword, or your grandmother's first hand-carved wooden doll, still dressed in tatty hand-made clothes.

I had been procrastinating and postponing the clearing out of our attic now for about five years. There always seemed to be something better to do with my time, compared with rummaging around on my hands and knees in the roof, deciding once again what is to be chucked out, or simply moved to a different area in the dark, dusty corners of our family heritage storage space. I know what is up there. After all, I was the one who put the stuff there in the first place. Our daughter's collection of Barbie dolls, a bunch of Kens, our son's action figures, boxes of Hot Wheels cars, their first rocking horse, about a dozen old suitcases, my teenage boy beer can collection, old Phantom comics, my LPs, all our children's sports trophies, and heaps of containers inherited from my parents and grandparents' junk that my siblings didn't want! How on earth did I end up with all this stuff? But there it all was. Sitting safely out of sight in the roof attic, and out of mind.

That eventual day came when my long-suffering wife had had enough.

"Angus. You said that you would clean out the attic this weekend."

I was trapped. It was October 2014 and I saw the metaphoric storm brewing. The weather was lousy, so I couldn't even mow the lawns. There was no footy on the radio because the finals were over. We had spent the previous month of weekends working in our garden, so there was little more to do. I had only just retired from full time work. No one was coming this weekend to visit. I was stuck. The only remotely philosophical utterance I could remember was my one and only Homeric quote — '*doh*'!

"Ok. I'll get into it...now."

The attic was the final resting place of our family's history up until this point in time. It contained everything we held most dear, or to be more precise, the stuff that we thought was not important enough to be kept downstairs. It reminded me of the underground storage bowels of a museum, where many artefacts are resting silently in packing cases, never to be seen upstairs in public again. Our children had grown up, left home, and taken some of their things with them, but we still held on to most of their valuable childhood treasures. I can't believe my son doesn't want to add his 'Round the Twist' book collection to his own bookshelf.

Reluctantly, I lowered the hallway roof ladder, and climbed into the spider-infested territory that we call our attic. This is also the space where I keep my LP collection, a TEAC stereo and a 'record player'. With much reverence, I selected an original Australian Crawl album, removed the black disk from its plastic sleeve, placed it gently on the turntable, being careful not to touch the grooved sides, blew the fluff from the stylus, lowered it in position, and then James Reyne's unmistakable voice filled the void. I still have no idea what the words of 'Beautiful People' actually are, but that doesn't matter to me. I was transported back to 1980, when I had hair and my knees could bend. If I had to do this work, at least I was going to be serenaded by Aussie music legends.

After about an hour reminiscing with my LPs, which really meant that I spent time only looking at my record collection, I decided to move onto a large chest, placed right at the back of the neglected space next to the old brick chimney. It is a box of stuff I placed here after my father died. For some reason, my siblings and I divided up the family trinkets, and I reluctantly agreed to take this box. At the time, I simply hid it in the attic and thought I'd go through it one day soon, someday. Truth be told, I just couldn't bring myself to go through his stuff at the time, so I thought, after all these years, it was now time to dive in and see what was there.

Inside the big chest were many smaller shoe boxes and what appeared to be old hat boxes. The first box I opened contained a collection of black and white photographs of us kids on the family farm with mum and dad, cousins galore, lots of animals (mostly sheep and goats), and many Kodak envelopes stuffed full of photos of us next to, on and in Lake Learmonth. I sat cross-legged there for hours going through each memory, and remembering happier times. These photos contained our lives, our fashions, places visited, the various family cars, and tables piled high with all kinds of food. The photos gave me the impression that our family camera only ever came out of hibernation in summer.

It was a joy to travel down memory lane again, handling family photographic treasures, and being transported further back in time than Australian Crawl. Back to when the Seekers were travelling by train from 'Morningtown'.

"How are you going up there?"

"Really well. Just looking at some old photos."

This little verbal exchange must have happened all day.

"Still looking Angus?"

"Not long to go now."

I hadn't actually done anything apart from re-arranging boxes of photos and listening to LPs. I had the thought of buying a scanner and having them all digitally scanned, but realised that it would take months! Then I found hundreds of colour photos, and we kids were older now. More memories flooded back. Skyhooks and 'Living in the 70's' blurted out from the stereo and I had to laugh at the sight of mum and dad hearing 'You just like me 'cos I'm good in bed' for the first time. Mum was moved to yell "Angus. Turn off that rubbish!"

I was almost ready to descend the ladder when I noticed something odd at the bottom of the box; a tatty black satchel containing four dark brown folders, each bound together by string hiding under the last box of memories. My interest was piqued, as I could not remember ever seeing this before. I carefully untied the string from the top folder and discovered what appeared to be about 100 pages of text inside. Clearly, this had been typed on a very old typewriter, and the paper had a yellowy beige tinge to it … coupled with that familiar musty aroma. It looked like a manuscript of some kind, so I decided not to read any of it until I was safely sitting at the kitchen table. As well as pages of typed sentences, someone had made copious notes in beautiful hand-written black ink.

"How's the clean-up going?"

"Yeah, going really well. But I have found this bunch of folders in Dad's stuff. Remember that big box of his that I said I would go through one day? Well, today is that day. Look at this."

Leaning precariously out of the hole in our roof where the attic ladder folds in, I showed Rita my discovery.

"What is it?" she asked.

"Looks like a manuscript of some sort."

"Well, don't just lie there, get down here, open it up and read it!"

I didn't need to be told twice. The first folder had a front title page, and it said 'George's Café, by Mr. A. Harrison'.

"Hey, I think this is from my grandfather, not my father."

"Why do you say that Angus?"

"Dunno. I just have this feeling."

I can't explain it now, and nor could I at the time, but I intuitively seemed to know that this was special. I never knew my grandfather, and I did not know many stories of his life. Yes, I had inherited his name, his war medals and a few other sundry items, but this felt different. Although we had his photo on our mantle, and his framed 'Discharge Papers' were on our loungeroom wall, my father didn't really talk to me much about his father. All I knew of grandpa Angus' life was that he was a multi-lingual farmer/teacher who was an ANZAC soldier in WW1, and he had survived the carnage right through to the end. He came home, started a family, grew the family farm, went into teaching, retired and died.

Growing up, I was much closer to my maternal grandparents, and they were really the only 'old' family members that I knew. They both died in the late 1980s and then my parents passed away in the early 2000s. When dad died in 2004, my siblings and I decided to sell the family farm and move to Ballarat; the farm didn't somehow seem right without them around. As much as we loved this farm that grandpa Angus had started on his return from WW1, we received an offer to sell that we couldn't ignore. Sadly, the farm is now a housing estate — *sic transit gloria mundi* … Anyway, many of the old trees planted by Angus and my parents surprisingly still remain. They are the same species of trees that line the road out of Ballarat and stretch all the way to our farm, or should I say, our old farm. That section of road is now called The Avenue of Honour, and was constructed with trees planted in honour of local soldiers who participated in the Great War.

As I looked at the George's Café folder, I saw that the typed pages were divided into chapters, with the last chapter being headed "Olympic Games — Melbourne 1956". On further reading, it became clear that the manuscript was a story regarding certain, but not all aspects, of my grandfather's life. It began in 1915 with a chapter titled 'On the farm', and finished in 1956. Notwithstanding the hesitant typing and the idiosyncratic lay-out, within only a few pages, I was captivated.

"What are the other folders, Angus?"

"Well, hang on, let me have a look."

Placing grandpa's typed story aside for a moment, I unravelled the string binding from the second folder, and noticed it had loose papers of beautifully hand written Greek. My Greek language skills being somewhere between ordinary to woeful, I passed it down to Rita, who was a bit more familiar with the language. The front page had only one word, written in English, in the middle of the page. 'Maroula'. Who was she? And why is a Greek manuscript included here with grandpa Angus' things?

The third folder was similarly confusing and surprising in equal measure. It too started with a single page with only one word, or to be more precise, one name, written in English — Mustafa. Both names appeared to be hand-written by the same person. After the 'Mustafa' page came a sheaf of handwritten pages in Turkish.

No good handing this one to Rita, since neither of us could read a word of it, so clearly, we had no idea of what the third story was about. Who was Mustafa? Who was Maroula? Why did Angus have these two other stories in with his? Was he planning three separate books? Forgetting about getting me to continue cleaning the attic, Rita excitedly shouted up and asked me to open the fourth folder.

The last folder contained only about ten pages of handwritten notes in English, which were most likely grandpa Angus' writing. We hoped that these notes would hold the necessary keys to unlock the secrets of the Greek and Turkish stories. In the dust of the attic, it began to emerge that in the fourth folder were his notes for compiling a book describing the important events of his life. It mentioned that the other two manuscripts were made by friends of his, and whilst the folders had their own chapters, about what, we were not sure.

Down the ladder I came one rung at a time, with the tatty packages in my right arm, clutching them tight to my chest. I placed them carefully on the kitchen table. We sat, and stared at the pile of old folders. I have to admit that at this point I was seriously confused. I had never heard of any stories of his, or about him, regarding Greek or Turkish friends. I had heard tales of some of his Australian war buddies, and as a young boy, I was told, I had met some of them. But, for crikey's sake, what 8-year-old can remember such things? And if there were Greek and Turkish mates, I most certainly was completely in the dark. But now I was curious — who were these other two, and why were they part of his life? Why did he consider these other people important enough to be a part of his life story?

I closed the attic ladder and mentioned to Rita that the roof junk will have to wait as we turned our attention to the folders. Rita is excellent at speaking Greek, but less confident when reading the handwritten language. She did try to read some of the story of 'Maroula', but had to abandon it after a couple of pages. I suggested she might find someone as soon as possible help her with the translation, while I would set about finding someone to do the same for the Turkish text.

* * *

At this point, it is appropriate that I make some comments on our background, because as grandpa Angus' story began to unfold, resonances with our own interests and experiences began to emerge and this explains some of the reasons why we were becoming so interested in grandpa Angus' material. Rita and I had been travelling with our two children to Greece for a number of years, slowly renovating Rita's family home on the Greek island of Limnos. Her parents migrated to Australia with one-year old Rita in 1960, settling in the Melbourne suburb of Coburg. Rita's father never went back to the island, and her mother only made the return trip once, to visit her dying mother. Whilst I could not understand why they didn't really want to return to their homeland, this was not an uncommon event with others who were in the same situation. They left a country racked by years of civil war and depopulated by a mass exodus to all parts of the globe.

Given the culturally matriarchal nature of Limnian society, Rita inherited her mother's house in Limnos, in the village of Paleo Pedino. Rita's mother Maria was from the village of Angariones, and her father was from a village called Plati, about one hour by donkey away. On the occasion of their marriage, Maria's parents did not own a house to give as part of her dowry, so they decided to purchase a house in a nearby village instead. The house chosen in Paleo Pedino was once owned and built by a Turkish family who gave it up in the 1912 exodus of all Ottoman citizens from the island. After the forced withdrawal of these people, the house was lived in for nearly 25 years by a family who ultimately abandoned it before WW2 when they left for a better life on the mainland. Rita's parents purchased the house in the late 1950s, and lived in it for nearly four years, when they too left for a better life away from the island. This time, the migration was to a foreign country, Australia, where many Limnian people were already living.

Between 2004 and 2014, we visited our island house every two years, spending up to four weeks at a time. We liked it there and were developing a quiet rapport with the village and the island. I had visited the military cemeteries on Limnos a few times, but didn't really know anything about the history of the WW1 rest camp or hospital sites. Slowly, I began to feel proud that Australians had been here all those years ago, but was saddened by the lack of detail beyond that available in the cemeteries. What had never clicked in my mind was that grandpa Angus *had been there*. I had known he was at Gallipoli and had been in other fields of battle in Europe, but that was about it. It never occurred to me that he might have *had to visit Limnos* possibly for medical treatment, rest or the final evacuation off the Turkish peninsula.

I also did not really appreciate the strategic importance of the island of Limnos to the whole Gallipoli campaign, it being only a few miles across the sea from Gallipoli. I certainly didn't know that I had a deeply personal connection to the island until the moment of reading grandpa Angus' story. As soon as Maroula and Mustafa's pieces unfolded, I was invigorated with a renewed sense of purpose. *His story needed to be told.*

* * *

My part of the translation was helped when I remembered that one of the old original clients from my business days still runs a family based Turkish restaurant in Melbourne. I rang Mehmet, the owner, to seek his advice. When I mentioned that I had a need for someone to translate Turkish handwriting into English, he came good with someone who confidently completed the transcription of the manuscript. Rita managed to obtain the assistance of one of her relatives to complete the Greek translation, thus in the space of just over two months, we had both of these additional stories translated to English. It became clear that my hunch was right. These two people were friends of my grandfather, and with the fourth folder, I had notes of how grandpa Angus wanted his story told. He had written very specific and clear instructions on the construction of how he wanted the chapters to appear, and in what order. These notes were apparently not directed at anyone, but were his developmental thoughts on how he intended to build his narrative.

The decision to publish my grandfather's story was not a difficult one. I consulted with my siblings, aunties and uncles and other members of my extended family, and they all agreed with Rita and I. None of them knew anything much of Angus' life story apart from him being a WW1 veteran, that he loved working with sheep, spoke many languages and ended up a schoolteacher. I was still confused as to why he went to all this trouble to write a story, obtain other chapters to include, and then leave it wrapped up and unpublished. What happened? Why was this so important for him?

Christmas 2014 passed by, and the celebration of 100 years of the ANZACs in Gallipoli was saturating the local media. To any outsider, it may have appeared that Australian soldiers only fought on the Turkish peninsula at Gallipoli. All TV, radio and newspaper stories seemed hell bent on publicising April 25, 2015. I was sadly moved when I saw that stories about nurses, medical staff, doctors, other battles and the tragedies of war were given short shrift. The media were glamorising this one specific day. We knew we had a story to tell, but we decided to wait until all the 100 years events were done and dusted. Now, having been retired for a few years, I had time to work on his story. I was determined to stay true to his original words and his hand-written suggestions. What you are about to read comes from the hand of my Grandfather Angus Harrison, and his two significant friends who were asked to add their words. This is the story of "George's Café".

CHAPTER 1

ON THE FARM

(1915)

Peeking through the dark rain clouds, a final gasp of sunlight smothered our farm in a glorious orange glow. I had finished milking the last of our sheep and was changing out of my work shirt when I stopped to catch a breath and stare longingly at the fading sunset. Lost in thought, I wondered out loud if this was to be the last time I would ever witness such a wonderous event here on the land. And I am not talking about milking sheep!

It is easy to become lost in the minutiae of daily life on a farm when there are so many important and necessary tasks to perform and so little time in a day to complete them effectively. There is always tomorrow if you haven't finished today's chores. But allow me to rewind a few days and I'll explain what transpired in order for me to become maudlin over a sunset.

It was late on a typically warm summer's afternoon in early January, 1915. I had just surfaced after a massive hangover brought on by far too much grog the previous night. Mum and dad had to conduct my agricultural duties that particular morning because I was apparently still asleep at 10 am.

An old friend of mine, 'Pickles', turned 21 the day before. We had been naval cadets a few years ago in Ballarat, and our grand claim to fame when we were young lads of about 13 — 16 years of age, was a walk to Melbourne to visit the American 'Great White Fleet'. The fleet consisted of about 20 all-white battleships and destroyers, and was to arrive in Melbourne on August 29, 1908. Naturally, we all wanted to go to see it, and asked the government at the time to help with assisted passage on the Melbourne train. When we were knocked back by the Victorian State Premier, we did what any bunch of lads would do — we walked with our leader Captain Adeney from Ballarat to Melbourne, about 70 miles, in four days. That journey on its own is worthy of a story, but maybe I'll keep that for another day. Anyway, during Pickles' twenty-first birthday party, there were drinking games and loud, boisterous celebrations, and someone said that it would be a grand idea if we all enlisted!

Pickles, Clarry, Billy C, Horges and a host of others were serious about this and decided to enlist so that we could fight the 'Hun' in Europe. A few good mates of ours from the cadet days were already in training and due to leave for the war any day now, so we thought we should do our bit. So, after the birthday bash, we responded to a notice in the local paper that asked for 100 recruits to join the 8th Battalion 4th reinforcements, and to meet in a place called the 'Orderly Room' at the Drill Hall in Curtis Street on Monday morning. If truth be told, I didn't really want to do this at all, but peer group pressure, and an unrelenting barrage of propaganda for young men like me to enlist was too much to ignore. A gut full of grog the day before may also have helped in that thought process.

The propaganda machine was relentless. Posters on trees, street poles, shop windows, trams, walls and anywhere paper could be nailed, hung or stuck was covered. The most irritating and possibly successful part of the campaign came not from these posters, but from the eyes of older people who walked past any young male. They would look at us and you could tell that they were thinking 'why is this fit young man still here?' The stares from these people spoke volumes — and it was not just the stares, but the questions to our parents like 'why is your son still here?'

Maybe deep down I wanted to enlist. Maybe I wanted to stop the questioning of my parents by these inquisitors. Maybe I had no valid reason not to go. Maybe my sheep wouldn't miss me. Maybe enlisting was actually quite simple. Maybe all these questions, mixed up with a few bottles of Ballarat Bitter, a 21st birthday party and a summer's day with mates of the same age, is a recipe for adventure.

So, hi ho, hi ho, it is off to war we go!

I could tell many stories about our training days at Broadmeadows Camp, but there are only two that stand out all these years later. The first one has made me laugh for years, and was the cause of many of my cobbers from the 8th to down beers at the RSL thinking about our training days. One particularly early morning, we were all dressed up wearing our full kit, rifle included. "Assume the push up positions lads for a lazy hundred" came the instruction. We dropped to the ground and started "One, two, three, four..." and then whack! The drill sergeant used his rather long cane and thumped one of the lads across his backside.

"No 'oller back push ups. Start again. The lot o' ya."

"One, two three, four."

Whack came another blow on some poor unsuspecting sap's leg.

"Start again. No 'oller back push ups. You'se boys deaf or somethun."

I had to whisper to my mate Pickles next to me. "What's an 'oller back push up?" I asked hesitantly. His reply made me, and all around us laugh uncontrollably. "I think he means "no hollow back push ups. Keep a straight back!"

For the next half an hour, we couldn't make it past five push ups before some bright spark started laughing, and 'whack' — start again. It took nearly an hour to complete 100 push ups. By the end, we were knackered!

The second memorable event happened early in our training too, and was the start of a lifelong friendship with my new mates. We Ballarat boys had lined up in our brand new, itchy woollen uniforms after about two weeks of training. A rather older, slightly overweight but still quite menacing staff sergeant was standing in front of us with his feet apart, chin out and hands behind his back.

"Right. I've heard from your boyfriends that some of you think you are pretty tough. I've heard that some of you pussy cats like it a bit rough inside the hessian sack. We'll see about that. Whoever thinks he can take me on had better take a step forward. NOW!"

Nervously, we all looked sideways to our left and right, straight ahead, and at our own feet all at once. Then something strange happened. I expected at first, for one of the boys to step forward and then have the shit kicked out of him by this scary Boer War veteran. But that didn't happen. This still makes me laugh. After he bellowed 'NOW', to a man, we all stepped forward.

From that infamous day in early January to the landing on Gallipoli three and a half months later, was indeed a wonderfully exciting time in my life. I promise I'll return to that part of my life soon enough, but let me take you on a brief journey and explain who I am and how I went from a being a humble shepherd to a Gallipoli veteran.

My father Charles grew up in Ely, a smallish town near Cambridge in England, but lived out of town. Dad's parents, Angus and Dorothy Harrison were farmers, who sold their produce to a number of stately homes in the area, and eventually were employed by a wealthy family and lived in their tiny, cramped forty-roomed house. My paternal grandparents went from being happy farmers to very happy farm managers in a house Grandpa Angus used to say to my father was "big enough to get lost in for a month".

Grandpa Angus and Nanna Dottie lived in the mansion when

they first arrived to work for the landowners, but later moved to a new two-storey stone cottage built by their employers, at the entrance to the estate. My father grew up in this wonderful environment, and spent his childhood years roaming freely around the large house with the children of the nobility, imagining they were kings and queens in waiting. Dad particularly loved examining the huge oil paintings in the old house pretending to be a famous art critic, but was totally enamoured with the collection of Greek and Roman statues strategically positioned around the front gardens, water fountains and of all places, the stables. On his first time walking the grounds, peering at these statues, he was reported as asking "did their clothes fall off in a wind?"

The estate owners only had one child; a daughter called Marjorie. Marjorie and dad were best friends, and inevitably her parents began to treat him as one of theirs. They were desperately wanting a son of their own, but it was sadly never to be the case. I think this was why dad was treated as one of the family. He didn't mind, and Angus and Dottie certainly didn't mind.

Dad was sponsored by my grandparent's employers to attend the King's School, and after graduating from that most prestigious institution, went to Cambridge University to read classical languages, where my father eventually became a pupil in the class of a tutor by the name of Herbert Sanderson.

My mother was Violet Sanderson, also born in Ely, to Herbert and Mae Sanderson in 1895, but being four years younger than dad, did not know him during her childhood. By all accounts, mum was a very bright young girl, eager to learn as much as she possibly could in the shortest period of time. I know that because my Grandfather Herbert, (who was the tutor in classical languages at Cambridge University mentioned above), said that mum could understand everyday kitchen conversations in Latin, German and both ancient and modern Greek before she attended school. My grandfather spoke to mum as a young girl all the time in the languages he taught at university, whilst my grandmother spoke only in English, although she could understand some French. Apparently, mum could swear in at least six languages at her sheep, goats and pet dogs. To this day, I don't know what that 6th language was. This greatly amused my grandparents and other family members, that such a sweet young thing could have a mouth that suited an English sailor!

Grandpa Herbert moved into a rented cottage on campus with my grandmother and their three children when mum was about 10. For the next decade, mum learned how to read the languages Grandpa Herbert taught, and was good enough to speak to his students in their chosen language on just about any topic. Mum loved it and couldn't wait for the day that she too could be a Cambridge University student, but alas, that day would never come. Mum could have been a great student at Cambridge, but it was not until only recently in the late 1940s that females could actually graduate. Mum could have taken lectures, but only if the dons allowed it, and even if she could, would never have been allowed to take an exam. She also didn't want to put Grandpa Herbert's position in jeopardy, so she never really pushed it and kept her mouth shut, which was totally out of character for her. I have never known my mother to be stuck for words, or not to vocalise her opinion, whether it was asked for or not.

Mum loved the structure of language, and could not only discuss everyday matters in any of her chosen languages, she revelled in the grammar, structure and etymology of each language. Apparently, she delighted in meeting new students to her house and asking them if they knew the meaning and origins of the Greek word 'ετυμολογία' or the French word '*etymologie*'. To mum, this was her idea of a joke!

Violet became as knowledgeable and as capable as any Cambridge male graduate in classical languages. But my familial connections could render me just that little bit biased. As luck would have it,

Grandpa Herbert often let mum loose on one of his top students, a bright young man called Charles Harrison.

Charles' first time in the house to receive tutoring from Grandpa Herbert was a major event. Mum found him sitting in the library waiting patiently for his tutorial and proceeded to interrogate the unfortunate Charles on grammatical issues in Ancient Greek, German and French. She fired so many questions at Charles, he barely had time to think. One family legend says that he loved these sessions with mum eventually, but that first pre-tutorial session frightened him enormously. By the time he was asked to see Herbert, he was already sweating profusely.

"Who was that girl Professor?"

"She is my daughter. Pretty intimidating, don't you think?"

"Will she be doing this every time I come here?"

"What do you mean Charles?"

"I mean the hundred random questions, in any language, on any topic?"

"Do you want to improve your knowledge and proficiency in these languages Charles?"

"Yes Professor. I most certainly do."

"Then you had better get used to it. I thought today she was particularly gentle with you. Most of the students who have been here once, never come back. They are too frightened of her."

The second time dad was invited to the house to study with Grandpa Herbert, mum was lying in wait like a leopard waiting to pounce on its unsuspecting prey. She was pretending to read a book with her eyes peering over the top to wait for the hapless student. I can just see mum licking her lips, ready to move in for an easy kill. But before she could ask her first question, dad fired off with some of his own. Apparently, mum was flabbergasted at this, and wasn't used to being quizzed in such a fashion by Grandpa Herbert's students. Even though she had grown up with him doing the very thing to her on a daily basis, she was ill-prepared for

Charles' inquisitorial nature. When he finally entered the inner sanctum of Herbert's study, he had a smile on his face bigger than any cartoonists caricature could possibly draw.

"Well done lad. You can give as good as you take. I think you'll go far. Loved your question on endings in Latin and Greek of a gerund. Brilliant!"

"Thanks Professor. I have been rehearsing all week! Actually, the more I thought of difficult questions to ask her, and you of course, the more I learned myself."

"I think you have a future Charles, in these languages, as a professor like me. You have a gift. Don't lose it."

After about a month of these meetings at the house, sometimes up to five visits a week, mum and dad, although remember that they weren't my parents at this stage, both prepared for the visit by trying to outdo each other. Grandpa and grandma would listen intently in the study to the pair of duelling linguaphiles in the library and chuckle quietly at the tactics each participant chose. In attempting to surpass the other with obscure questions and topics, their score so far was simple — love all!

Herbert suggested they try a different location for these verbal jousts, and said that taking a punt along the river Cam was possibly a good idea. Each Sunday afternoon for about six months, they would meet up at one of the punt mooring piers, hire a punt and proceed to argue in any language that they deemed necessary to attempt to win at whatever the argument of the day happened to be. It was not uncommon for them to switch languages mid-argument to try to put the opponent off. How I would love to travel back in time to witness one of these epic, grandiose scenes of love played out under the bridges on the river Cam.

Dad excelled at languages and on graduation in 1885, became a schoolteacher. He married mum in 1888, and soon after accepted a position in the far-flung colony of Victoria to teach at Jolimont Grammar School, a newly created school for boys in Melbourne.

For no other reason, mum and dad thought that travelling to Australia would be an adventure. How right they were. Maybe they thought they might pick up another language — Australian!

Settling originally in a small rented weatherboard cottage in Carlton, it was not long before they realised that with the advent of a family, a move to a larger home was necessary, and by 1891, they moved into the newly constructed Drummond Terrace, not far from their first Melbourne home. Fortunately for mum and dad, they had enough in savings and a family inheritance for them to purchase the property.

Dad taught classical languages at Jolimont from 1889 to 1896, but with three children and a desire for both my parents to return to an agricultural community, moved to the Ballarat area to become a farmer and part time tutor at the local Grammar school. Mum was busy with us littluns; me 1, Daphne 3 and Rosie 6, and it wasn't long before we became country kids. But the farm would have to wait just a few more years.

Our first house was a modest little four-roomed cottage two streets back from Lake Wendouree. Dad would take the tram to work each day, and I remember spending an inordinate amount of time playing by the water's edge, attempting to build rafts with my mates. The cottages near our house smelled constantly of home cooking and fireplace smoke. Boys and girls played on the streets as well as by the lake. It was a wonderful environment to grow up in. I loved the lake. As I mentioned earlier, I even joined the naval cadets for a few years and met lots of other boys my own age. Later on, I went to war with many of them, and sadly, some did not make it back home.

When I was 15, we moved away from the city cottage and purchased a larger house on 20 acres due west of Ballarat, near where a golf club now stands. Mum and dad decided they still wanted to be farmers, so the move to us seemed like a huge undertaking, but actually, it was only about eight miles from where we lived originally. Anyway, we were now sheep dairy farmers, and at first, I didn't like it. My sisters loved the farm from the first day, but it took me a while. I missed my mates.

Dad remained teaching at the Grammar school, eventually becoming more and more a farmer, but he did cause a stir in the local dairy community. Given dad's love of all things European, including languages, he once travelled with mum to Greece and Italy before coming to Australia, and noticed farmers milking sheep. Whenever they came across a farm with sheep or goats, they would try to buy any cheese made and milk produced. Instantly falling in love with the non-dairy cattle milk products, they both vowed to one day own a herd of sheep or goats to milk for cheese and yoghurt. Now, that opportunity was a reality, and we became the first people in our area to attempt the farming of sheep and goats for milk. When I reflect on those days, we were probably the first in the state!

Growing up, we were not very religious, and as a result of our 'non-attendance' at church on any given Sunday, made us into outcasts of a sort. That didn't seem to worry mum and dad, but it was a minor problem for dad at his school. Although I can't remember going to church as a boy, dad told me he pretended to sing hymns at school during services. I remember listening to a choir singing once, about soldiers marching onwards to war. If only I knew then what I know now about war. I'll tell you one thing about marching to war — we blokes certainly did not sing any bloody hymns. A heightened heart rate, sweating palms, the knot in my guts and lump in my throat just before the moment my mate next to me lost his face to a sniper bullet certainly sharpened my survival skills, not my singing voice.

I didn't really learn much at school. Having a schoolteacher father, and given the subjects he taught there, I had a head start over the other kids, and at times, the teachers. At home, with multi-lingual parents who loved history, languages, culture and mythology, meant that we had many books to browse whenever we liked. It was nothing for conversation at the dinner table to start with verb conjugation in German or Greek, and then talk about our neighbour's apple trees, finishing with a discussion on Pliny the Elder and how he talked about yoghurt in the first century!

I remember learning Latin at school, or should I more accurately say, I remember attempts to teach me Latin at school. I was clearly bored with the content because I could hold half-decent conversations in the language, and here we were learning words for cat and dog! After a few canings from my teacher, Mr Crafter, for open disobedience in class, I learned how to shut up and hide my obvious superior knowledge to him! One palpable mistake of mine was being sent to the principal's office and telling the truth.

"Young Harrison. What brings you to my office? It says here that you were disobedient to your wonderful Latin teacher Mr Crafter. What exactly did you say to him?" I think I said something like *"Domine, Magister Crafter amentis est."*

The principal had absolutely no idea what I said, but he gave me 10 of the best anyway, probably because he rightly assumed the true meaning of what I said. It was the best 10 canes I ever received. I couldn't wait until I got home to tell dad. I remember him laughing so hard, he patted me on the back, and then corrected my grammar!

I left school at 15 and began to work on the farm with mum. I was given responsibility to look after our sheep. I loved walking around the paddocks with them, talking in languages other than English, and having them answer back in their own language. I'd pretend that I understood what they were saying, and to an outsider, it would have certainly seemed very odd indeed.

But my quiet farming life crashed to an end in 1914 when war came to Europe, and thousands of young lads like me joined 'the big adventure'. None of them who enlisted in those first few months had any idea of what they were in for, and I was no exception. I held off joining at first because I really didn't want to go, and my parents thought it would be all over soon and encouraged me to stay on the farm. But, as I said before, the pressures to join became too much, so my best friends and I, along with nearly a hundred other young and not so young lads, found ourselves at training camp in Broadmeadows, in what would be known as the 8th Battalion 4th Reinforcements.

From mid-January 1915 to early April, we trained, laughed and joked our way through learning how to be soldiers. On April 13, it suddenly became real, and for the first time, we felt a little nervous, but still excited, as we walked up the gang plank onto the *HMAT Wiltshire* in Melbourne. I'd never seen a ship as big as this. I'd never even been on a ship, before. I hated swimming! Even though I had been a Naval Cadet, we rarely went swimming.

For the next five weeks, this was our home, and I was seasick for the entire first week. I wasn't alone. Many of the lads were miners, used to being underground, and to be on a ship sailing above the ocean was as far out of their comfort zone as you could imagine.

I won't bore you with life on the *Wiltshire*, but I will say this. We got to know each other a whole lot more, and became friends, cobbers but most of all, mates. None of us knew of the ultimate destination of this leisurely ocean cruise, but there was a late strong rumour that it was some Greek island called Limnos. Being the only Greek-speaking person on board as far as I knew, I was bursting for a chance to talk to some of the locals, but alas, that was not to be. Within two hours of arrival, we were shunted off onto smaller boats on our way to a place we came to know as ANZAC Cove.

CHAPTER 2

MAROULA

The first 20 years of my life were most exciting. Many things happened, not just to me, but to the island of my birth, Limnos.

I think I was born in the winter of early 1895. No one in my family could remember exactly when it was, but it could have been late '94 or early '95. I don't know any of my friends who know their exact birth date. Record keeping of such dates in those days was not done on a daily basis. My parents only officially registered my birth with the Turkish officials several months later. Birthdays are not that significant in our culture because name days are considered far more important. My name day is August 15, which for me is the most exciting day in the Orthodox calendar. I have many happy memories of going to church in Tsimandria on the night of August 14, then treating ourselves to food and dancing in the plateia until early morning. If we were lucky, the moon would guide us back home to Portianou, but more often than not we simply bumbled our way home in the dark. We weren't alone at these times, as others from the village walked together with us. Even our donkeys came along for the entertainment and celebrations.

Our Turkish overlords tried half-heartedly to dampen our

enthusiasm on occasions such as these, but they were not going to win this mini battle. The first August 14 after the Turks left Limnos was a night to remember. We danced, sang and ate until we could hardly move. As if to especially mark this new-found freedom, the walk home that night was aided by a brilliant moon. I remember that within two short years, we had foreigners again with us in Tsimandria, but, in contrast to the previous years, these visitors were most welcome.

Like my parents and their parents, I was born in the sitting room at home with the help of a μαία (midwife) from the village who was present at more births than I could count. She told mum that I was a difficult delivery, and had really made her work hard. Not like my three older sisters who were apparently easy births. After me, mum could not have any more children, and therefore, I don't know what it is like to have a brother. That didn't bother me at all because there were many boys in our village to play with who were my age or close to me in age. I didn't fully realise the implication of Ottoman rule was when I was growing up, but only that the Turks were the rule makers. Notwithstanding this, they seemed to not really interfere with our lives at all. After all, they had been in charge for over 400 years!

Our house in Portianou was near the village square, and was no different from any other, consisting of a kitchen and cooking area downstairs, separate sitting area, and two bedrooms upstairs, with a barn next to the house with chickens and our donkeys. Considering my life now, you could say it was rudimentary, but we loved it. Within yelling voice distance from outside our home, I had nearly 50 friends living just like us. Life seemed magical then. We had no cares, no worries and no concerns about anything. Our parents and grandparents were there to worry for us. We didn't even know we were poor!

Let me tell you a bit about my name. Most girls at birth, or at the time of baptism, are given the names of their grandmothers.

But not me. My paternal grandmother was called Maria, and my maternal grandmother was Fotini. I couldn't be called those names because I am the fourth girl in our family, and my grandmothers names have gone to my older sisters. I was lucky enough to be given a new name which had not been used in our immediate family.

Maroula is a famous character from our history. Legend has it that there was a girl of that name who helped defeat the invading Turkish army in 1478. Her story goes something like this. In about 1462, the Ottoman Turks invaded Limnos in their quest to control the Aegean, and remained for several years until the local population, with help from a Venetian army, expelled the invaders. Not to be outdone, the Turks returned in 1478 and mounted a new invasion at the castle of Kotsinas. General Isodoros Komminos was the local leader of the Greek militia, and together with more Venetians, tried once again to oust the pesky aggressors. Things were not going well for the good guys; officers and soldiers were lying dead and dying all around, and then General Isodoros was killed. With the death of our leader, the Venetians thought a swift retreat to the centre of the island was called for, and begged the Greeks to follow. The Turks were winning and soon had full control of the castle, which at that time, commanded an important strategic position over the bay of Pournia. Observing from a safe distance, young Maroula, daughter of Isodoros, saw her father killed and noticed the urge to fight had evaporated from the local militia. Picking up her father's sword, she rushed into battle, and encouraged others to do so as well. Not to be outdone by a female, the Greek soldiers, together with the Venetians, fought off the marauders and won the day.

I was named after her. But what is usually left out of this legendary battle is that only one year later, the Turks came back and stayed until 1912!

While the original Maroula may not have seen the backs of the Turkish intruders for good, I can say that I did see them leave.

In 1912, on October 8, the Turkish occupiers finally departed from Limnos, never to return. I was standing on the beach near Tsimandria where the Greek flag was raised for the first time as Limnos became part of Greece. It was a proud day. I have some idea how my namesake ancestor must have felt, torn by her mixed emotions at gaining freedom from oppression and the same time as the loss of a father.

Life for my family, my parents and grandparents did not change much after that auspicious day. There were so few Turks on the island at the time, seeing them leave did not change the way we did things. The Turks had become part of us, and we had taken some of their culture and adopted it as our own. Many words, clothing, food, music and habits we still use come from a melded Greek/ Ottoman history. On that separation day, I lost a friend, a young boy of about 16 from the village of Pesperago, near us. His name was Mustafa, and his family had lived on Limnos for hundreds of years. I knew that he considered himself Limnian, not Turkish. Whilst he spoke Turkish at home, he used Greek with me and our friends when not around his family. I learned Turkish from him. All my friends from Portianou spoke Turkish. It was just the way it was back then. It was a very sad day for me when Mustafa and his family left forever. We all cried. He wasn't going 'back home', as he had been 'home' all his life.

Why do we have countries that want to take over another? It doesn't make sense to me, and never did. Having Turkish authorities on Limnos for so long was not always a bad thing. For one, they taught us how to keep accurate records and pay taxes. My parents always said that they taught us how to be good managers. All over Limnos there are water fountains and βρύσες (taps) built by the Ottomans. There must be hundreds of them spread out all over the land, so they did do some good for us.

One of my favourite things to do since I was about 10, was to ride my donkey to the top of Mount Elias, imagining I was Queen

Hypsipyle looking out over my kingdom. When the family donkeys were not being used as beasts of burden, the other kids in the village and I would pack some figs, water and bread, and head off with our four-legged transport towards Mount Elias. The village elders from Portianou, Tsimandria and Kontias built a church on top of the mountain some years ago, and it became a site of pilgrimage for all sorts of people, including us kids. It was up there that we first saw the strange, khaki-coloured foreign ships arriving one day in March 1915.

Coming down off the mountain, we gained a closer look from our farmland on Pounda and these ships gliding gently into the harbour and anchoring over in Moudros. Our main block of family land was on the western side of Portianou, down by the water and before Pounda. My father also had the use of other land at Fakos to run our sheep, but he didn't own that land. Like many other shepherds, he used communal land for most of summer, only bringing the sheep back closer to home at the start of autumn. At the same time, while taking our flock to Fakos from the land close to home, he caught a closer view of these ships across the bay in Moudros.

Within days, there were about 50 vessels in the harbour, and none of them were either Greek or Turkish. From near our village and from the 1912 pier near Tsimandria, our men took their kaiki's out of the safe water and over to Moudros to see what was happening. I am sure many of our elders must have thought that we were being invaded yet again.

The men returned in an hour or two with a mixture of feelings ranging from excitement and dread. Excitement at the prospect of selling these newcomers food and supplies, and dread because the foreigners were preparing for a war with our old overlords, the Turks. From that moment onwards, my life changed as I and all my friends prepared the best we could for the unknown. But first, and not waiting for an invitation, we had to gather food, supplies and souvenirs to try to sell to the foreigners in these ships. Our parents sensed an immediate trading possibility.

CHAPTER 3

GALLIPOLI

(1915)

The 8th Battalion 4th Reinforcements were kitted up and weighed down with our equipment, then loaded onto a number of smaller personnel craft. We were packed in like sardines and sweating with nervousness as we headed due east to the Turkish coast. I can't be sure if we were officially told where we were off to, but I remember being two parts excited and three parts shitting myself. I was on edge because midway across the Aegean, we crossed paths with a hospital ship coming the other way, and all I could focus on were the number of men standing by the rails or laying on stretchers, with bandages on their legs, faces and arms, either shaking their heads or just staring at us. Some of them made an effort to wave, but most didn't. We all waved ferociously, but that didn't seem to matter to them. I've never forgotten that image of men with blood-stained head bandages and rolled cigarettes hanging loosely through the cloth.

One particularly distressing image has always remained with me from the time of passing that ship. Our vessels had almost quietly passed each other, when we noticed a sack, about the size of a person, being carefully dropped over the rail into the water. Not really thinking about it at the time, we later learned that this was a 'burial at sea' of one of our blokes.

Now only half an hour away from dry land, we anchored off the coast and made our way on to even smaller landing vessels which were nothing more than rowed lifeboats. As we were getting aboard, a barge loaded with wounded soldiers was waiting until we got off our boats so they could transfer them to the hospital ships. Looking down at these poor unfortunate chaps made all of us very quiet. What were we in for? About the only thing I knew for certain was that I was in it with my mates. If I was shit scared, so were they.

It was about this time, rowing to shore, that we first heard the unfriendly sound of a bullet whizzing close to us and fizzing as it hit the water.

"Oh Shit! What was that?"

We were being fired on. Bloody hell. Couldn't the bastards at least wait until we made it to the beach? Two seats behind me, Tommy Carter copped a bullet in his left arm. Jesus H. Christ — welcome to the war, mate!

CHAPTER 4

A STRANGE
INTRODUCTION TO WAR

At around 7.30 am on the morning of May 24, we arrived on shore at Gallipoli. It was the strangest of introductions to war you could possibly imagine. We were trained to be soldiers at Broadmeadows, and on board our vessel we had endless drills. However, none of us had ever fired a live round at any living person, none of us had ever seen a Turkish soldier, and none of us had ever been to war. But, on the positive side, at least most of us had shot a rabbit or ten.

We could see men running about everywhere. There seemed to be little or no order to the activity, but looks were deceiving. It had been raining very lightly for over an hour, but strangely none of us even noticed we were wet. Not surprising perhaps when you are about to get off a cockleshell boat into the water, loaded to the gills, and ready to head off into the unknown of war. We were taught in training camp not to think, to follow orders without question and do what we were told. It didn't seem real at that time, but now we were here, let me tell you we were waiting to be told something. Reality was about to strike like a thunderbolt.

Holding my rifle and worldly possessions above the water line, we made our way from the landing boat to a safe dugout on shore, following the instructions of a very loud sergeant. He told us to place our kit down in what looked like a child's sand pit surrounded by carefully stacked sandbags, and then to follow him. The gunfire that had welcomed us earlier on the boat, given way to a deathly silence. Not at all what I had thought our first day would be like. It was quiet because unbeknown to us, a burial armistice had been declared for 7.30 am this particular day so that both the Turkish and our side could bury the dead without any recriminations. About five days before, there had been terrible losses on both sides after a rather intense battle. In-between the two opposing combatants was an area called No-Man's-Land, and the stench of thousands of dead was overbearing. Soldiers had to smoke continuously just to mask the stink of rotting, bloated bodies lying in the heat.

The first informal armistice to bury the dead from the May 19 battle was made on May 20, when the Allies raised a 'Red Cross' flag. This was shot down by the enemy, but a Turkish runner coming from a German Officer's trench came out with an apology. So, an informal armistice took place under 'Red Crescent' flags raised at various intervals along enemy lines. Some wounded were saved, but there were many misunderstandings between both sides, and fighting started up again after the Turks began to pick up rifles, not bodies. One of our generals said that if a truce were to be established, it must be done formally.

During the back-and-forth negotiations for the informal truce, our side suggested that if a burial armistice was to be achieved, the Turks should send an envoy along the beach from Gaba Tepe. Terms were accepted, and the day was set for May 24.

Burial rules had been carefully negotiated over a period of a few days, and this is what I remember being told before we started work. A line was to be pegged out down the centre of No-Man's-Land with the Turkish burying parties to work their side of the line, while we worked on our side. Any dead belonging to the Turks on our side of the line were to be carried on stretchers to the centre line. The enemy was to do the same for us, so that each side would bury its own dead, after first trying to identify them.

No-Man's-Land was opposite Quinn's and the Nek, and was a perilously narrow strip. Being recently arrived fresh soldiers, we were instructed to hastily dig pits so that hundreds of corpses could be buried. Sadly, we didn't have enough time to bury our blokes with dignity, but we did all we could do given the time constraints we were under. We found many bodies that had clearly been left out in the open for over a week, so our task was unimaginably heart breaking for us. I remember picking up a dead New Zealand bloke with my mate 'Horges' so that we could place him on a stretcher, but his right arm came off. Horges was instantly sick, and I wasn't feeling too good either. Things like this happened time and time again.

One of my miner mates from Ballarat, Charlie Greaves, was also part of the 8th Battalion 4th Reinforcements, and due to his mining background, joined the mass grave digging group. They were given a patch of land to dig in a hurry, and shovels to do the job. Charlie and some other soldier-miners got to work like they were digging for gold back home. I remember that these blokes were later digging tunnels under enemy trenches, but on this day, tunnels were not necessary. But that didn't stop Charlie from yelling out *'eureka'*. He had come across some old pottery at a depth of about 10 feet, but couldn't call a halt to examine his finds more closely. They apparently had come across an ancient village, and had to ignore the amazing artefacts *'in situ'*. He showed me a piece of pottery and a broken stele with some Ancient Greek letters. Not knowing I spoke any Greek, I asked him to pass it to me for a closer look. The artefact appeared to be a carved stone stele from a burial of some village elder. How ironic!

I remember that early in the day, when surveying No-Man's-Land, I bent down to pick up a rifle, which looked like it was one of ours. I was told by an overzealous sergeant in no uncertain terms to put it down. I did as I was told and asked what I should do with any rifles of our boys, and what should I do if I found any of theirs. Apparently, one of the terms of the armistice was that rifles found in No-Man's-Land were to be immediately placed on stretchers. No man was to carry a rifle in his hand. Each side was to carry off its own rifles found near its burying area. Enemy rifles were to have the bolts removed and then all parts placed on stretchers and taken away.

Standing in this charnel house called No-Man's-Land, it had the strange appearance of a sporting competition. Officers from both sides stood in little groups pointing at things, flags had been placed at differing intervals in what looked like an obstacle course, and a line of sentries gave the impression of being match officials. I wondered when the umpires would enter the playing arena and toss a coin with the captains of both teams. But this was no game.

At one time I remember walking aimlessly towards a dirt parapet, looking down at the ground, trying not to see too much, when my right foot landed on a piece of soft mud and immediately some iridescent green muck oozed up from the dirt either side of my boot. Lifting it out of the squelch, the black flesh of a Turk's head came free. I wanted so much to run back down to the beach, but somehow, I managed to ignore it. The entire parapet was constructed of swollen, hideous, dead Turkish soldiers held together with bloodied dirt. The end result of machine gun fire and high explosives became evident. Entire companies wiped out. Not wounded, annihilated. This was my baptism into this hell on earth.

I lost all track of the time of day, and just concentrated on getting as many as possible of our dead buried. I remember looking up at one stage and seeing a young man just like me, but wearing the enemy's uniform, picking up the remains of a Turkish corpse, and placing what was left of the dead soldier onto a stretcher. The young soldier was crying and trying to be brave, but I could see he was really struggling. He caught my eye, and I wandered slowly towards him to lend assistance in any way I could. He accepted my offer of assistance, and together, we located pieces of his former comrades, and took them to where they would be taken away. I would never find out if those poor buggers were buried in a mass grave or an individual one.

This bloke seemed to be just like me in every possible way. We were about the same age, same height, weight, and complexion. The only difference was the uniform worn and language spoken. After sheer exhaustion overtook us, we sat down and shared a cigarette. No words, just two cobbers having a smoke. We were two young men bound like brothers in the business of war. We were two loved sons experiencing the brutality and futile existence of soldiers from opposing sides, yet plainly the same in every respect. I cursed myself for not being able to fully explain to him how I felt, and I know he was thinking the same. Looking around, this was happening on both sides. Some of our men were swapping things such as souvenirs and badges with the Turks, and I even heard two enemies speaking in French while they stood no more than a yard apart, sucking on a shared cigarette! I cursed my parents for not teaching me any French!

A particularly interesting thing to add to this bizarre event was happening away to our left. There were some high table-topped hills not too far distant, and they appeared to be covered by thousands of intrigued Turkish civilians who had come out to watch the burials. We found ourselves waving at them, and they to us. Then I heard one of our officers yelling at us to 'stop waving at the enemy'.

While the lower-ranked soldiers were actively burying the dead or swapping gifts, the higher-ranked officers on both sides were surreptitiously attempting to spy on on each other's relative positions and make surveys of strengths and locations. One of the rules agreed to before this armistice was that both sides would not try to spy on the defenses of the other side. Yet, to my amazement, there were Turkish and British photographers hard at work! Then, at about three o'clock in the arvo, we were given final instructions to hurry up and return to the beach.

One final event of that very strange day occurred soon before we were due to head back to the trenches. This image has remained with me all these years. I found myself on corpse recovery duty working alongside a New Zealander who had been on Gallipoli since landing on April 25. We were looking for bodies under a shrub and came across a dead Aucklander still holding his rifle with his bayonet firmly embedded in the body of an equally dead Turk. We agreed to bury them together. What more could we do for them?

From this moment on, and until I left the Peninsula some months later, the enemy became known as 'Johnny Turk'. We didn't hate him. We respected him, and he respected us. As strange as it seems, a kind of brotherly bond began on that day in May 1915 that would remain with me for a lifetime.

One day in early June, Pickles copped a bullet in the leg, and had to be evacuated down to the beach by a couple of athletic stretcher bearers. I didn't see it happen, but as he came past me, heading for the regimental aid post, he said "See you later cobber. I'm OK, but my knee feels like wet shit! Say goodbye to the lads for me, will ya'. I may not be back for a while." He wasn't wrong. I had never seen so much blood on a living person before. The next time I saw him was in 1919, back in Ballarat.

CHAPTER 5

SOMETHING IS BREWING

Late July 1915 saw the Gallipoli campaign grind to an uneasy stalemate. We weren't gaining any real ground, and the Turks could not force us back into the sea. We noticed a lot of new, fresh British troops land in early August filling up any trenches and gullies above ANZAC Cove, and straight away, we could sense something big was about to happen.

And happen it did. A major operation was to take place at Suvla Bay, and the ANZACs were tasked with creating a diversion at Lone Pine. We were pretty excited at the thought of this, but our joy was short lived. Instead of getting into the thick of it, the 8th Battalion were to lend support to the 6th Battalion in their direct raid. Although we were disappointed at not being involved in the direct attack on Turkish trenches, many of the enemy shells still landed on us. Poor Clarry must have been blown to bits because we could not find anything left of him after one shell burst right near where he was standing. Billy C was also killed, along with about 20 of our mates that day on August 6. Some we managed to bury, but some we had to leave out in the heat, dust and flies for days. In an attempt to help an injured British soldier, I managed to get shot in the leg, and had to be evacuated to a casualty clearing station on the beach by very eager and nervous stretcher bearers.

The trip down to the beach with our mad, brave, athletic medics, dodging bullets and exploding bombs was more harrowing than being shot. When you cop a bullet, it happens so fast, you just feel it and then you start to become dizzy with the loss of blood. But lying on a stretcher, being carried down to the beach when you know men have been killed doing what you were doing, you feel a bit of a cheat. You have cheated death sure, but you are left to feel like you are letting down your cobbers by not being killed and getting away just wounded. I now know how the wounded men felt when we saw them on our first day coming into ANZAC Cove on the boat. They were looking at us and thinking "those poor buggers have no idea".

It wasn't until my leg was wrapped up in a makeshift bandage that I realised how lucky I was at being alive. It was also the time I was told officially about Clarry and Billy C. I think I was just numb. No thoughts. No feelings. Nothing.

In what felt like a few hours, my stretcher was loaded onto a flat-bottomed boat with a hundred or more other wounded in far worse condition than me and taken offshore to a hospital ship bound for Limnos. On the way to the ship, the digger next to me stopped screaming, and I thought he was asleep. Sadly, he was very deeply asleep — never to wake up again. Conditions were OK on the hospital ship as far as I can remember, but like my 'sleeping' mate earlier, a few more didn't make it all the way, and they were quickly and silently buried at sea.

Conditions on Limnos were not much better than on the hospital ship. I think I am being nice when I say that, but the main difference was that we were now on *terra firma*, not rolling about on the open sea. I was coming in and out of consciousness and missed the actual moment I was transferred from the ship to a dry hospital bed. When I awoke in some sort of agonising pain, I noticed that my hospital bed was a piece of canvas on the dusty and stony earth, with a piece of canvas above me keeping the afternoon sun from my face. There were about 10 of us in that open tent hospital, all with varying degrees of wounds. Some had nasty head wounds, and the rest of us had bullets that had ripped parts of our bodies away. Like I said, I was the lucky one. My bullet had gone clean through my leg, just above the knee, missing bones and anything that might cause me long term agony, but I can tell you, it still hurt like buggery!

Soon a revelation of loveliness appeared in my vision — a nurse asking me my name.

"Hello soldier. Can you hear me. Wake up sleepy head. Wake up. What is your name?"

I mumbled something, and she apparently understood and asked me "and where are you from Angus?"

"Ballarat."

"Just try to relax and I'll be back soon."

Then she went to ask the bloke next to me the same questions, and so on and so on. Whilst we had landed at Limnos in a new hospital, we quickly learned it lacked a few of the everyday normal essentials of a regular hospital, like beds, wards, medication, bandages, water, toilets, washing up facilities and doctors. But we did at least have nurses and a canvas roof over our heads to keep the sun off our faces. Luxury when I think about it now, considering my mates were getting the shit blown out of them back at ANZAC Cove and Lone Pine.

Apparently, we landed a day after the hospital was supposed to open, but the buffoons who organised this had forgotten to let us soldiers know. How rude! Anyway, the nurses were fantastic. If not for them, many of us would have not survived. They managed to find bandages and give us a drink, and some of us even had our wounds cleaned. But for those first few days, the bandages used were torn up pieces of their own nursing uniforms. Fair dinkum, but you would think that if you plan a war, you plan for dead and wounded, and plan for hospital care. How hard is it? Not long later, supplies did trickle in and we were at least able to lie off the ground on a stretcher bed.

Let me tell you about those nurses. Soldiers at least had some training at the Broadmeadows camp — training how to be soldiers. Nurses did their training in hospitals back home, and many were not well prepared for nursing in a war zone. But in all my time as a patient during my war years, I never once heard a nurse complain. If they ever had issues, the last people to hear about them were their patients. That is why I still call them our 'angels'. They got sick like us, and many Aussie nurses died on active service, so they had plenty to complain about.

Luckily for me, I did not require any major surgery, just a bullet wound that healed soon enough. Many of my friends sharing the hospital beds next to me were not so lucky. While surprisingly few died once they reached this level of care away from the front, for quite a few, their war was over, and returned as soon as they could to a sort of civilian life, busted and heartbroken at leaving their mates behind, both alive and dead. I never truly understood how these poor buggers must have felt when told "you are going home soldier". It was when I got back home myself many years later, and spoke to some of these boys, that I realised that their misery was only just beginning. For many years, they hated the thought that they had let their mates down and hated leaving them — alive or even dead. This feeling of abandonment never left them, and sadly, some of them could not control these feelings, and they ended their lives. Only a soldier or a nurse who was there amongst the shambles can truly understand how these men felt.

When I had recovered sufficiently to hobble around a bit, I managed to fashion a pair of crutches out of some broken wooden tent poles and pieces of torn canvas. That was another of the missing pieces of medical equipment that some clown should have organised. Once these fine examples of walking aids were skilfully crafted, I was permitted to leave the hospital grounds and go off wandering, as long as I promised to return soon.

With my newly created walking aides, it was time to explore the local villages to see if I could use any of my language skills. I hadn't told my mates that I could speak some Greek, or that I even knew any of the language. Up until this stage of my recovery, I hadn't even seen any local people up close, but I could see them at a distance. Two of my wounded mates and I decided to make our way on foot (with our crutches) to a village we had been reliably informed was nearby, where a coffee and tea house was rumoured to exist. The weather was very warm, and not a breath of wind blew on the morning of our big adventure — a three-mile promenade along a dusty track into town!

Hobbling along the well-worn dirt path, we noticed a young woman about 50 yards ahead walking with two donkeys laden with produce. Without even blinking, I said to her *"καλιμέρα"*. She just looked at me with a sympathetic smile, laughed a bit and continued on with her work.

"I didn't know you spoke the language mate."

"Apparently I can't, as it seems."

"How come you can speak another language? I have enough trouble with English."

"What did you say to her Angus" asked the other of my wounded companions.

"I think I said good morning, but I may have mucked it up a bit. I've never actually spoken to a Greek person before."

"You've offended her mate."

"I just said *καλιμέρα*, it means "good morning", I think."

The young lady in question was now out of sight, and we followed some officers ahead of us making their way into the village. We ambled along quietly taking in the surrounding fields, the sights and smells and within a few minutes, found ourselves in the middle of a beautiful, stone-built village with the most magnificent shady tree in the centre of the town square. Only it wasn't square, but rather oddly shaped. Local men were sitting outside these stone buildings, smoking and drinking what appeared to be a strong coffee in a tiny porcelain cup. The three of us shuffled over to the building we figured was the coffee shop, because the officers were now seated there and one of them, an Aussie I remember, was gesticulating to a local man and his companions. I couldn't hear what they were saying, but it sounded like 'coffee'.

My two mates and I carefully eased ourselves down at a table, and a waiter, a man about 20 years older than us, walked over, and I thought that I would attempt to use my language skills again. In my best and most proper Greek, I said this.

"Good morning sir. May I have a cup of coffee and could you please give my friends two cups of tea."

"What did you ask for, Angus" inquired one of my mates.

"I think I asked for a coffee and two teas."

The waiter looked at me, and then disappeared inside the shop without saying anything.

"That went well mate."

I had no way of knowing at that time, but my parents had taught me a very formal and old style of textbook Greek. I had never ever spoken to a real Greek person before, and I don't even think my parents had, so I was a bit nervous at my potentially archaic, proper language skills. I had only ever spoken to my parents in Greek, and maybe a sheep or two back home.

Just then, the waiter came over to our table with a coffee and two teas.

"Thank you very much sir, and here are your drinks", or that is what I thought he said.

I understood him enough to respond by thanking him. The other local men sitting nearby were now looking at me, and so too were the officers. My two tea-drinking cobbers were very impressed.

"Say something else Angus. Go on. Say something."

Not wanting to create a scene, I did manage something very formal.

"My name is Angus. These are my friends, Mr William and Mr John. What name are you known by? Where do you live?"

The waiter said his name was George and that he lived in the village of Portianou, and this was his café. I could hear some of the old local men laughing, and I wasn't sure if they were laughing at me or George's response. Probably a bit of both.

I said to one of the laughing local men *"Good morning sir. The weather is very nice today."*

The old man mumbled something, and I thought my language may be a little heavy with accent, or that I had no real idea what I was saying, which was more than likely. He mumbled some more and I heard him say *"It is summer you donkey!"*

One of my wounded mates noticed some men eating cakes, and he asked me to order some.

"Excuse me waiter. Could we please have some biscuits?"

"Biscuits?"

George looked a bit puzzled at my request, and I pointed to the cakes being eaten.

"You want some cakes?"

"Cakes, yes. Not biscuits. Sorry George. My Greek is not very good as you can see."

George brought out some beautiful, sweet cakes for us, and carefully placed three small empty glasses in front of us. Then, pouring a clear liquid into each, he said to me *"to your health"*.

Looking around to the seated patrons, the local men were looking directly at us, raising their glasses also full of this rich smelling aromatic liquid, and gulping them in one shot.

"I think we are to do the same. Bottoms up lads."

We upended these drinks in our eager throats, and it wasn't long before the impact hit us. I had never tasted ouzo before, and

I was hooked. It was beautiful. My drinking cobbers were not that impressed, but they did have a second glass, just to be sure. One of them said "at least this is better than the medicinal pig's piss they force us to take."

George asked me where I learned his language. I told him about my parents teaching me, and this was my first time speaking to a Greek person. He congratulated me and said I was the first foreigner he had heard try any words in his language. He was very proud and happy that I tried and said that he would pay for the drinks. It was to be his treat. At this point, the officers looked at me differently, and one even came over to sit with us. He too asked me about my language skills and said that he would remember that in case he needed a translator. I even tried to teach him some phrases, but his accent was rat shit, so he gave up before I did.

We left the village later that morning, one hot drink, some cakes and two ouzos later. The journey back to our hospital beds was more difficult, as it was mostly uphill. Limping back to our hospital tent, our sleep, on less than comfortable beds, was a bit more enjoyable due to the two fine shots of the Olympian liquid that we had downed.

Some of the hospital staff were talking that night about the thermal springs on the island where you could take a hot bath. Considering it had been nearly five months since my last bath, this seemed like an excellent, if overdue, idea. They had overheard some officers and doctors discussing a place called Therma, but no one had actually been there. I decided to try the next day to locate this mythical hot bath venue.

One thing about the summers on Limnos that I can confidently say is that the weather in August in Limnos was much better than the August mornings in Ballarat. Now my two new friends were waking me up early asking me for another trip to the village as soon as possible. Due to our wonderful medical care, our injuries were healing nicely, but the downside of this was that we could be sent back to the front anytime soon, so we agreed to make the most of our leisure-time in hospital. After morning rounds by the nurses checking our wounds, redressing, and rebandaging, the three limping cobbers once more shuffled along the dusty track to Portianou. It was obvious that our own hospital, the 3rd Australian General Hospital, was still looking like a tent village, but the new Canadian hospital site which was nowhere near ready, had roads and the tents were being lifted into position. Nurses were there to prepare the wards, and I remember speaking to one on the way to our ultimate destination. Nurse Mary was very keen to get started but was bitterly complaining about the conditions. She asked about our hospital, and I told her that it had only been there for a week or so and was still lacking many resources. I wasn't to know, but the next time I would meet her would be at her grave in Portianou cemetery.

About 400 yards from the village boundary, I saw the young Greek lady once again with her donkey's baskets loaded on each side with fresh daily produce. I didn't want to speak again for fear of making a galah of myself, but the boys convinced me to give it a go one more time. So, I did.

"Good afternoon. What a beautiful afternoon it is."

This time, she didn't laugh, but responded with *"yes, it is. But it is still morning, sir."*

Progress! I spoke to my first Greek woman, and she understood me. Well, apart from messing up the time of day, at least she understood me. I couldn't believe I made a mistake with 'good morning' and 'good afternoon'.

When I explained to my mates, they laughed, and never let me forget it. That night, back in our hospital beds and long after lights out, they both delighted in saying to me "good morning Angus" at least ten times each, laughing harder after each time. Eventually they stopped, and I was almost asleep when I heard a whisper — "good afternoon Angus".

The next time we were out, I was able to speak to the lady again. I asked her who she was and where she lived and found out that her name was Maroula and she lived in Portianou, and that George, the café owner, was her uncle. She giggled and said my accent was funny — one she had not heard before. I explained my background, and she seemed to accept it.

"*Maybe I can teach you proper Limnian*" she said.

"What did she say" quizzed one of my walking friends.

"I think she wants to teach me how the locals speak Greek!"

"*Where are you going now?*" I asked hesitantly.

"*In to see Uncle George to sell him some of our food.*"

My mates were no longer teasing me. They kept asking me to ask Maroula if she had two sisters, and they could teach them anything they wanted to.

"*What did your friends say?*"

"*Oh, nothing much, but they are asking if they could sit on your donkeys.*"

Maroula laughed but shook her head and said '*not on these ones*'.

I wondered a bit about this, but then said "*Have I seen you and some friends with bigger donkeys near our hospital?*"

"*Of course. I suppose we could take you on these donkeys to Therma, where you can have a hot bath. The water is beautiful there. The baths were built by the Turks many years ago. Would you like me to take you and your friends?*"

This was very tempting, but I said "*Maybe when we don't have bandages on, but thank you for the invitation.*"

When I told my injured cobbers, they of course wanted to go straight away to the hot springs, but when I said we all had bandages and un-healed bullet wounds, they said "Oh yeah. Not a great idea just yet."

We hobbled into the village with Maroula, and her donkeys, and sat down at George's café. Maroula led her animals away because apparently, they were not welcome at the café! George approached our table and we ordered a Greek style coffee with sweet cakes. I was beginning to like George's coffee — much better than the billy boiled, tasteless muck we called 'tea'. Nor did his cakes need a sledgehammer to break them into bite-sized chunks, and they did not break our teeth when trying to chomp down on one. At the café, we felt like officers taking afternoon tea on the green! The only thing missing from our bliss at being here, was the sound of a willow bat striking a red leather ball for four runs, with a polite handclap and some chap saying 'jolly nice shot, what?'

After completing our morning tea duties, and not really knowing when we would be leaving for the front, the three of us walked 200 yards to the newly constructed military cemetery immediately behind the village church.

It was an all too familiar sight these days to see a funeral procession pass by on its way to this cemetery. Unlike the hastily constructed burial grounds over at ANZAC Cove, this one at Portianou was well away from bombs, snipers and bullets, so a proper burial was able to take place with a padre, mourners and a gun salute. This particular morning, we formed part of a guard of honour to one of the poor chaps who came over from the front with us on the same boat, but sadly did not recover. There was one nurse present this day at the grave site, and I recognised her as one of the Aussie nurses who first cared for me only a week ago. Her name was Madeline, and she said she was from South Yarra in Melbourne. After the service had concluded, we four walked back through the village to the hospital together. On the way, we walked past George's café in Portianou, and I asked Madeline if she had been here for a tea. She said no, so I mentioned to George to please make these nurses welcome if they came in for a cup of tea or coffee.

"Do you speak Greek, Angus?"

"A little bit. My parents speak many languages and they have been teaching me ever since I could crawl."

"My brother speaks a bit of Ancient Greek. He went to

Melbourne Grammar, and then Geelong Grammar where he learned mostly Latin, but did a year or two of Greek, I think. He's in the Light Horse somewhere in Egypt at the moment. I haven't heard from him since I got here a few weeks ago."

Many years later, I learned from a Ballarat nurse who served with Madeline in France at the end of the war that Madeline did meet her brother Martin only a few months after I met her. Of all places, they met on Limnos! The story goes something like this. Martin's unit, the 4th Light Horse Regiment, were evacuated from Gallipoli, roughly the same time I was, and of course, ended up on Limnos. He and his cobbers were camped in the tent city at Sarpi when he somehow heard that Madeline was across the water, about 200 yards away as the crow flies at the 3rd Australian General Hospital. Martin and a mate purloined a small, oared boat and rowed over to the other side and walked around looking for Madeline, until they eventually found each other. Because I had told Madeline about the coffee shop in Portianou, she took Martin, his mate, and some other nurses down to partake in afternoon tea with George. Apparently, Madeline had learned to order tea and cake in Greek, and her brother was most impressed with her.

Sadly, this was the last time Madeline and Martin would ever meet. He was killed in action at Mount Kemmel in Belgium in April 1918, and like too many of our cobbers, his body was never found. Probably blown to a million pieces. I may have walked past him in Sarpi during our time after the evacuation, but there were thousands of men camped in that space in December 1915.

After my five years in the military had concluded, I have lost count of the number of times the island of Limnos has popped up in stories, anecdotes, and memories, both good and less so. When I least expect it, I find someone who was there, had tea with George, was patched up by the wonderful angels in the hospitals, camped in the freezing tents of Sarpi, or who like some of my now best mates, were there to practice the Gallipoli landings before April 25. Limnos in Greece had become a major part of my very existence.

CHAPTER 6

THERMA

(AUGUST 1915)

My mates and I had recovered from our wounds sufficiently enough to attempt a donkey trip to the bath house. Given permission to leave the hospital grounds one final time, we limped off towards Portianou to find donkeys and perhaps, if I was lucky, a chance to chat with Maroula.

It was late August, and the weather was absolutely wonderful. Perfect, in fact, if not for the war just a few miles away in Turkey. I later thought that this might be a nice place to visit for a holiday, come better times. By mid-morning, we had walked into George's café and ordered a coffee. The same two old men were sitting at their table, smoking a shared shisha pipe, mumbling away in a form of Turkish/Greek.

George brought us our coffees and cakes, and I asked him if Maroula was around so that we could hire her donkey service to the hot baths.

"I think she should be home by now. I'll send a boy around to ask her to come immediately."

"Angus — your Greek is getting better" said one of my wounded mates.

The two old codgers were still staring at us, but at least by now, I didn't get the feeling they wanted us to leave. Maroula arrived with four donkeys, and we quickly finished our morning coffee.

"Are you ready now, Angus?"

"Yes, Maroula. We are ready. Let's go."

I had only heard about these baths, and now we were finally going. My mates and I were so excited. The trip out of the village took us past many farms and vineyards. Although the journey would only take an hour or so, we had to stop to water the donkeys because it was still summer, and quite hot.

We stopped at what appeared to be an old stone constructed tap. I thought it might be Turkish because the carved writing on a headstone above the tap was written in what looked like Arabic script.

"Do you know what this says, Maroula?" I asked.

"No, not really. I remember someone saying it contains the names of the workmen who made it. George seems to think this tap is over 400 years old. The water here comes from the same underground source as the Thermal springs."

The water was particularly nice and warm, and the donkeys slurped up enough water from the large carved stone troughs to fuel them for the next part of the journey.

Maroula and I were travelling at the front of our little tour group, and my two mates were to our rear. Until we reached the hot springs, Maroula and I talked non-stop. We talked about family, farming, and sheep. She was most impressed that I knew about the sheep they had, and that I knew how to milk them and make cheese.

Talking with her was totally different to learning Greek with my parents. For a start, she was a natural-born speaker, and spoke the language of the village, where my parents learned mostly from textbooks and other academics. She corrected me as I went, not by saying I was wrong, but quite masterfully repeating what I said, but in the more natural way. She was a marvellous teacher. On the way, we also met other soldiers and their guides on the return leg of their bathing odyssey.

On our arrival at the bath house in Therma, Maroula took care of the donkeys while we entered the modern looking stone building. There were already a number of other donkey tour groups here with soldiers from all sorts of places — Britain, France, New Zealand and of course, Australia.

The bath house was constructed many years ago. No one could tell me how old the baths were, but these current buildings were only about 50 years old. Like the Turkish tap at which we refuelled our beasts of burden on our way here, these baths had most likely been used in some form or another for hundreds of years, but surely water had been bubbling its way to the surface for a lot longer.

My mates and I could have stayed in the water for hours, but after about 30 minutes, we decided it was time to make our way back to the hospital. Maroula was waiting for us at an outside tap which was a much grander structure than the one in the valley. This one had carved letters on it saying it was built in 1908, and there was a soldier taking a photo of some locals scooping water from a stone trough below the outlet.

We felt clean and refreshed. Having a warm bath tends to do that to a man. I asked Maroula if she had ever been to the bath house herself to bathe in the water, and she said that she had only once taken a bath there. I didn't ask any additional questions, because I suspected it was too expensive for her. However, during war time, she was happy making trips with her donkeys to carry soldiers, officers and nurses and making some money for her family.

She told me that many donkeys had come from all over the country for the war in Turkey, but her donkeys were not destined for the front. Local village elders had convinced the Allied army command that about 30 donkeys would be better off remaining in this area travelling to and from the bath house.

The return journey to Portianou was exactly the reverse of the first — via the Turkish tap in the valley for a water stop, and then down to the village. I gave Maroula enough money for her donkey transport service and said my farewells to her and George outside his café. Even the two older human table ornaments waved as we left for our walk back to the hospital. I didn't know how long it would be before I returned, but I felt that it might be a long time away, if at all.

"Hey Angus. You have feelings for that girl, don't you?"

"Shut up."

"Nothing to be ashamed of mate. If I spoke her language, I'd talk to her as much as you did."

I didn't say anything more to my two bullet-wound recovered mates all the way to our hospital tent. We walked in silence. They were thinking about going back to their battalions. I couldn't stop thinking about Maroula!

CHAPTER 7

SARPI REST CAMP
(SEPTEMBER – NOVEMBER 1915)

I was only back at ANZAC Cove for a few weeks, when our battalion received instructions to proceed to the rest camp at Sarpi, on Limnos. Some of my cobbers had been on the peninsula for months, and were beginning to fade, physically and mentally. On the night of September 9, eight officers and 278 men of the 8th Battalion boarded the minesweeper *Sarnia* and once again, I was off to the island. This time though, not as a patient, but as a rest camper.

We disembarked in Moudros onto a jetty chock-a-block full of tired, exhausted men clutching their meagre belongings in calico bags. We were told not to move, and as the *Sarnia* departed, its place was taken by the launch *Water Witch*. This next water trip was thankfully much shorter, over to the other side of Moudros Harbour, near where I was dropped off as a patient only six or so weeks prior. We were then told to march five miles with packs, through the hospital lines, around the small bay at the edge of Portianou, turn right and past the village of Pesperago. When we were nearly four miles into our march, most of the lads were on their last legs. Four months with lack of exercise, poor diet and sickness, was taking its toll. We were well and truly knackered and ready for a rest. Just one more mile … and the tents of Sarpi beckoned.

To keep us amused, we imagined out loud what our new accommodation might look like.

"I reckon we will have feather pillows on a soft bed, sleeping under a light, fresh, woollen blanket, in silk sheets."

"Yeah, and room service each morning to bring us breakfast."

"Warm showers and fresh clothes each day."

"And no lice!"

At that comment, there was laughter from everyone.

"I'm going to miss those little buggers."

Immediately prior to walking across the stretch of shallow, ankle deep water near Pesperago, we stopped to remove our boots. Most of us rolled up our trouser legs as well, but some of the lads removed their trousers altogether, revealing a lack of proper attire in the underwear department! Lots of comments were made regarding the new look 8th Battalion uniform, but it didn't last. One of our sergeants could be heard laughing so hard, he could hardly bring himself to order the immediate installation of proper attire once safely across the water.

"Put your gear back on lads. You don't want any of those local ladies having a stroke."

"But Sarge, the little soldier needs some fresh air too."

"Be that as it may Jacko, but we don't want him sunburned!"

More laughing, but we did return to proper uniform for the final walk around the little bay. To help with the last few minutes, someone broke out into song, and we walked into camp singing our hearts out. For the life of me, I can't remember what we were singing, but it felt great.

We were allocated 17 marquees, and we simply fell onto our beds and slept for a day. Considering the quality of our sleeping accommodation over on ANZAC Cove, this was the height of luxury. But, fair dinkum, some bozo had mucked up our booking! Half the marquees had apparently been pre-booked by another unit, so next day half of us slept on the ground until our new digs were allocated. There were no feather pillows and silk sheets for us!

To help overcome the disappointment of our double-booking arrangements, the paymaster gave us our pay, and some of the boys decided to explore the island. For most of them, they hadn't been to the island since the start of the campaign, so this was their first leisure time without having someone trying to shoot them. We found that there weren't many villages near Sarpi, but for those that were, they had certainly stocked up on supplies to sell to soldiers like us.

After a morning of forays into the closest villages to purchase a range of edibles, we returned by early afternoon to the delight of the camp kitchens firing up their stoves. Unlike the poor water supply for the hospital areas across the shallow inlet, water at Sarpi was slightly more accessible. We were given strict instructions not to splurge on the water supplies of the closest villages, because if we did, they would soon run dry. Water carts pulled by horses were always busy ferrying water sourced from wells on farms not in use by farmers. All the potable water on the island is underground, so it is impossible to gauge how much is available. To combat this potential problem, water rations were strictly imposed. Then again, coming from Gallipoli where water was as rare as rocking horse shit, being in Sarpi was a minor luxury for us.

On arrival back in camp, we compared notes on what was purchased and how much the price was. Soldiers who came with me were shocked at how much their comrades had to pay for the items we bought at village prices.

"How come you guys got the apples for that price?" was a common question to me.

"It helps if you speak the local language!"

"Next time, you're coming with us Angus."

I could have sold my services as an interpreter for more than they could save, so I declined their generous offer. As it turned out, I didn't have to offer my language skills at all because word got out in the nearby villages that someone in the Australian camp could speak Greek, and from then on, the boys paid just slightly more than market rates.

On my next free morning, I took a bunch of fellows to George's café for coffee, cakes, and maybe some of that fine local liquid that knocks your socks off. I explained to George why we were suddenly back on the island, but he didn't seem to be listening to my explanation. He seemed genuinely excited about something.

"Angus. I am happy you are here. Do you mind if I ask you for a favour?

"No George. What can I do for you?"

"It is not just you I would like to ask. Can you and your friends come to my farm nearby and help me pick grapes?"

I translated for the boys, and to a man, they all eagerly agreed. Some of them were farmers back home and were itching to see how the Greeks did things.

"If you all agree, this coffee will be my treat, and I promise to find a bottle of my ouzo so they can try it for the first time. What do you say?"

My mates were asking me what George said, and when I told them that we were going grape picking, and that we were going to sample some of his fine alcohol, they jumped up at once and said 'Too right. Let's go'. Three days before, we were trying to shoot Turkish and German soldiers and they were trying to shoot us. And now we were off to pick grapes! This war could not have been more ridiculous.

George already had some villagers in his paddocks hard at work picking the ripened grapes, and when we arrived, they stopped what they were doing and looked up at us. I noticed that all the pickers were young women, and one of them waved at me. It was

Maroula. I waved back. I secretly thanked George for giving me this gift. None of the boys I was with from the 8th knew I was friendly with anyone at all on the island, apart from George of course, who by now, was busy himself placing grapes in a woven basket. I strategically manoeuvred myself over to where Maroula and her friends were and casually started to fill my first basket. The boys could see what I was doing, and they were waving at me.

"Why are they waving at you Angus?"

"I think they would like to be shown by your friends how to cut the vines properly, and to know which grapes to add to their baskets."

"I understand."

With that, Maroula spoke to each of her friends and told them to show the Australians, how to cut the vines and pack grapes. For the next few hours, there were pairs of grape pickers hard at work — one Greek girl, and one Australian boy, not knowing anything of what the other was saying, but not caring much apart from being happy doing some farm work for a change.

George had a cheeky, sly grin on his face. I taught the boys how to say 'Hello George' in Greek, and every now and then, you could hear the thickest of accents yelling *"Yar soo Yorgoe"*.

Then I was hearing from the girls *"Hyello Dsorj"*. We were all in hysterics at the antics. Random comments were being thrown out now in really poor English and woeful Greek. It was difficult for the girls to wrap their mouths and tongues around our broad accent, and near impossible for the boys to roll their 'r's. But that didn't stop them from trying.

In the meantime, Maroula and I were busily trying to outdo each other in filling the greatest number of baskets. I had never before seriously picked grapes, and asked Maroula to explain to me how Greeks went about making the wine. I loved listening to her explain the whole process of filling big wooden barrels, stomping on the grapes to make juice and the fermentation stages later on. I managed to understand most of what she said but didn't dare let on that some of the words and expressions went straight over my head. I just loved to hear her speak.

Before long, the fun ended when we ran out of vines to pick. The sun was almost directly overhead for this time of the year, which meant that we had to start heading back to the campsite very soon. Instead of giving us a taste of his ouzo, George gave us some bottles to take back, together with six baskets of grapes. We tried to tell him that it was too much, but he said he had now over 200 full baskets thanks to our efforts, and that was more than he and his customers could drink in a year at the café.

Waving goodbye to George and Maroula was difficult for me. I had only met them on a few occasions, and really struggled with the language enormously. But they treated me with kindness and respect and didn't mind me mangling their dialect. They were bloody good teachers. George knew I liked Maroula, and I think she knew too. But there was nothing I could do about it, because I had a job to do, and could not stay here and pick grapes, milk sheep and drink coffee for the rest of my life. The boys were happy for the few hours of distraction too and appreciated getting to know just one tiny aspect of farm life in a Greek village, far away from what they were used to in Australia. They all wrote letters back home later on that night waxing lyrical about the girls, grapes, shitting over a clean pit, swimming and village coffee.

Luckily, the walk back to our camp site was not an arduous one. But carrying six full-to-the-brim baskets of grapes was a little tricky given that we were dead tired. Walking along the shoreline from Pesperago to Sarpi, we helped ourselves to grapes, and anyone we came across from our Battalion having a dip in the water, received some honestly worked-for fresh grapes. When we finally staggered into our tents for a well-earned rest, the lovely local fruit had commenced to work its way through our guts, and the latrines beckoned our attendance before our heads could strike a pillow! Our mistake — after an army diet of tinned beef, rock hard biscuits and billy tea, fresh fruit cleans out your intestines in a matter of minutes. Many of us had diarrhoea over in the trenches, but this bout of self-induced 'runs' seemed much more enjoyable.

To help with our medical problems, we were comforted by the arrival of about ten bags of mail, as news and letters from home were a blessing. It was a truly wonderful thing to hold in your hands a letter written by a loved one back home. It didn't matter that the news was old by the time it reached us, we read and re-read those letters dozens of times. We even read our letters to each other. I had received two letters from home and was swimming in the knowledge of gossip and news of mundane family matters.

The rest of that day was a wonderful blur, but between trips to the latrine trenches, reading our letters quietly and out loud to my mates, and a casual swim down at the shallow beach, handing out fresh grapes to all who wanted some, I truly felt like I was on holiday! For many of the others, this was just the start of a much-deserved rest, to be nursed carefully back to mental health, and to regain some woefully lacking physical strength. For the next eight weeks, we marched, drilled, marched again, lined up for inspections dozens of times, and wrote lots of letters home.

Soon after the grape-picking day, rain set in for two full days. That didn't seem to bother our officers, who at once set about designing and carrying out our drills and march routines. On many days, men were taken ill, and left for the hospitals. This was a constant daily event. We were always checked by medical staff to see if any diseases were around, and at times, we would lose some to the hospitals, while gaining ones who had recovered. Visiting our mates in hospital was a chance to cheer them up and take over some hijacked rum, found in a storage area for the Pommy officers.

The rum came in simple ceramic jugs and had been imported from England for use by English officers. One day, when a shipment arrived by barge at the jetty down from Sarpi, our tent of eight Australians was ordered to help with the unloading. This was not a particularly clever idea, since we quickly found out what we were unloading. In the day, we carried and pushed boxes and boxes of rum to a storage area nearby. At night, raiding parties of light-fingered soldiers would nip down to off load some of the rum bottles. We became very good at relieving the English of their drinks and sharing it with our mates banged up in hospital. How we weren't caught, I don't know, but it was one of the highlights of our army lives up to that point.

Apart from the daily drills and marches, we were enthusiastically practicing for some athletic events planned for October. The 8th Battalion were ultimately the camp champs in the tug o' war, beating the 7th Battalion on November 9. The reason for such a late date was simple. We were meant to be going back to the Peninsula on October 29, and we had attended a concert on October 26, inspected by General Munro on October 27, all in readiness to leave on October 29. But the weather was so bad, we couldn't leave Limnos safely, so the return voyage was postponed indefinitely. We were getting heartily sick of training. All we wanted to do was to return to the fight and be there for our mates still on the Peninsula.

But something didn't seem to be quite right, as many of us thought we could have easily gone back to ANZAC Cove. The unexpected visit by General Munro set tongues wagging, and rumours began to fly that we were set to evacuate soon. Rumours such as these were best kept quiet, but they spread like wildfire, nonetheless. On November 11, we were still at Sarpi, and inspected yet again, but this time by Lord Kitchener, General Maxwell, and General Sir William Birdwood. I was sick of hearing how good the war effort was going, and a win was surely imminent. But we all knew that the situation over in the trenches was still probably a hopeless stalemate.

When visiting our mates in hospital, we also saw many new arrivals of sick and wounded from across the water. News from them was always the same. No progress. Stalemate. Death all around. Pointless! Of course, we couldn't ask our officers about any of this. As a soldier, the first lesson you learn is to follow orders without question. Questions lead to disaster. Questions lead to your mates copping a bullet.

Anyway, the party on Limnos finally ended with our return on November 21, albeit minus our baggage! Arriving at ANZAC Cove at midnight, we disembarked and made our way to Shrapnel Gully. Within 24 hours, our baggage arrived, and we had moved to Bolton's Ridge and found some lovely earthen support trenches to sleep in.

Weather was turning poor with snow and frost. We had fortuitously been issued waterproof coats, which were a blessing from the sodden woollen grey coats now rendered useless in this weather. Instantly, as if we had never been to Sarpi, life returned to its tragic normality. Sergeant Anstee was killed, and we found ourselves back in the thick of things once more.

CHAPTER 8

MUSTAFA

I never wanted to leave my home in Limnos, but political circumstances dictated that I and my family had to go. I was only 17 years old and had never left the island. My family had lived and worked there since anyone could remember, but to the Greeks, we were still Turkish, and the reality was that they wanted to govern themselves and see the back of us.

I spoke Turkish at home with my parents and cousins, and when I was younger, with my grandparents. I was born in the village of Agios Ipatios, just outside Repanithi, and near the spot where my ancestors attacked the Limnians in 1478 at Kotsina. As a kid, I remember playing on the ancient castle site and re-enacting the battle where our side lost. My friend Eleni, who was from Repanithi, played Maroula, and pretended to kill me. I have fond memories of overacting my dying scene when her stick sword pretended to stab me in the guts. Many Greek kids from her village played with us, and we all went home afterwards as friends.

One of our favourite things do at the castle was walk down the stairs to the well at the bottom, take a drink, and walk back up. That doesn't sound very exciting I know, but we did it in the dark — no candles allowed. The entire site didn't look much like a castle, but underneath the grass, you could still see stones that once were rooms. We played in them, pretending to fight off pirates attacking from down below. My friends didn't see me as anything other than a friend who they played with. I wasn't 'the Turkish kid'. I was simply one of the village kids. Our village was only a 10-minute walk from Repanithi, and then another five minutes to Kotsina, our favourite playground.

After a few years, my family moved to a different house in Pesperago, near Portianou. I missed my friends dearly, but it wasn't long before I was playing with different kids. I didn't know as a child that we were considered outsiders to the Greek population. I spoke their language fluently, and they even gave me a Greek male name — Michali. One of the first friends I made was a girl of about my age, Maroula. When I told her of playing the game at Kotsina where I was always being killed by a Maroula, she laughed.

Growing up in this village was just as nice as the old one. Our family kept to ourselves, but I and my brothers and sisters tended to go out more and mingle with the 'Greek' kids. But our idyllic world soon came crashing down in 1908. There were tensions on the mainland to our north, and growing tension on Limnos itself. Even though I was only 13, I could sense that something was about to happen. Parts of Greece had been independent from the Ottomans since 1821, but the islands of Limnos, Tenedos and Imbros were still under Turkish control right up to 1912. I didn't really know what my father did for a job, but essentially, he was a fulltime builder and stonemason and parttime tax collector. All the Turkish families had someone whose job it was to collect tax from Greek farmers and pay the government in Turkey. While there were many Greeks who did object to their hard-earned income going to a foreign government, some did not mind as there had never been any real problems.

By mid-1912, my father could see that something was not right with the political world, and commenced arrangements to have our family moved to a village in Turkey called Madytos. He had some obscure distant relatives living there, and the village was essentially a Greek village, so he thought it might be a good enough place to make a fresh start.

Maroula and her family were friends with my family. Her father often did some work for the monastery outside our village, and when he did, I would go and help him. He was a stonemason, and I became his labourer when he was repairing stone fences, walls, wells and doing other odd jobs. In fact, it was her father who taught me to build a drystone wall by the time I was 12. Many of the walls around our village were made by him and men from Portianou, when they weren't on their own farms tending their sheep.

There was a girl in our village I was going to miss. Eleni was the first person who spoke to me when we moved to Pesperago. I am sure others did not want to talk to us because to them, we were Turks, not Greeks. It didn't matter to them that we were all born on the same island, spoke the same language, and worked the same land. We were Turks, and that is all that mattered to some. But not to Eleni and her family. It was through her that our two families became friendly. I hope it wasn't to their detriment, but they were nice people. Her father Niko and my father would often spend long periods of time discussing the world of politics, and I can remember them agreeing on most matters.

Leaving Limnos was traumatic for my brothers and sisters, but surprisingly, was equally as traumatic for my parents and cousins. Limnos had been our home, and now we were leaving. Luckily, Madytos was a very nice village, and it soon became our new home.

In Limnos, we were considered 'Turks', and in Madytos, we were called 'Greeks'. The population of this village at that time was mostly what you would call Greeks, or people with Greek ancestry. Fitting in was not a problem for us. Although newcomers to the country, our family were welcomed with open arms and before long, we had fully integrated into their way of life. Funnily enough, we came to see ourselves as being 'Greek', even though our first language at home was Turkish.

Sadly, the war on April 17, 1915 came to our doorstep, and some of the Greek people from our new village decided to leave their homes in Madytos. It was the last time I ever saw many of them again. Because we were essentially Turkish speaking, we were spared the ignominy of leaving, but inwardly, we were heartbroken yet again. By this stage of my life, I was 20, and had joined, or should I say, forced into the army. The British were apparently trying to attack the Straits, and the Turkish army was prepared for that attack. How well I remember the day on April 25, 1915 when I heard that soldiers had landed on a beach nearby, and our unit was rushed to the area. I had never fired a rifle at a living person before, but it wasn't long before I had to. It was shoot or be shot. To this day, I don't know if I actually killed anyone, but I probably have. It still haunts me.

From that morning in April right up until late November, my unit was involved in direct combat in several places, as well as helping to carry wounded soldiers back to our makeshift hospitals. Many days of combat were spent crawling around trenches, firing a few shots each day towards the enemy, digging more trenches, and setting traps for the enemy. My memories are of the heat, flies, stench of rotting human flesh, the sound of fizzing bullets and exploding bombs. Our food was terrible, our sleeping was impossible, and our weapons and clothing were in drastic need of repair or replacement. I tried as hard as I could to abstain from any fighting, and soon mastered the art of faking an injury — thanks to Maroula and all those years ago when I had to fake my own death on a daily basis at Kotsina.

The battle with the British and their allies was at a stalemate by November, and all we could do was to wish they could see it and go home. Then one day I was given a task by my commanding officer. When I say I was given a task, what I really mean is that it was told to perform a deadly task, whether I liked it or not. He told me to try to recover the bodies of two of our men who had been killed near our trench at *Bomba Sirt* a few days prior, who were still lying out of range.

'You're kidding', was not what I said, but it was what I thought.

"I'll do my best", I said, or something like that.

So early the next day, when the coldness of the night was still hanging in the morning air, and it appeared that the enemy was still asleep, or at least having breakfast, I had an idea. I grabbed a parcel of our cigarettes and attached a note to it written in French *"take with pleasure our heroic enemies. Send some milk."* I wrapped this note to the cigarettes with some string and lobbed it as hard as I could into the enemy's trench.

Soon after, another parcel was thrown towards our trench, and we ducked for cover immediately on hearing the dull thud. It didn't explode, but to our surprise, it was a similar parcel to the one we threw over, but this one had a packet of Australian dried milk powder. We laughed.

Ignoring all that we had been told, I poked my head above the parapet for a split-second, and then straight back down. No bullets. I did it again for two seconds, and I'm sure I saw a soldier on the other side do the same. Next time was for approximately five seconds, and in the enemy's trench, I could see a soldier standing up, with a white rag in his left hand. I stood up with a similar rag. We slowly walked out in full view of each other, still clutching our white rags. I said with my hands clasped together "thank you for the milk" in my language, and he said something in his. I noticed him smoking one of the cigarettes we sent over.

He was joined by another soldier and I motioned for one of my friends to come with me. We told them who we were by pointing to our chests, repeating our names, and they did the same. The first man said his name was Angus. We pointed to our two dead comrades and gestured to the enemy soldiers a desire to take our men away for a burial, and they nodded their heads. I called out for some help, and a minute later, our two dead brothers were back behind our trench lines. Angus and his friend stood and watched.

I walked over to them and asked *"Est-ce que tu parles français?"*

Both men looked at each other and shook their heads, then looked back at us.

"Parli italiano?" I asked in nervous anticipation. I don't know why I chose Italian, but I was now out of languages that I thought they may know. Angus shook his head at the Italian question, and then he asked me something, and I recognised a German word, and I shook my head.

He mumbled something else like *"blah blah blah Latine?"* and I shook my head again.

Not giving up, Angus tried one more time. *"Μιλάς ελληνικά?"*

Yes. Yes. I couldn't believe it. He spoke Greek. *"Yes, I do. How come you can speak this language?"*

He told me that his Greek wasn't that good, so I said to speak slowly and I'll do the same. He explained about his parents' language learning and teaching, and I was impressed that this Australian could speak so many languages. By this time, some more of my comrades joined us with more cigarettes, and Angus' friends did the same. You have to remember, but this was the first time we had seen each other up close and alive. We all shared cigarettes, and they had more gifts for us, like tins of food and we gave them more milk. In the meantime, the unfortunate dead comrades were taken away, but not before Angus told me something that made me very emotional.

He said that he had visited the island of Limnos for treatment on a gunshot wound inflicted by one of us. I pointed to a wound on my left side and asked him if he was responsible. We both laughed. Then he said that he visited the village Portianou in Limnos and drank a coffee before being taken by donkey to Therma for a bath.

I asked him if he drank his coffee in the café owned by a man named George, and he said yes.

"Mustafa. How do you know this? How do you know the villages on Limnos and how to you even know who lives there?"

"Angus, my siblings, my parents, my ancestors were all born on Limnos. My family had been there for over 400 years. I'm as Greek as the next person, but because of politics, I am now Turkish by ancestry and recently, by necessity. We had to leave three years ago, and my new village is not far from here. I'd love to take you to meet my family, but I don't think that will happen."

Angus told me more of his time on Limnos, recovering from a gunshot wound. I don't know if he understood all that I asked, but he was nodding as I spoke.

"I met George one day when I drank a coffee in the village, and I asked him if we could go to visit Therma for a bath. He asked me how many in our group, and when I said about six, he sent a message somewhere for a person to find transport. It wasn't long until a group of donkeys were heard baying outside the café, led by a girl about my age."

Angus and I stood and talked for what seemed like hours, but most likely was only about half an hour. All around us were our buddies looking at us, wondering how we could be so friendly.

Then Angus told me that he thought they would leave soon.

"What do you mean, leave soon?"

"I mean that I think we are going to evacuate soon."

"How do you know this? You are only a private like me."

Then he told me that very important military personnel from his side were visiting, having photos taken with the men, and the talk around the camp was that something big was planned. He'd seen them in Limnos when he was resting at Sarpi. I remember Sarpi as a village of about 10 houses, but he told me that the Allied Forces had built a temporary rest camp there. He said that top Generals had visited and walked around the camp site, but the talk was that they were planning for a withdrawal. Later that day,

I told my superiors this story as soon as I could, and they didn't say anything. I think they expected such news.

Before Angus and the rest of his group went back to their trenches, I asked him to deliver these important messages for me.

"Please find a special friend of mine, or at least, her family. The girl is Eleni, and she lives, or I hope she still does, in Pesperago, the village where we used to live. Tell her I am good, and we still think of her and her family always. But do not use my Turkish name. Say the message comes from Michali, who had to leave."

"One final thing. If you go back to Limnos, please also find George and especialy his niece Maroula who was a very good friend to me, that I am well, our family are well and that we miss them terribly. Especially Maroula's father. I left the island, and I never got to help him finish building a stone wall. Tell him — sorry."

When I mentioned Maroula, Angus seemed to be most interested in my request. But I could have been wrong. I desperately wanted to give Angus a gift to remember me by and this very strange situation. I only had one thing to offer, so before he finally returned to his trench and me to mine, I reached inside my jacket and carefully withdrew a pistol. It was a spare one I gained from the body of one of our dead soldiers. I know I could have been shot for doing this, but I was sure noone could see what I gave him.

It was at that moment that one of our officers yelled out *"finis"*, so we all retired to our own trenches and recommenced the battle. I had been so enthralled at meeting one of the 'enemy' that I completely forgot our mission — to repatriate two dead comrades, but that seems to have happened. My immediate superior officer, in his gruff manner, thanked me for my initiative and told me to get back to work — the work of firing at the enemy; the enemy we had only moments ago, shared cigarettes and tea with.

I thought I'd never see Angus again, but I was wrong. For some time now, since the middle of November on the Peninsula, it appeared Angus was right in that his troops seemed to be less interested in fighting us, and more interested in massing on their beach. We were told to conserve all ammunition, and to only use it if absolutely necessary. Sure there were random shots fired, but the number of casualties dropped to almost none on our side. The only casualties were caused by frostbite and freezing conditions making some of our soldiers slip in the mud and injure themselves. The hardest part for us was not facing a dwindling enemy, but taking an injured soldier back through our lines to the hospitals.

We became fascinated at a game they were playing on a flat ground near one of their landing beaches. In the middle of the bare ground, one person appeared to throw a ball at another person about 20 yards away, who had a piece of wood in his hands. The one with the wooden stick hit the ball being thrown at him, and then ran away to a spot near where the person who threw the ball was originally standing. All around them, other soldiers cheered, and casually looked up at the hills where I'm sure they knew we were watching. I couldn't help thinking that this game was most strange. At one stage, the soldier with the stick hit the ball very hard, and didn't run. All his friends standing around waved their straight right arm with palms faced down and yelled out at the top of their voices 'four'! One of our officers had spent some time in England as a young man, and he told us that it was an English game called cricket, and that it was the most uninteresting, pointless activity of all time. He attempted to explain the rules to us, and even after he did that, and we were watching 'cricket' being played, it still didn't make any sense. He then tried to explain the game of 'golf' to us. By then we had had enough of these strange English games.

By mid December, it was very obvious to us that the enemy was leaving. I don't know if I was elated, overjoyed or just blissfully happy that this invasion of my new country was finally coming to a close. I did see Angus one more time. It was the day or two before his countrymen left our shores. I saw him in the distance waving at us, or possibly waving at me.

Their evacuation seemed to go smoothly. It was clear to us they were leaving, but their ingenious methods of giving us the impression they were still there were wonderfully inventive and even funny. The first method was to have a few days of silence. Late November, we went for three days without a shot fired from them. So, we simply did the same — not wanting to waste any precious ammunition. They didn't even throw any tins at us. We sent an aeroplane up to spy on them, and all they could see were men lying in trenches, looking up and waving at our plane. I ventured out one night, or early morning — I can't remember which exactly, to walk around No-Man's-Land, and still no one fired at me.

Some of our soldiers ventured too close to the enemy trenches one morning and were fired on immediately. These stupid comrades of mine were convinced the enemy had left, but they were soon proved wrong. Fortunately, the enemy shots were aimed to scare and not kill.

Their best tricks to convince us they were still there were the self-firing rifles. They had two variations of these. The simplest one was a kerosene tin filled with water, with a slow leak hole punched in the bottom. Underneath it was a secondary tin attached by string to the rifle trigger. When the tin above leaked enough water into the tin below, it would slowly become heavier, and when heavy enough, pulled the trigger and fired the rifle. I loved it. What inventive combatants they were.

The other method was more elaborate. A candle was placed inside a wooden box and lit. As it burned down far enough, it burnt a string attached to a stone. When the stone dropped, it too set off a rifle shot. Luckily, the rifles were not facing us, but most were firing towards the sky.

Far more visually noticeable were the number of enemy soldiers visiting the graves of their comrades in early December. Now that I have had time to look back on this moment, it was a sad and emotional farewell by those living to those who had perished. I always felt the same when passing a grave of one of my countrymen.

Eventually, the Allied forces departed our beaches and most likely made their way towards Limnos before continuing on somewhere else to fight. When we were completely convinced that they had gone, we cautiously approached their trenches, mindful of any unexploded bombs or booby-traps. That is when we found the self-firing rifles. They left precious little for us to salvage, but we were lucky enough to find some items useful to our efforts. Little things like tins of food, the odd rifle, some ammunition, blankets, cigarettes, and the saddest of all were photos and letters pinned to walls in trenches reminding soldiers of their loved ones.

I hoped Angus managed to deliver my message to Eleni and her family, and also to Maroula and her family, that I was alive, that we were well and thinking of them. It was clear that we would never be able to travel back to the island of our birth, but the knowledge that they are alive was enough for me at the time.

CHAPTER 9

WHERE TO NEXT?
(DECEMBER 1915 – JANUARY 1916)

As I reflect on these times, I think that the most bizarre moments in my time with the 8th Battalion on Gallipoli were the 'official' burial armistice in May and the 'unofficial' version in November. However, without doubt, meeting Mustafa in No-Man's-Land was one of the truly memorable and moving moments of my life. What sort of cosmic organiser was able to bring two non-entities together in such a way!

Many soldiers who came home brought with them obscure and strange objects found on battlefields, purchased in shops, stolen, or simply being in the right place at the right time to acquire them. I knew that many of my cobbers had souvenired pistols and various other objects obtained from dead soldiers, but I bet none of them had the 'enemy' voluntarily offer a pistol as a farewell gift! I decided not to tell anyone the circumstances of how I acquired my pistol. I also kept quiet about how a Turkish soldier had information well before his officers on our eventual departure from the Peninsula.

Our evacuation from Gallipoli was planned well in advance of any of us soldiers knowing officially. But we, even as simple war fodder, could see it coming a mile off. By December 14, it was official — we were to evacuate.

Sometimes in war, stupid decisions are made that have the potential to cost lives, or at the very least, serious injury or disease. Here is an example of one of these ridiculous situations. I'll pose it as a question: If the top brass of our side had made the decision to evacuate, then why did they allow hundreds of sick and wounded soldiers to leave the confines of hospital beds on Limnos to be transported to the muddy, freezing, stinking, disease ridden trenches of Gallipoli, only to be returned a week later?

Here is another one. On December 10, there was intense shelling over our heads from a warship supported by artillery fire. What for? We were leaving soon! The Turks knew we were to leave. Mustafa was more informed than most of the idiots in charge on the Allied side. The final few days was spent silently packing up any supplies that could be taken away and destroying any equipment too large to take with us and too important to leave in the hands of the enemy.

By December 18, we were due to farewell this god-forsaken place. We felt like rats deserting a sinking ship. But what got under our skin was that we were leaving our mates buried here, and that our efforts were all for nought. Well, that is how we felt! To make the charade even more farcical, we were told to cover our boots in sand bags, so that the sound of our boots could not be heard by the Turks as we said our goodbyes at cemeteries all over the place.

One last task given to some of us in the 8th was to lay a trail of rice on the ground from the trenches down to the beach for others to follow at night. The reason given to us was that it was thought that some men filing out of their trenches in the night might get lost along the way. It must have been a great trail, as we didn't lose any men at all in the whole evacuation. When it was my turn to finally board a little boat to take us from the beach, the unmistakeable sound of a bullet fizzing past broke the otherwise stony silence. I immediately thought of Mustafa, and that he had sent me one last sound to remind me of our brief time together. Or most likely, it was a bullet from an unknown Turkish soldier telling us 'good riddance'!

We departed ANZAC Cove onboard the *SS Abbassia* and set steam for Moudros Harbour. In almost an identically planned event as our 'rest' some weeks ago, we once more found ourselves marching through the Aussie hospital lines. This time, it was different because they were bunking out too. No singing of songs as we crossed the shallow waters near Pesperago, but I did manage to look up at the billowing smoke from kitchen fires. We trudged silently towards our tents at Sarpi. Years later, one of our Corporals wrote and described us as a 'grim silent crowd of old young men, each with his own thoughts'. How true. Equally as silently, we just flopped down on a bed and slept in the gear we were wearing.

The next morning's greeting as we resumed tent life, was a severe dust storm that lasted all day, followed by rain bucketing down on the next. Back home in Ballarat, I could read rain cloud formations well. I knew when to bring my sheep in, and when to ignore the threatening clouds and stay out in the paddocks. But in Limnos, it was a different world. I was clueless as to the direction of rain and how much we would get. Thankfully, it only lasted the morning. Our reward in the afternoon for only a half morning of rain was the usual route march. That was about as welcome as 'three cheers' at a funeral. However, on our return we came 'home' to new socks and shirts, so it wasn't all bad. Given two hours off before dinner, I walked briskly along the beach to Portianou to say *'για σου'* to George. He was packing up the café when I approached the plateia.

"If it isn't the Australian, again" said one of the two old blokes sucking the life out of their shared shisha pipe.

"Do you two live here?"

One turned to his mate, then looked at me and said *"pretty much, yes. Nothing much else to do around here."*

I couldn't go on thinking of them as being two nameless old geezers that I had seen outside the café every time I happened by, so I asked them for their names. That is how I came to know Petros and Vaiyos just that little bit more. I sat down, smoked a cigarette with them, and we talked for about half an hour. I learned that they had been shepherds all their life. Both men were from Tsimandria, but married women in Portianou, so they now lived in their wives' village. That may seem like a strange situation to anyone not from this particular Greek island, but let me tell you something about Limnian property rituals. When a girl became hitched, her parents usually provided a house as a dowry item. Inheritance of housing in Limnos was mostly given to females. So, it was not uncommon for men to move away from home to live with their new wife in the village of her birth. The two villages of Tsimandria and Portianou are only a mile apart, so it was not a big deal for Petros and Vaiyos.

But fair dinkum, these two old blokes could talk! I heard about their families going back about four generations, who each member was, where they are buried, who married who, what their children's names were and anything else they could think of. I understood most of what they were saying, but every now and then, their liberal use of Turkish words completely stumped me. I tried so hard to remember some of them, if only to relay them to mum and dad.

I asked them if they remembered Mustafa and his family, and they said that they were amongst the 'nicer' Turks. When I told them about meeting him only a month ago, they were stuck for words. After a minute or so, they reverted to mumbling about various family members and how many sheep they used to milk each day.

When they finally stopped talking about themselves and heard that I was also a sheep farmer from Australia, they couldn't believe it. But when I told them my name meant a breed of cattle, coming from Scotland, they violently disagreed.

"*No Angus. Your name is Greek, and it means unique, or superbly strong.*"

Well, there you go! I thought my name was Celtic, and had been told it meant strong in that parlance, but to find out that I have a name that is both ancient Celtic and ancient Greek, left me a little amused.

I had to leave the two wise old sheep farmers to their discussions on the meanings of names because I had to see George. I entered the café as he was closing all the windows and placing the tables and chairs under cover, out of the expected rain. I wanted to speak to George privately, but two Aussie Sergeants sitting at an indoor table could see that I had some language skills, and one of them said something to me in a rather crude manner.

"You speak this language young man?"

"Just a little. My father is a teacher of European languages, and he taught me some polite conversational phrases in Greek."

George could see that I may have been playing down my language understanding and he said something that made me laugh.

Nodding in the direction of the two sergeants, he said "*Your Greek is just fine Angus. None of these sheep shaggers can even say hello, goodbye, please or thank you in our language.*"

"What did he say?" asked the more abrupt officer.

"Oh, nothing much. He just hoped you like his coffee and cakes."

I ignored the two officers and turned to speak with George.

"*George, I have some news for you. Remember a Turkish family who lived nearby in Pesperago?*"

"*There were many Turkish families who lived in that village Angus. Which family do you mean exactly?*"

"*I don't know the family name, but the young man is about my age — Mustafa, but people may have called him Michali.*"

"*Oh yes. I do remember them. They lived for a while there before leaving in 1912. How did you know that Angus?*"

"*You are not going to believe it George, but I met Mustafa not long* ago. *He is a soldier in the Turkish army, and our meeting was very strange."*

George was totally taken by surprise at this news, so I explained to him how I met Mustafa. I also told George to let people know that he is doing well, and his family are living in Madytos now, a village where there are many Greeks.

He sat and listened to my story and I thought I noticed a tear in his eye. It appears that George and Mustafa's father had become very good friends over the years and was very sad to see them leave Limnos. George fully understood the circumstances of Mustafa's family's departure, but was sad, nonetheless.

Darkness was quickly creeping in, and I was overdue at the camp, so I bid George a good night. Before I left, I asked George one final favour.

"Could you please pass this information on to Maroula for me George?"

"Of course, Angus. Maroula and his sisters were great friends. They also helped me pick grapes, just like you and your friends did some months ago."

I asked George if he knew of Eleni, Mustafa's friend in Pesperago. He said that he knew them well, and when I told him I had to find them, he said that I should simply ask anyone I see at the fountain next to the plateia. There would be so many people there who could help me.

Leaving George, I made my way on foot to the nearby village of Pesperago, which happened to be on the way to Sarpi. Stopping at the fountain, I could see some older men sitting outside a closed café, so I approached them. Seeing an Aussie soldier walking their way, they started to get up out of their wooden chairs and move away, probably not knowing if I was friend or foe.

"Don't go away. Please, I am looking for Eleni and her family who live near here. I have a message from Michali. George from the café in Portianou suggested I come here."

"George! Why didn't you say so? Follow me" said one of the two men. He led me to a house just near the village square and called out to an older man inside.

"Hello Niko. This foreigner here has a message from Michali. George from Portianou sent him."

I was half expecting to be told to go away, but Niko came outside, and the two men had a very quiet talk, and I could not hear what they said.

"Come inside young man."

The house was the typical stone construction style that seemed to be prevalent all over the island. Being late Autumn or early Winter, the weather was exceptionally cold, and inside had a rather nice fire burning in a stove. I was offered a chair near the oven and Niko spoke.

"You have a message from Mustafa, no? I know that outside this house, everyone knew him as Michali, but we called him Mustafa."

I explained who I was and the circumstances of me meeting Mustafa at Gallipoli. He was so delighted at hearing this news, he called for his daughter to come inside the kitchen, so she could meet me. Eleni walked into the room and I could tell why Mustafa wanted to get a message to her. She had a beautiful smile, bright green eyes, and pitch-black hair; she was gorgeous! More importantly, Eleni was overjoyed to hear that her childhood friend was alive.

It was at this stage that they suddenly realised how strange it was that I spoke their language. Again, I had to further explain my parents, and my rather unusual childhood.

"No Turkish person ever did our family any harm Mister Angus. They had only ever been good to us. We know that others were very unhappy with the Turks here, but Mustafa's family were very nice."

I got the impression that they may be Turkish sympathisers, and therefore possibly in the minority on Limnos, and desperately wanted to keep this news private. I understood them perfectly and thanked them for trusting me.

"Would you like to see where he lived?" asked Niko.

Agreeing to this request, Niko, Eleni and I left the warmth of the kitchen and walked the 40 or so yards to where Mustafa had lived with his family in the village. I remember the house well, because on entering through the front door, it appeared that the family had only just left. There was crockery still on the kitchen table, glasses on shelves, and two beds made up waiting for someone to lie in them. A cupboard under the stairs had items stacked inside, and there were some homemade objects, like a leather fly swat hanging on the wall, shoes under the table and some clothes on a chair. Kitchen utensils were still hanging on metal hooks from beams of wood above our heads. It certainly did not look like a house where a family hadn't been living in for over three years.

I thanked them for showing me where Mustafa lived, and wished them a good evening. I could easily imagine him living here, and I wondered what may have happened if Mustafa and Eleni had been able to stay together. Bloody wars and conflicts. They get in the way of normal people getting on with lives!

I didn't know how long we were scheduled to remain on Limnos, but I was beginning to like this place. Even though the island and its people were considerably poor, much poorer than I was accustomed to, there was a simplicity about their lifestyle that I liked. I had an increasing urge to return here one day, but the pragmatic part of me knew that this was highly unlikely. Probably because I would have to survive the war first, and that was not yet a done deal.

One day before we departed this island, I accidently bumped into a Padre from the 22nd Battalion casually walking around Sarpi, a chap by the name of T. P. Bennett. I normally wouldn't take any notice of the religious leaders, but there was something strangely familiar about this man. I asked him where he was from, and I remember him saying Learmonth and Ballarat as well as some other places. I had heard about this man from some of my mates and some of the boys I met from the 22nd who said this man lived with them in the dugouts at Shrapnel Gully. We got talking, and I said that I was also from Ballarat, and I had heard of his heroics on the battlefield. According to many sources, and although he was not on active service, this Padre actually went out into the battlefield to check on the names of the recently dead. He did this in full view of Johnny Turk, and they didn't shoot at him. I asked him if he buried some of these men at night, and he said "yes, I did." Later that day, I walked with 'TP' to George's Café and bought him a coffee, some cake and a small plate of sour cherries. I asked him why he wrote down the names of the recently departed, and he said that he had to know who they were so that he could write letters home to their families.

A few days prior to Christmas day, our company was given orders to prepare for a departure at very short notice, so any chance of leaving the camp area was virtually impossible. The weather was lousy, and all we could do was sit inside our freezing cold tents and wait. Writing letters home was out of the question because it was impossible to hold a pencil. Then, on Christmas Eve, we discovered the plans for leaving had been scrapped, so we were issued with our Christmas 'billies'. This package contained a much-loved pudding, some Melbourne biscuits, shirts, knitted socks, handkerchiefs, pencil and paper, tobacco and cigarettes, a pipe, razors, pickles, tinned fruit, sauces, cocoa and coffee. The ironic gift in this package was a map of Gallipoli around the tin saying "this bit of the world belongs to us". For some of the men in our battalion, this hurt very much, as we had to leave so many of our mates buried in Gallipoli. Those poor buggers would not be celebrating Christmas, so we shared many quiet moments thinking of, and talking quietly about, our departed comrades. I think the people who originally packed these 'billies' thought we would be opening them on Gallipoli, not in some tent on a Greek island waiting to go somewhere else. The 'billies' contained just enough of home for us to really think we were back in Australia. For me, the best gift was the new woolen socks. Our feet were nearly frozen, so an additional pair of new socks was heaven-sent. We felt like kids around a family Christmas tree opening the contents of our stockings. Apparently, over in the hospitals, our nurses gave each soldier in their care, a 'billy' in a stocking.

To replace the usual hats of a Christmas celebration, we wore the 'billy' lids on our heads as long as we could, until being told to remove them by an overzealous sergeant. Bah, humbug!

Christmas day was spent in a parade, a march past a General, and a half day holiday. Our tent buddies just sat in and around our tent, smoking new tobacco in a new pipe, writing the odd letter home, and starting an improvised game of cricket down by the beach. Until the New Year, we did pretty much the same thing each day. Route marches, half day holidays and cricket. We still had to be ready to evacuate. That day arrived soon enough. Orders to leave came on New Year's Day.

On January 4, 1916, the 8th Battalion departed Limnos aboard the *Empress of Britain*, bound for Cairo in Egypt. Nothing too alarming about the seas, but something we were warned about scared the 'shit' out of us. We had been told not to smoke on deck after sunset and don't show any lit matches, and to muffle all lights. Some brave private dared ask 'why', and casually, the answer was equally short — 'submarines in the area'!

CHAPTER 10

YOUNG CHARLIE

(AUGUST 1916)

I should say at this point that I did not plan that this story would be a personal diary explaining all my war experiences. Mostly, these deeds were extremely pedestrian, and indeed there is no way that I could satisfactorily paint a meaningful word description for you that would do the profundity of the occasion true justice. I have never read anything about war that in any way describes the true horror of what people can do to others in the name of a righteous cause.

Why I am writing this account is that rather than dwell on the events of the time, I want to record what stands out for me, all these years later, of the people that I have met along the way. They just sort of stick in my memory. Some of these people I have known now for over 40 years, and then there were some who I barely knew for 40 hours. Charlie Church is one such character I met. Charlie, sadly, is not with us anymore. He is buried somewhere in France near *Pozieres*, where the 8th Battalion was fighting in August 1916.

Pozieres was the stuff of nightmares, and in truth, to many of my cobbers, it still is. It took me a long time to forget most of it, but from time to time, I remember bits of it like it happened yesterday. It is not only the sights, but the sounds and smells are the things I can't seem to shake. The sounds of heavy German bombing, gunshots, explosions and blokes screaming. The smell of the dead and decaying in stinking, hot conditions. The biting from lice and our uncontrollable urge to scratch unreachable part of our bodies. Later on, we were told that the *Pozieres* battle was a victory to our side. It sure as hell didn't seem like it at the time.

In late July, the 8th was ordered to seize, occupy, and take control of *Pozieres*, at least as far as the cemetery to the north. I'm sure *Pozieres* would have been a beautiful village in its past, but what we saw of it was a fair dinkum disaster. Buildings, roads, and houses were no more than a pile of construction rubble, occupied by unfriendly Germans, who were trying to keep us out. There didn't seem to be a local in sight.

It was early August, and I found myself relaxing with my back to a trench wall, bombs whizzing overhead and bullets fizzing past every few seconds. Next to me was a rather fresh-faced young lad in what appeared to be a clean, new uniform. He looked like he had seen a ghost.

"Don't worry mate. It will be all over by teatime, and then we can go back to the farm and take a dip in the dam. Might even have time for tea and scones."

"How can you joke at a time like this?" he nervously screamed at me. Obviously, he was a new chum, and hadn't seen a battle before. I quickly calmed him down by asking mundane questions like 'who are you', and 'where are you from?' He said he was from the 15th Reinforcements and they only arrived yesterday.

"Don't worry cobber. We'll look after you."

I couldn't help but notice how young he looked to me. It may have been that I was now a veteran of over a year of fighting and I must have seemed to him to be as old as his father. I hadn't looked in a mirror for a while, but I must have aged. Having your mates blown to the shithouse and Germans trying to part your head from your neck does things to a man. It ages you.

Anyway, Charlie, as he was called, said he was from Port Melbourne, but originally from the 'old country'. "My parents are dead, and I thought I might as well do my bit over here." I had a sneaking suspicion that maybe he wasn't being truthful with me, but I was in no position to have a detailed, in-depth conversation. First, we had to get back to our main trench without being killed.

"Follow me mate, and for god's sake — keep your head down and don't look behind when I say 'run'. Got it?"

"Yeah. Got it."

"Run!"

He took off at a rate of knots and I had to yell at him to keep going, while I dragged my sorry bum behind by a few yards. We made it to our trench, and I found Charlie sitting down grinning from ear to ear.

"Try to keep up old timer."

I immediately liked the boy, and I introduced him to the others. But introductions soon turned sour when we couldn't find one of our officers. Normally, we wouldn't be too concerned, as he could have been 10 yards away and we wouldn't know. But something didn't seem right.

Captain Heydon was always the one who survived, and he was the one who managed to get us to safety. About two hours later, he was found, buried but still alive in a trench not far away from us. No one could believe that he could survive such an internment, but within a few minutes, the medics were working frantically to get him to a dressing station. The blokes who found him said that he was lying alongside a group of others who had died. That about summed up Captain Heydon. Not even being buried alive could kill him. We all felt a little better about ourselves, thinking that we too could be immortal.

All this didn't seem to faze Charlie at all, because he hadn't formed any lasting bonds yet with those of us who had been here a while. That night, we slept where we sat, and thankfully, the bombs were kept to a minimum.

For the next week or two, our jobs were to dig jumping-off trenches near Sausage Valley in preparation for an all-out attack. Charlie and his crew from the 15th Reinforcements took to it like a duck to water. The assault was to use a new method of attack called a 'creeping barrage'. None of us had ever heard of it, and to this day, I doubt many of our officers had ever heard of it either, let alone having practiced it.

Let me explain my understanding of the difference between a 'standard barrage' and a 'creeping barrage'. The standard barrage was when our heavy artillery bombed the shit out of the Germans for as long as the supply of shells lasted, in order to demoralise them so that we could waltz in and take their land. The theory was that they would be so startled at our tactics, they were supposed to simply throw down their guns and run away. However, someone clearly must have given the Hun our bombing manual because they were doing the same thing to us! End result, stalemate!

Some genius in command, probably 15 miles behind the front line who slept in a feather bed, thought it would be a good idea to make a variation on that theme, much like the third movement of a symphony really. They would limit the barrage to a minute or so and concentrate in a small area near the front. The Germans would move back to avoid the barrage, and we would creep forward a set distance, about 150 yards. The barrage would then focus on the next area, and this was to be repeated until we had taken and occupied their trenches and before they had time to react. Bloody great in theory don't you think? For it to work, you need a whole lot of circumstances to fit neatly in place and nothing to go awry.

We didn't know it at the time, but no Australian troops had ever advanced under a creeping barrage before that day. I suppose when this was planned and practiced, the soldiers who were part of the practice were doing so on a neatly manicured lawn, all running 150 yards and lying down again, while some toy bombs were sounded to imitate reality. Then on a whistle, they would all get up, run in a straight line and after the required distance, fall flat on their faces on soft grass. It is one thing to run with a bayonet stuck on the end of your rifle at an imaginary enemy, but try doing it when that enemy is real, and wants to shoot you in the head, or worse, in the meat and two vegies!

OK. Now for reality. For the creeping barrage plan to be successful, all officers had to know when to run, how far to run, have trenches ready to fall into, and the artillery had to know exactly when to stop, readjust their aim, and start again. We poor bastards, running for our lives also had to know these things.

Here is what happened. First, the ground was littered with holes, dead soldiers, unexploded bombs, uneven surfaces, bits of trees and exploded buildings. We were dodging bullets and the barrage was not timed exactly to plan. Some men were slower than others, some faster. The slower ones were picked off by the enemy, some of the faster ones arrived at an enemy trench to be immediately taken prisoner, and the barrage ended early, allowing the enemy to re-group. If a whistle had been blown, it probably couldn't have been heard, even if the bloke blowin' it was next to you blowin' it in your bloody ear!

All the while, Charlie and his new chums were probably thinking, 'who came up with this brilliant plan?' I know this because I was thinking the same thing. Charlie actually said that to me during a lull, but I told him to keep his private thoughts to himself, keep his trap shut, and to trust the officers and those whose orders they were relying on, at all times. I told him that we aren't allowed to question anything. I might say that the first time we tried to creep up on the enemy, it failed dismally, and we lost a lot of men.

One of our platoon sergeants yelled at the top of his voice "Come on back lads, it's no good." We didn't need to be told twice. Charlie and I had reached about 200 yards from the German trenches. We heard the retreat order, but others didn't, and advanced at a pace. It was a shemozzle. Charlie, myself and two others found ourselves stuck in No-Man's-Land. All I could say to the others was "keep yer heads down lads, and maybe we'll make it through the night."

I don't know what the official instructions or orders were now, but I knew we were trapped. Then our barrage started up again. In a shell hole next to us, with their bayonets facing towards the enemy, some of our boys jumped up and ran into the thick smoke hovering over the German trenches. At least our bombs were landing in the right places.

Charlie asked me if I thought we should go too. Within a heartbeat, we four lads took off like we were on the blocks at the final of the Stawell Gift. The next I remember was diving headfirst into the German trench, head butting a German in the guts. I don't know who was more startled. I elbowed him in the face, catching him on the chin and he fell back, unconscious. His startled mates sat about three yards away and were equally stunned to see five or six of our boys join me in the trench.

One of our boys lobbed a bomb straight at them, and it seemed that they didn't want to stick around to hear the bang. Many of the Germans took off as fast as we ran at them. Some stayed to defend their trench, but met with stiff resistance from the Aussies, and of those who stayed behind, sadly, none would ever see their mothers again.

I remember, when my heart slowed down to about 200 beats per minute, I looked for Charlie. He wasn't in the trench. I could not look for him or the others outside because putting your head up was a sure bet that it would soon be detached. Call me old fashioned, but I had grown rather attached to my head! We could peek out a few inches above the top of the trench, but it was not a pretty sight. No-Man's-Land was littered with dead and dying from both sides. Some of the Germans were so disoriented, they ran the wrong way, and were accidently killed by their own fire. I spent the next few hours cradling my rifle, half expecting Charlie and his stupid grin to come diving over the wall.

Just before sunrise, we decided we had to make it out of that German trench and make it back to our side. On a standard three count, we made a beeline for our side and ran as fast as our fading legs would carry us before diving into a shell hole once more. This time, no one was hit, but one of the lads did get a nasty ding on the side of his helmet.

It was then that I saw Charlie. It was the same shell hole we had left from a few hours earlier, only he was going no-where. It looked like as soon as he jumped up, machine gun fire put him straight back down again. Now he had two mates lying with him, both Germans who had made the mistake of running in the wrong direction. One was clearly dead, but one was still barely alive. Speaking some German, I asked him if he was OK, and he said, *"No. Not really."* I could see that he had a big hole in his guts, and his uniform was now oozing bright red.

"Don't worry mate. I'll make sure you get back home."

He managed a little smile, followed by a stifled laugh. *"What's so funny?"* I asked him.

"I'm dying in a trench with an Australian asking me if I am OK, and he's speaking my language. You can't see the funny side of that?"

Before I could ask him his name, he coughed up a large bile of blood, and breathed his last. His head was on my lap, and now I was wearing his insides.

Within a few days, our battalion, or what was left of it, bivouacked overnight at *Brickfields*, were billeted briefly at *Warloy*, and then marched on to *Rubempre* and *Amplies*. Poor Charlie was still probably lying in that shell hole in No-Man's-Land. I didn't get to know him very well, but in that time, we had a laugh or ten in the face of death all around us. It was years later that I learned his body was located and now lies buried in the military cemetery on a hillside at *Ovillers*, just outside *Pozieres*, near where he fell. I was happy with this knowledge, but the next bit of news deeply saddened me. Like hundreds of others, Charlie had lied to get into the army. He wasn't from Melbourne, and his parents were not dead. They were very much alive and living in Adelaide. Charlie is listed as having died on August 18, 1916. On September 15 of that year, he should have been home in Adelaide with his parents and mates, celebrating his 16th birthday!

CHAPTER 11

THE END

(SEPTEMBER – OCTOBER 1918)

All of us could see the end of this conflict coming soon. However, why the Germans would not recognise it I will never know. Why did they continue to fight, kill, and be killed when they could not possibly win?

It was late September and the second group of men who had been in the 8th Battalion since the beginning were given furlough to Australia. These were the remaining men who enlisted in 1914. We called them the three figure men, and they deserved to go home. How we wanted to be going with them, but it was not meant to be at that time for us.

The departure was not handled well, and we never really got a chance to farewell some of our mates. We had been through so much together, and now they were gone. But it was no different to losing a mate who one minute was next to you, and the next, he copped a bullet in the guts. This had happened so many times to all of us, I couldn't see why some of the men were upset at not farewelling live mates. Maybe it was because they were alive, and we knew we may never see them again. I don't know. Much uneasiness was now spreading. After this latest group to suddenly depart, those of us remaining were put on a train for *Longpre Les Corps Saints*, which is so close to England, you could almost smell the bangers and mash. The Germans, bless them, tried to bomb our train, and they very nearly succeeded. After one such bombing alarm, the train stopped, we checked out any possible damage, and when the 'all clear' was given, we were told to re-board. For some unexplainable reason, I stumbled a few yards away from our carriage when I slipped and fell into a small, year old bomb crater. Not thinking I was hurt and hearing joyful guffaws from my mates who were belly laughing so hard that I thought they would burst a collective hernia, I somehow got back on board my carriage.

"You don't look too flash, Angus", said someone. Indeed, I wasn't too good at all, having managed to dislocate my right shoulder. A nurse on the train looked at it, strapped on a few bandages and a sling and told me to get it checked by a doctor when we arrived at out next stop.

Bugger me, but it was so bad, that the doctor said I had to go to hospital in England, which thankfully was not far away geographically. It was still an epic journey by train and ship, and there was still a war raging around us. Now it was my turn to farewell mates as I started on the next leg of my life's adventure, which was to start in Lindfield, a Red Cross Auxiliary Hospital in Sussex.

I thought I only had a dislocated shoulder, but doctors at Lindfield managed to find a whole litany of other medical problems with me. I won't bore you with my medical issues, but I was destined to stay in the ward for a month or three, and not the week or two originally imagined.

The hospital was the ground floor of what was the King Edward Hall in Sussex. Given the places I had slept in over the previous four years, this was a bloody palace. If I could only ignore the moaning of the blokes next to me in our ward in their iron beds on wheels, and not more than two feet away from me, then this was luxury. Our angels, the nurses, attended us with all the skill and care you would expect, and the doctors were also nice. In the middle of our ward was a wooden table that seated about a dozen. Those of us who could get out of bed would eat there, and those that couldn't, we'd take their food to them in bed.

Conversations were wonderful. Who are you, where are you from, where have you been, and when are you going home? What we didn't talk about were the mates we had lost and horrific things we'd all experienced. On good days, we were allowed to sit outside the Hall, watch and chat to passers-by, and enjoy the view of the pond. On bad days, we'd just sit up in our beds, or at the community table playing card games and chess.

My recovery was progressing well. All my minor ailments were clearing up and my shoulder was now almost able to withstand lifting a few pounds of weight over my head. OK, when I say minor ailments, I had pneumonia, and had lost a lot of muscle, I had chills, a cough, ringing in my ears, laboured breathing, body aches, chest pains and blue skin, but who in my battalion didn't? I thought I had battle fatigue, but it really was much more serious. On a number of occasions, I was told by the nursing staff that I was a very lucky lad to have been sent here when I was. I even remember one morning in the early days waking up to a couple of doctors standing over me, and one whispered to his mate "he should be dead".

As each man progressively improved, one by one we departed, saying our goodbyes, and offering hopes and wishes for the future. Soon enough, the hospital was to be returned once more to the community as a village hall, thus ending its contribution to the recovery of men like me. I would not be sad to go. However, I had one more duty to perform in England before sailing home to Australia.

CHAPTER 12

GRANNY MAE

(OCTOBER 1918 – NOVEMBER 1918)

My Grandmother Mae, wife of Herbert, still lived in Ely. Sadly, Grandpa Herbert was no longer with us, but I desperately wanted to see Mae. We had never met in person. I had written to her and received countless reply letters throughout my life before the war, and even received a letter or two from her during my service to King and Country. I felt as though I knew her intimately, through the stories told by my parents. I would have loved to have met Herbert, but that was not to be.

The trip by steam train from Essex to Ely took two full days. After trying to sleep on train platforms and inside waiting rooms at stations, I had this sudden urge to go back to Essex and find my warm ward bed. Arriving in Ely in the early morning, I made my way on foot to the Cathedral and asked for directions to Mae's house. Luckily, it was not far away, and after a brief walk around the church and its grounds, within 20 minutes I was standing at the front gate of a small home with smoke billowing from a chimney. The sweet smell of home cooked something was wafting through the air, and it was impossible to tell which house or houses it was coming from. Mae was not expecting me, and I had no way of knowing if she would be home. Hitching up my trousers, I opened the creaking gate and carrying my swag, walked about 10 paces to the front door.

A big brass knocker echoed throughout the house, and I heard the shuffle of footsteps coming down a corridor towards the front door. The door opened inwards, and I stood behind a screen door looking into the eyes of my Grandmother Mae. We stood and stared at each other before I got up the courage to open the screen door, and then received the biggest, warmest, and strongest hug of all times. I knew then where mum got her hugging ability from. We were a family of huggers, and proud of it.

Granny Mae finally released me from her vice-like grip and asked me to follow her to the kitchen. A fire was burning in the oven, and she had made scones. She could see that I was salivating and pulled a tray of freshly baked ones from the oven and made me a cup of tea. I could see where mum got her looks from as she was the spitting image of my oldest sister Rosie.

She wanted to hear about mum and dad and my sisters, and I wanted to hear all about mum's family. We talked for the rest of that day. I think I ate all but one or two of the scones, and drank so much tea, I thought I'd burst. I had not been this happy since before leaving Melbourne. I stayed for two days, and in that time, met a number of my extended family. It was wonderful. One of mum's brothers came to visit Mae, and so it was that Uncle Raymond was to be my family tour guide for the next few days.

I haven't told you much about my father's family, apart from his mother Dorothy and father Angus. Like Mae, I had never met my father's parents, but sadly I was unlikely to see them on this trip as they had passed away some five years ago. I asked Mae if she knew of the family they worked for nearby, and she said Uncle Raymond would love to take me to see their old house.

Dad had told me about this place, but it in no way was it like his verbal description. It was so much grander! We entered the main gates and turned right to the house next to them where my father once lived. Luckily, someone was home. I enquired if they remembered the people who had managed this property many years ago, by the name of Harrison. They said yes, and I said that I was Angus and Dottie's son. They asked us to come inside and we sat at the kitchen table where my father had so many meals, and where my grandparents lived for many years.

I wanted to learn about the landowners, and they asked me if I would like to meet them. I said yes, and within a few minutes was standing, gazing up at a house bigger than King Edward Hall in Sussex. The grandeur of the house was breathtaking, and looking around the front garden, I could see the statues where dad played as a child, and where the seeds were sown for his future.

Knocking on the front door, and might I say, the knocker made Granny Mae's look decidedly insignificant, a rather mature woman of about the same age as my father came to the door. We introduced ourselves and we were ushered inside. Uncle Raymond and I entered and followed the lady who greeted us at the door to a sitting room. She disappeared and a short while later, another lady of about the same age came to meet us, beaming from cheek to cheek.

"Are you Charles' boy?"

"Yes, I am."

"I am Lady Cynthia Fotheringham-Smyth, and I am guessing your father has not told you about me!"

"I'm sorry, but alas, no."

"Your father and I grew up here. Even though his parents were employees of our family, I saw Charlie as my dearest friend. We used to play outside for hours, and he loved coming inside to view the family paintings and read books from our library."

I was hearing stories about dad as a boy which he seemed to have glossed over somewhat. I was fascinated by Lady Cynthia.

"My husband has not come back from the war yet, but we are expecting him to be here any week now. Were you in the war Angus?"

It was at this point I told her about my experiences, or a severely abridged version anyway, and she told me about Captain Smyth of the British army. He fought at Gallipoli in 1915, and like me, was wounded there, spent time on Limnos recuperating, and in various other theatres of war. I immediately liked him but could not help thinking that her descriptions of him made him seem an awful lot like my father.

We talked for hours, and after my third cup of tea, Raymond and I had to make a retreat before the night light evaporated for our trip home to Mae's house. Before we left, Lady Cynthia took us for a quick tour of the 40 roomed home, and I could now picture my father here as a goggle-eyed boy in Wonderland. While we were walking towards the door to leave, Lady Cynthia put her hand on my shoulder and whispered into my left ear.

"Tell your father that 'Cyn' has not forgotten."

Not really knowing what to say, I agreed, and waved our goodbyes as Uncle Raymond and I descended the stone steps to an awaiting carriage. Lady Cynthia must have loved dad!

"I think she had the hots for Charlie, Angus!"

"I think you might just be onto something Uncle."

I remained in Ely with Mae for a few more days before I reluctantly had to leave to secure a passage home to Australia. That week with Mae was the best medicine a young man could take. Ely has a bush telegraph better than anything country Victoria could offer, and I met countless cousins, uncles, aunties, and old family friends from Cambridge University. One of the old dons who Grandpa Herbert taught with must have picked up on mum's questioning ability and he too grilled me on languages just like mum would do with dad when he visited all those years ago. I was living and participating in my own family history. Not only mum's family but meeting distant relatives of my father's and Lady Cynthia's made me appreciate much more where my parents were from, and where I was from. Strangely, I felt like I was home.

The morning before I left Ely, I was taken to the University of Cambridge, which is strange to say really, because the whole village is pretty much the university. The old don I met the day before had arranged for one of his students to show me around the campus, and he pointed out the house where mum lived.

"Would you like to see inside Angus?"

"Yes please. Will it be possible?"

"I don't see why not."

The house was now lived in by one of the professors in the European language faculty who knew my father and who also studied under Grandfather Herbert! He agreed to show me the reading room and the study where my father would have duelled with Herbert. The professor told me he only came once to the house, due to the questioning of a particularly feisty young woman — my mother.

The second highlight for me was taking a punt on the Cam River. To be in the very places where my parents first met was a wonderful experience. Considering what I had witnessed in the past four years, this was memorable for all the right reasons.

Parting from Granny Mae was difficult, as I knew that we would never meet again. She gave me one more big, warm family hug to go on with. Now, my focus was on getting home to Ballarat to see mum and dad, my sisters and my sheep. Would they remember me — the sheep that is! I bid my farewells to Uncle Raymond and made my way to the Ely train station for a return trip to London.

At this time, I had almost completely forgotten it, but the war had not officially ended. My cobbers in the 8th would probably still be in France somewhere, and here I was swanning around the English countryside on trains, carriages, visiting palatial mansions, cathedrals, talking to relatives and taking tea with freshly baked scones! On the journey into London by train, the jolt I needed to remind me once again that we were still at war was the soldier in a seat not far from me. He obviously had a leg missing, bandages on both arms and head, and was accompanied by a nurse. I asked him where he had been, and he told me that six months ago, he was blown up in France somewhere. He couldn't tell me exactly because he'd forgotten all about the incident. He had a huge head wound, and I'm sure it affected his memory. His nurse told me he forgot many things, but his outlook on life was surprisingly good.

"He knows he has lost many mates, but he seems to have lost none of his will to live. I'm taking him home to London now to be with his wife and child, who he hasn't seen in over three years."

He then blurted out "Hey Australian. What are you doing on this train?"

I told him that I too had spent time in a Red Cross Hospital in Sussex, but I have just been visiting relatives in Ely. Once he found out that my heritage was English, he opened up about all sorts of things, but the one that stuck with me was his association to Ely.

"My father once worked in Ely, as a stableman for a Lord and Lady. He loved the work, and once he had saved enough money, moved to London, met mum and had us kids. He loved working there and once a year, he returns to visit them."

"Do you remember the name of the family?"

"No, sorry, but he said the house had lots of statues all over the front lawn, and what got him was that they had some in the stables area!"

It was at that point I mentioned that my father once lived on site of a house just like the one he described.

"Was his lordship a Captain Smyth by any chance, married to Lady Fotheringham-Smyth?" I asked.

"Don't know about Captain, but Fotheringham sounds familiar. Dad used to tell me stories about the daughter of the house and a boy whose parents managed the estate, who played a lot in and around the statues, especially the ones around the stables. They would often get in his way, but he loved hearing them make up stories of famous horse battles of ancient Rome and Carthage and pretending to ride chariots around the Circus Maximus."

"Did he ever mention the boy or girls name?"

"That's easy. His name is the same as mine. Pleased to meet you. My name is Charles, but please call me Charley."

I couldn't even get my name out because I was choked with emotion.

"Angus. My name is Angus."

"My son is Angus. What a coincidence. My father suggested that name because of the man who lived at the house in the farm manager's cottage. He always told me that he was the most kind, fair and generous man he had ever met. So, we named our son Angus."

I asked him if I could give him a hug, and he didn't seem to mind, but was slightly suspicious. At this time, the nurse, who had remained quiet the whole time, spoke.

"My brother here is a little lacking in manners. My name is Dorothy. Pleased to meet you Angus from Australia."

Shit. This couldn't get any weirder.

"Don't tell me. Your father suggested a name for you too, maybe after Angus' wife?"

"How could you possibly know that?"

"Charley, Dorothy. You are not going to believe it, but you are referring to my grandfather Angus and my father Charles, and my grandmother Dorothy, or Dottie as everyone called her."

Now it was Dorothy's turn to give me a big hug. I'm sure the rest of the people on that train thought we were nuts. By now, we were all crying. One thing Dorothy told me about her brother's condition was that he often would cry for no reason, but he didn't appear to be sad. Well? He was certainly crying now. We all were. He had a reason to cry.

For the remainder of the trip to London, we constantly chatted about family, but conversation drifted into war matters. As it turns out, Dorothy was a qualified nurse who spent time in military hospitals in Egypt and France but was medically discharged a year ago after a bout of severe dysentery. Her brother had been badly wounded and was repatriated home. After she had recovered, Dorothy volunteered to look after him and let him recuperate before he returned home. She was used to seeing soldiers in his condition, but Charlie's wife and children weren't. She didn't want them not to see their husband and father so badly disfigured. But after nearly six months, she thought that it was now the right time for him to go home.

I wished so much that my father was here right now to hear all of this, and to meet these two siblings. He would be so proud. So too would my grandparents. They'd be tickled pink!

Charley showed me all his wounds by asking Dorothy to undo his bandages. His injuries must have been bad, but at least now, the skin had scarred, and the healing process was well under way. He proudly showed me where his left leg used to be and told me that he was quite attached to that leg. I laughed so hard, I nearly cried. I don't think Dorothy quite understood a soldier's humour, but then maybe she just didn't think it was funny. I dropped my trousers, lifted my shirt and showed him my bullet wounds.

"Here is where the bullet went in, and here is where it had done enough damage and decided to leave."

He laughed at how pathetic my scars looked compared to his. I laughed again and told him that he was the wound winner. I told him I had just recently recovered from a dislocated shoulder and a minor bout of pneumonia that nearly killed me, but that didn't leave any scars to show off in this game of *'mine's bigger than yours'*.

The train porter walked past as I was undressing and tersely asked me to put my clothes back on. But when I told him that I received my wounds in the line of duty, bugger me if he didn't drop his dacks, bent over to touch his toes, and showed us a wound to his bum.

"Got this courtesy of Jerry in France a year and a half ago."

"Thut's noothin! Check this out" said Charlie in a fake northerner accent as he once again showed us his left leg stump."

Try to imagine the scene on the train ride from Ely to London, where three war veterans, in various stages of undress, were showing their wounds to each other. By now, Dorothy was laughing, and so too were some of the other travellers. One of the other passengers, an older man approached us, loosened his belt, lifted up his shirt and showed a huge scar on his belly.

"Boer War boys. Bayonet in the guts. But you should have seen the other chap! All I can say is that he'll never play the violin again! Come to think of it — he'll not be doing much ever again."

The porter left in a hurry, and just as quickly returned with four glasses and a bottle of rum. The bottle was a ceramic jug with the letters SRD embossed below the lip, and underneath, a maker's mark from George Skey in Tamworth, Staffordshire. Bugger me, but it was the same bottle type we used to pinch from the British at Sarpi back in 1915! Apparently, the letters on the bottle mean 'Supply Reserve Depot', but we all called it 'Soon Runs Dry'.

"Lads, I shouldn't be doing this, but here's something to make the last few miles go a bit quicker."

By now we were all dressed, and sipping on a rather strong rum, courtesy of Ken the porter, and drinking to the memory of lost mates. Morty the Boer War veteran had joined us, and he was a lovely older man with stories not unlike ours. Dorothy joined in as well and had quite a few stories of her own. We hadn't really thought of a nurse's perspective before, and to be perfectly honest, they were as horrifying as ours.

"Here Charley. Give me that glass. Ken — some rum please. Here is to my mates, gone but definitely not forgotten. Cheers."

Pointing to her scalp, Dorothy said something quite profound.

"In here are the scars I'll carry for the rest of my life. I think you all will too. No one can see these, but we know they exist."

With that, we clinked our glasses and stopped to think of all the women killed in the war, and the nurses like Dorothy who had put their lives on the line helping us. I had visions through my tears of that first angel I saw on Limnos when I was brought in from the hospital ship and lying on a sheet of canvas over a rock and pebble mattress. I remembered the Canadian nurse Mary, whose grave site I visited in Portianou.

We were all respectful of each other, and to the passengers around us. Morty quietly reminded us that some of these people may have lost sons and daughters in the war, so we should always think of not only ourselves, but those around us too.

Ken took our glasses, placed the ceramic rum bottle back in his knapsack, and we returned to our seats for the final few minutes of the journey. Once the train eased gently into the station for its final resting place for the evening, we helped Charley out onto the platform where a wheelchair was found for us by Ken. Morty came up to us and wished us all the best, and he shuffled away. I will never forget him. Ken waved goodbye from the carriage door, and Dorothy pushed Charley out onto the street to catch a carriage. We hugged once more, and I promised to write to them once I returned home.

I know I grew up in Melbourne and Ballarat, but I felt strangely at home here in London, and even more so in Ely. Now I had my own memories of the places mum and dad talked about; my grandparents, and now my new friends. What could life possibly throw at me now?

It wasn't long — one day later in fact, that my philosophical question was answered in a most surprising way. I was in London when the Armistice on November 11th was signed by the Germans and Allies in a place where only two months prior, I had been with the 8th Battalion. I don't know if I felt happy or sad, which is a strange thing to say now. I should have felt happiness, but I truly felt sad at the tremendous loss of life on all sides, and for what? I felt relieved if anything.

It was not hard to find Australians in London after the Armistice signing. I found plenty of them in a pub one night, and conversation was flowing. I knew it was an Australian pub because some wag had made a new sign hanging over the front door. It said, *'The Amputees Arms Hotel'*. Would you believe that we were sharing a beer or ten and talking about our experiences? I overheard a conversation between some Aussie soldiers talking about going back to Gallipoli to help with some repatriation work, but that trip would not start until mid-January 1919. I asked them who was in charge, and they told me that Captain 'Carrot' was to be the leader of the official party.

Strange as it may seem, but I wasn't quite ready to travel back home just yet. All I could think about for the past four years was being back on the farm, but now the war had finished, I really wasn't so sure.

CHAPTER 13

THE MISSION
(NOVEMBER 1918 – MARCH 1919)

The next two months went by quickly. Considering it was now almost four years that I had been in the AIF, I wasn't used to having to think for myself. Being free felt good for a week or two, but then I longed for some certainty and discipline in my life. London was awash with people like me from all over the world. It should have been a great time, but more and more of us were drinking far too much. At the time, we didn't know how to feel or act. So many thoughts and so much time to think about lost friends and the sheer pointlessness of war. There are only so many fancy-dress, New Year, Christmas, or Armistice parties that you can attend.

One memorable event some of us attended was a fancy-dress party at a Canadian Military hospital on November 17 for wounded soldiers. One of my new Australian mates had spent some time recovering there recently, and he asked us to go back with him to this special party. Barry from Benalla introduced us to his friends still at the hospital. Many were a long way off leaving, but the sight of Barry and a few of us, lifted some of these poor buggers' spirits, if only for a day.

"How are ya' Bazza, me old china plate?"

One obviously recently blinded soldier said, "If I could touch your face Baz, you'd still be an ugly bastard."

"I've brought a few mates with me to meet you lazy bludgers."

We were introduced, and handshakes and stories flowed yet again for an hour or two before the staff asked us to help. The nurses suggested we should make costumes out of old bed linen, so they tossed us the sheets, some scissors and gave us a needle or two with thread. No one knew what to do next, so I piped up. I had an idea — togas!

"Splendid idea Angus", said Barry.

So easy to do, we became experts in making togas. Some of the costumes made wearers look more like ghosts, but we didn't mind. The soldiers didn't mind, and for a few moments, we all forgot about the war, our injuries and our lost brothers and sisters. A band was formed from half a dozen of the wounded soldiers, hospital staff, and recovered veterans, and everyone had a costume. For those lads who could not walk, no problems, we gently picked them up from their beds, plonked them in wheelchairs, and pushed them around and around. For some of these limbless, wounded souls, wearing a toga made from their old, but cleaned bed sheets gave them a boost in spirits. I think it was just the idea of wearing anything other than a military uniform or a bare-bum hospital tunic.

The party went well, and surprisingly we all had a wonderful time. For those who had to return to the ward beds, they at least had a moment of happiness and sheer stupidity. There needs to be more of that.

We returned the next morning to our city lodgings, and I could not help but think of the possibility of returning to Gallipoli one more time. These thoughts were now occupying all my waking hours. I couldn't quite work out why I wanted to go back, but the thought of once more walking peacefully around the area where so much slaughter and a senseless loss of life occurred seemed grotesquely appealing. Years later, I understood these thoughts: there was unfinished business to attend to at the place they called ANZAC.

I remembered Captain 'Carrot' Bean from my time on Gallipoli. He was called that because of his bright red hair. Why we never called him Bluey is beyond me, but Captain Carrot seemed to stick. He was an odd sort of chap. Kind of aloof, yet approachable. Even though he was a war correspondent, we heard a story that he rescued a wounded Aussie soldier crawling back to our trenches while under enemy fire at Krithia. He went out of his way to do this after a Brigadier General told him specifically not to. That act alone gave him the credibility to speak to us as soldiers and ask for our opinions and thoughts. We all respected him because of that. He also copped a stray bullet to his leg during the August offensive, so that made him truly one of us.

While I never saw him fire a rifle in anger at the enemy, he seemed to know an awful lot about what was going on tactically, politically, and more importantly, from the point of view of a soldier. He spent as much time talking to common soldiers as he did to officers. I only saw him a few times at Gallipoli, and later, saw him again in France on a number of occasions. To hear he was still around at the end of the war suggested to me that he also had some unfinished business.

Talk in the bar between drinking and waiting for transport home, was that Captain Carrot and members of the Australian War Records Section had been busily collecting artefacts for over a year now from the Western Front and France to take back home to Australia for a new museum. Things like guns, bullets, documents, pieces of clothing, bric-a-brac, even the "Roo De Kanga" sign one of our boys hung on a wooden street pole in bombed out *Peronne*, just south of *Mont St Quentin* where we liberated the villagers from the Germans in September 1918.

Captain Charles Bean had been asked officially to collect these items, and to write a comprehensive history of the war. No small task, which did eventually take him more than 20 years to finish.

Anyway, back in London during November 1918, Bean was starting this massive undertaking, but he did not have anywhere near enough 'stuff' from Gallipoli, considering that we evacuated in a hurry and blew up most of what we left behind! He desperately wanted to return to the original battlefields to collect any traces of war that remained, but much more importantly, pay homage to those souls still there and to what we achieved in that hell hole.

His guiding principles were to report on and document the truth, through gathering artefacts, taking photographs, and painting scenes whereby emotional approaches and the interpretation of reality could be achieved. To reach this goal, Bean selected some very fine men to assist on the project. The first obvious choice of a cameraman was George Hubert Wilkins, who at the time, was the official war photographer for the Australian War Records Section. Although everyone called him Hubert, I kept on calling him George, and he didn't seem to mind. He had been working with Bean since August 1917 taking photographs of men, battles, and landscapes.

Prior to his time as Bean's photographer, George had spent time as a war correspondent in the Balkans and was in Alaska on an Arctic expedition when he heard there was a war going on in Europe. Not wanting to waste any of his precious life, he quickly returned to enlist as a pilot in the Australian Flying Corps given his flying experience, but on arrival in Britain, he failed an eye test! He told me he had flown many times, and could fly very well, but all that he lacked was a pilot's licence.

"They refused me a bloody licence! Something about being colour blind, Angus!"

Because flying was officially off the agenda for him, and due to his recent experience as a war reporter, the Government thought he could be useful to them if he once again turned his efforts to reporting and photography.

I didn't know what to make of George at first, but when he told me this story, I instantly liked him. Wanting to get some great photographs of a particular battle scene in late 1918, George and his assistant took to the skies in a balloon to spy on the Germans and to take photographs from a place no normal man would think about in their wildest dreams. But George was no normal man. They managed to take photos and return alive. What was surprising is that they weren't shot down. How dumb were the Germans? Did they think they were some French locals scoffing on a baguette and sipping a wine enjoying a leisurely balloon ride? Oh, and the time he was caught in the Balkan wars of 1912/3 and had to face a firing squad — three days in a row! Avoided it each time. What is it with this man and his love of cheating death? To top off his wartime antics, George was awarded a Military Cross for saving hundreds of American soldiers. He never really told me the details of this, but that was George. His life was so amazing, something like being a certified war hero too seemed normal. I got to know George over the next few months, and thoroughly enjoyed his company. His stories made mine seem perfectly pedestrian.

Perhaps the main reason that I liked him, now that I am thinking of him, was that he grew up on a sheep farm, and we had many a long discussion about all things to do with sheep. He wanted to know all that he could learn about the quality of their milk and cheese products. With any other person I met at the time, and who I shared my passion for sheep, I was usually met with some very strange looks, and some not-too-nice anatomically and biologically amusing suggestions. George didn't fit those categories of listener. He truly was interested and had a passion for farming like me.

The other chap Bean wanted to have on this bold mission was the artist George Lambert. What was it with Captain Carrot and blokes named George? Anyway, this George was a brilliant artist.

His background was as cosmopolitan as you could imagine. Born in Russia to English and American parents, he spent his early childhood in Germany, went to school in Britain and migrated to Australia where he worked on a sheep farm. You guessed it. We had something else in common that had nothing to do with war — sheep and languages!

Captain Bean had seen George's work as a war artist capturing images of the Light Horse through paintings and drawings. Bean loved Lambert's work and asked him to join what was now being called the "Australian Historical Mission". Somewhat of a casual artist himself, Bean was very impressed with Lambert's technical ability to display truth in his work. Lambert did not hesitate and eagerly joined the team.

There were several other members of the mission who joined along with Lambert and Wilkins. Staff Sergeant Artie Bazley was Bean's personal assistant, and he was a stickler for organisation. He had been with the good Captain since they both departed Sydney in 1914. Lieutenant John Balfour was another assistant, and his pedigree was important. Johnny served at Gallipoli in HQ, and in my books was a good bloke. His knowledge of Gallipoli and its terrain was excellent, and he enjoyed talking to me about my experiences when we walked over that hallowed ground later on.

Bean desperately needed someone who had been present at the time of the landings on Gallipoli in April 1915. Lieutenant Hedley Howe, or Howie as he was universally known, jumped off a landing boat on that first fateful day, and he and I became quite good friends too. Although from a different Battalion, we had many similar experiences. I was drinking beer in a pub in London when he told me about the mission.

Bean had asked Howie to find a few other soldiers who had battle experience, and who wouldn't mind going back to the scenes of horror, but this time for a completely different reason. On getting to know him better after three or four warm English beers, he asked me if I wanted to join the team, and that it might take a few months. I said yes immediately.

Howie introduced me to Captain Bean, and within a few minutes of meeting him again, he remembered me.

"I believe I spoke to you on Gallipoli" he said.

"Yes sir, you did. You spoke to me and my 8ᵗʰ Battalion mates for about an hour one day. I think you were interviewing us...."

I didn't even get a chance to finish my sentence when Bean said "...bomb making. I remember you teaching me how to construct bombs with the bits and pieces you had to hand."

"Let me see if I can remember. You used 18 pounder fuse boxes, jam tins, detonators of course, rags, shrapnel made out of .303 cartridges with the bullets clipped out, and gun cotton with ammonal for the explosive. Ingenious."

"You spoke to Johnny Turnbull and a few of us who were part of a 20-man bomb making team down on the beach."

"That's right. I did take notes, and I'm sure I'll find them again one day. Welcome to the mission Angus" he said, as I stopped to pinch myself. Meeting people like this and having them remember you was very important to me.

"Captain Bean."

"Yes Angus."

"Apart from surviving this past four years, I also speak a bit of German, Latin, and Greek. Will that be of any use to you?"

"My word it will. I don't think you'll need any Latin, German may be helpful, but Greek you say?"

"Yes. My father is a teacher of classics and I have grown up speaking all the languages he teaches. My mother also is quite fluent in them as well."

"Useful indeed."

"As you know sir, we spent some time recovering at Sarpi on Limnos, and I also spent time in the hospitals there due to this little flesh wound courtesy of Johnny Turk. I had some spare time, and I was allowed to travel to nearby villages, so I had some opportunity to practice my language skills. I have a question for you Captain Bean."

"What is it Angus?"

"Do you know the Greek meaning of the word 'Gallipoli'?"

"No, I'm afraid I don't. Do you know what it means Angus?"

"Sir, it means good (*kali*) city (*poli*), or even *beautiful city*."

"Angus. I knew there was a reason we had to have you on the mission team. We will be travelling to Limnos on our way through to Gallipoli, if all things go well."

At the sound of this, I was so extraordinarily happy. I was not sure if I contained my enthusiasm successfully, but the thought of going back after three years was very pleasing to me. I couldn't really explain my sudden rush of happiness. Why did I feel this way about a Greek island? I had hardly spent any time there, yet I felt something. Maybe I could see Maroula again. Maybe she would be married. She might have kids. Didn't matter. I was going to Limnos!

In the month prior to departure, Captain Bean was flat out with preparations for the mission. He wanted to gather as much information as he could from the men before they finally set sail for home. He set all of us a target to interview as many members of each Battalion as possible before they left for Australia. I helped Artie and Howie locate volunteers to interview every day. Bean would often leave for a day or two to visit important battlefields across the channel in France to make detailed notes. I didn't accompany him on any of these excursions, but he would come back with pages and pages of notes, drawings and some artefacts to help in his overall understanding.

I mentioned before about our experiences in *Peronne*. We helped liberate the town in September 1918, and Bean visited the site before Christmas. Taking some men with him, he managed to find the sign put up by the Aussies of our name for the street, so that is how the "Roo De Kanga" sign managed to find its way back to Australia. If my memory has not completely failed, I believe Bean celebrated Christmas in *Peronne*. While this was going on, Howie, Artie and a few of his lackies were finding more returning soldiers to interview. In-between the parties and general mayhem of London awash with thousands of emotionally drained and worn-out young men, we managed to prepare finally for the trip. Lambert was not quite ready to travel with us as he was completing a commissioned piece of work for the Australian Government. The painting was to depict the charge of the 4th Australian Light Horse at Beersheba on October 31, 1917. Lambert was not present at the actual event, but his research into it included visiting the site on horseback, talking to men of the 4th Australian Light Horse, watching a re-enactment in Egypt by actual participants, and studying one very dusty unclear photograph taken after the event. In his London studio, Lambert engaged his son Maurice and a few of us to wear the uniforms while he sketched us in pencil. I was fascinated by his attention to detail, and it was at this moment I realised why Bean wanted him, and why he was prepared to wait until this very important painting could be completed, or to be as close to complete as was possible.

I have seen the painting since those days, and I tell all who see it that I am one of the soldiers riding into battle. This was not to be my last time working for Lambert as an artist's model.

Finally, the day arrived to leave England, and on a cold, wet and drizzly Sunday on January 19, we crossed the English Channel and commenced our journey to Paris. Quite a contrast to my last French train ride, where I was headed in the other direction to become a patient in an English hospital. Now, the war had finished, and our whole retinue of returned diggers, artists and correspondents were slowly adjusting to life during peace time. I have to be honest here. It was not easy. For me, it took a while, and later on, I came to learn of digger buddies of mine who never did adjust to this life and could not function back in peace time Australia. For me, being a part of the mission allowed me to see the battlefields one last time, without the sounds of screaming men, the stench of rotting bodies, explosions, bullets and terrifying silences waiting for the next big bang. However, I did still wake up each morning expecting to hear the sound of a bugle.

Mum and dad visited Paris many years before I was born, and now I felt as though I was walking in my ancestor's footsteps again, like I did when visiting Granny Mae and Lady Cynthia. Paris was abuzz with excitement and hope. Only days prior to our arrival, the Palace of Versailles was the centre of world attention, due to a peace conference being held there to decide how the world was to look as it moved forward. Bean found his old mate, the recently re-elected Prime Minister Billy Hughes, and introduced me to the PM. I felt important to be in his company, and also to meet the other Australian representatives. I even managed to have a brief chat for a minute with Mr Hughes, and with Joseph Cook, another former Prime Minister.

I liked Hughes. He wasn't afraid to tell people how he felt, and he was proudly Australian. At the conference, he was discussing the League of Nations with the American President Woodrow Wilson when Wilson said something like 'Hughes only spoke for a few million people whereas he spoke for many more'. Hughes, ever the feisty orator and not afraid of the American said something like "I speak for 60,000 dead. How many do you speak for?" I was so proud of him after that moment.

The real highlight for me was visiting the famous music hall at *Folies Bergere,* and let me tell you — the women singing there had magnificent lungs. And they could also sing very well. I had never heard nor seen a performance like it. We culturally backward Aussies were mightily impressed. George the painter wanted to invite all the girls to be models for him, but we had to leave town the next day. Even he was awe-struck.

Leaving Paris, the next stopover was Rome, where we suffered the unfortunate loss of some vital luggage. Captain Bean was most concerned at the loss of several documents, but soon discovered his copies were safe and well. In addition to Bean, Howie had his luggage stolen. I was lucky, and nothing of mine went missing, but from that moment onwards, we watched our luggage, bags and cases like a hawk watches a field mouse.

Artie became sick with what we thought was pneumonic influenza, so we had to leave him behind in one of Rome's rest houses for British troops. Luckily for Bean and Artie, the wife of Bean's friend, Colonel Mason of the 59th, looked after him until he was well enough to join us two months later in Egypt. To me, it seemed that Bean had friends and acquaintances everywhere we went.

"Couldn't die from a bullet, but bloody influenza nearly got me", Artie said to me later in Cairo when we next met up.

From Rome, I remember the first major work location for the mission was in the southern Italian town of Taranto, where George Lambert picked up his brushes and easel to paint the military rest camp where we were staying. The camp had been an important Allied base during the war, a place Bean wanted to visit. However, tension between the British West Indian Regiment soldiers still evident in the camp and British military was simmering, and we all felt extremely uncomfortable being there. Recruited as soldiers, these men of the BWIR were never allowed to fight alongside British soldiers as equals, yet served with distinction when permitted. When we arrived, many of them were becoming ill due to poor treatment and the lack of adequate food. The tension was intense. Once the West Indian soldiers realised that we were not British, but Australian, we were left alone. Now I look back on this episode, I should have understood their plight much more than I did at the time. I regret not being able to do more for them, or at least voice the concerns they had with our British hosts.

Our Taranto tasks were completed in a few days, and then it was off to Malta, where the weather turned nasty and led to a shuddering boat trip. Most of us fed sharks with our fruity yawns over the side, and the eventual appearance of land was a sight for sore eyes and rumbling bowels. Wilkins, who by all accounts survived the Alaskan wilderness for months, could not stomach the boat trip and we voted him 'best in show' at vomiting. We remained in Valetta, the capital of Malta for three days, visiting graves of over 200 or so of our mates from the Gallipoli campaign. Before hospitals had firmly been established closer to the front in Limnos, many sick and wounded soldiers were sent to Malta. On a personal note, it was very confronting as I saw the graves of men I'd known and fought with. Somehow seeing the graves of officers and the men buried side by side and thinking how close it could have been to me being buried here, was a somewhat sobering thought.

Bad weather dogged our Maltese stopover, and Lambert could only start one painting. His choice of scene was a view of Valetta from the dark bay surrounding lighter coloured buildings, contrasted with dark skies above. It captured our mood perfectly.

On our way to the Dardanelles, the next brief stopover was to be in Limnos aboard the *HT Princess Ena*. None of the group, apart from Captain Bean, knew I had some Greek language skills, so we kept that tasty morsel of information for after his onboard lecture on the ANZAC campaign.

Bean was a master communicator, both aurally and in the written form. When he spoke, his voice was one of knowledge, but with deep understanding of the human spirit and desires. He told us of his time spent as a war correspondent on the Peninsula, but principally of the people he met, interviewed, lived with and the experiences they shared in the trenches, canteens, casualty stretchers and officers' tents. He wanted to fully understand the entire campaign, from the generals all the way to the stretcher bearers taking wounded, dying and dead soldiers away from the front. He wanted us to help him find out more and was very appreciative that

Howie and I had first-hand experience. After his talk, Bean had one final thing to say.

"Before we get to Gallipoli, we'll be stopping off at Limnos, where I know some of you have experienced the delights of the island. Angus here says he has some Greek language knowledge, so he will be taking over the translating duties should we need them."

Howie said "I remember Limnos. We practiced our landings there. One thing that was missing from these practice drills was Johnny Turk trying to take our heads off! Now that would've been realistic."

I told the group that I had spent about two months on the island, over three separate occasions. "My first time was in the 3rd Australian General Hospital after a gunshot wound to my leg. The second time was some much-needed rest at Sarpi. The third time was after the evacuation."

Howie said "Me too. First time was in April '15 for landing practice. Then in November '15 when they promoted me to Corporal. We were resting at Sarpi camp, and all I remember of that time was how bloody cold it was in those tents; but at least no one was trying to shoot me."

Howie then stood up and started to remember stories as if they were yesterday. He hadn't rehearsed any of this, and no doubt had not much time to really gather his thoughts in public on any of his experiences.

"After the evacuation six weeks later, I ended up in hospital. Whilst it was freezing to everyone else at ANZAC, my temperature was literally through the bloody roof. A doc took one look at me and said I needed to rest, so I was admitted to the Number 3 Australian General Hospital. I tried to resist, but two burly medical orderlies had an arm each, and my strength had evaporated. They were right. I needed rest and treatment. Pyrexia they called it. I was admitted at the very time they were packing up! Not long after I was forced into a bed, the bloody tent disappeared, and off

I was to the Number 3 Canadian Stationary Hospital, not far away if I remember right. Stayed a few days, then off again to the Scottish Lowland Casualty Clearing Hospital. Talk about travelling all over the world. I liked it so much, I stayed for a week."

Captain Bean had not heard Howie's stories, and let him talk.

"But I know ANZAC. I was there from the start, and all the way to the evacuation. In a strange way, regardless of the cobbers I know who are still there, buried in a cemetery or lying under some layer of blood-stained dirt, I want to go back. I owe it to my mates to help with the story our country needs to know. They need to have their lives and sacrifices remembered."

"What is your main memory of it all Howie?" asked Captain Bean.

"It was how bloody matter of bloody fact it all was. Like going to work. Apart from seeing my mates blown up, shot, and going quite mad, the officers and us had our jobs to do. For example, and I've never really spoken of this. I remember one day having to drag a couple of our blokes away from the trenches, some dead and most wounded. My CO just said to us 'make sure you get their unused ammo', and we did. We had no time to think about what we were doing. We had a job to do, and if we didn't do it, you could lose your bloody head, or cause your cobber to lose his. We looked out for each other."

Howie sat down, as his own words finally hit home.

"I remember dragging a bloke down to the clearing station, and when we got there, an orderly told me that my mate was dead. No. I said, he's just a bit tired. He'll be right in the mornin'."

Howie was now staring into the night's sky, not really looking at anything in particular, deeply lost in his own thoughts. Then as calm as he could be, he said "As for Limnos, I must say I don't know much about the place." Howie's full recollections of ANZAC would bubble to the surface soon enough, but for now, he was quiet again. Lost, no doubt, in his deeply personal memories.

Our vessel was entering the harbour, and I thought I'd lighten the conversation a little. "When I had a few days to myself on Limnos after my unfortunate bullet incident, I did venture out a bit from my hospital bed and found some interesting places. Did you know there are thermal springs where you can get a hot bath?"

"You're kidding me," said Howie.

"If I can organise it with some people who have donkeys, we can all go there to have a hot bath. What do you say?"

Captain Bean piped up and said that if we had any time, he would love to partake.

"Let that be your one and only official duty on Limnos, Angus. Make sure we get a good price for the donkey trip, and a good hot bath at the end of it."

"I'll do my best Captain."

I had been tasked with the responsibility of organising a bath! Sounds funny now that I look back, but at the time, remember having any sort of a bath in fresh, warm water was practically impossible, and the stuff of dreams. I don't know how many soldiers like me often dreamed of warm baths, with a nice fresh pot of tea at the end, followed by a long comfortable sleep in a feather bed, just after dousing the fire in the hearth. Instead, we were lucky to splash a little rancid water on our faces, make tea in a billy behind sandbags in a trench, and sleep in full kit slumped up against a dirt wall!

Landing in Moudros Harbour once again for some of us was most welcome after another rough sea voyage. Camping in the remnants of the Allied officers' tents at the Australian Stationary Hospital, the sudden wintry blast of Aegean wind certainly made us feel alive.

First duty was to make our beds and set up George Lambert's temporary studio in the only remaining wooden hut. Over the next few days, George painted some beautiful scenes of Moudros Harbour from many angles and perspectives. Being with him, and also with George number two, helped us all appreciate the final products of their labours when you are with them during the decision stage of what to paint, where to paint it, what to photograph, and how the light will affect the images. Amazingly talented men.

The tent hospital at Moudros had been in existence since March 1915 and was still treating severely ill and wounded soldiers. Some medical staff had remained behind, and due to their dwindling number of patients, we were permitted to stay in some of the recovery ward tents. None of the nurses were there, but some male orderlies were happy to look after 'well' people for a change. We were treated splendidly by the medical orderlies. In his usual fashion, Bean quizzed these men in relation to the injuries they saw, illnesses and other medical complaints that afflicted the men they patched up over the last four years. While Bean was doing that, Howie and I took a short walk around to the main pier and found a seat. All we did was sit and stare at the water, remembering that just short of four years ago, this place would have been teeming with soldiers, boats, supply vessels, animals for transport and local traders trying to get that last-minute sale. No words were necessary for this contemplation.

After our quiet moment, we decided to go for a short walk into what was optimistically described as 'town'. Walking past some closed waterside cafés and the grand church, there was not much else to see. The weather was rather cold thanks to a biting wind, and whoever was living in the stone cottages were comfortably tucked up inside given the number of smoking chimneys. On this particularly dull, grey day and not meeting a living soul, we returned to our canvas homes.

Next morning, after a brisk February wind nearly blew us into the Aegean, we breakfasted and walked to the military cemetery just out of town. It was there that we attended some of the grave sites, repaired crosses, and helped in a general tidy up of the whole area. Both Bean and Wilkins took some photographs, and I found the graves of some of the men I served with on Gallipoli. I didn't get a chance to farewell them in 1915, but on this day, I stood at each of their graves and shared some quiet and personal thoughts. My overriding emotion was one of 'this could have been me'! I wished Artie could have been here with me. Some of these poor buggers were his cobbers too. I have to say to you, I did shed a few tears in that place, just like I did in Malta.

After lunch, we took a boat across the bay to Sarpi, and all the way across those freezing waters, I could only think of seeing Maroula. Would she remember me? It had been just over three years. Thinking of the others, I wondered if we could still locate enough donkeys to take us to Therma for that much promised bath. All would be revealed. I only had one job to do here, and I didn't want to make a mess of it.

I bounced off the boat onto the jetty at Sarpi and couldn't help but wonder where all the people had gone. Last time I was here, there were thousands of tired and grateful men milling around, not quite knowing what to do, yet still fearful of what lay ahead for them. We had no idea of where we would be sent next, but I do remember hearing France mentioned in whispers many times.

Anyhow, Johnny Balfour, the Georges and I walked into Portianou, a distance of about two miles, and found the café open. Being winter, the locals were huddled around a fire inside the café, when in we walked. Instantly, George the owner recognised me. And yes, I know, we have another George, but you already knew about him.

"Hello George. Are you well?"

"Of course, my young Australian friend. It is good to see you again."

We hugged Greek man style, kissed each other on the cheeks, and slapped each other's backs.

At this stage, some of the local farmers and old coffee drinkers had stopped their coffee drinking and Turkish pipe smoking and looked at us, wondering how George knew me, but then, one of the old timers said in a rather gruff and totally incomprehensible way that he too remembered me, or at least I think that is what he said!

Without going into too much idle chat, I asked George the Greek if he could find us about eight donkeys to take our party to Therma. He seemed a bit slow in accepting the offer, but then I produced some gold coins, and four of the old men immediately sprang into action. Within five minutes, we had our donkeys.

"Bugger me dead" said Johnny, as he finally realised I spoke Greek, or at least enough of the language to order our luxurious transport to the hot baths.

"And here's me thinking that you were just another sheep-shagging farm boy."

"I think he means that as a compliment, Angus", said Lambert.

The donkeys stood in the town square outside the café, munching on some grass and tree branches. Johnny left with three animals to get Bean and the others who were still at Sarpi. Within about half an hour, all of our party were on our way up and around Mount Elias, heading into the unknown for some, and the known for me.

There were seven of us in the group, with a local farmer named Petros leading the way. He and I talked, and to all of my colleague's surprise, we talked all things sheep. I told him I was a sheep farmer from back home, and all of a sudden, he became my best friend. Both Georges were asking me for translations all the time, and I tried my best, but Petros's language was heavily influenced by Turkish words. My parents never once told me that classical Greek had any Turkish influence, but then again, these farmers and Limnian locals were not classically trained. He also had the habit of chopping off his verb endings, and it took me a while to figure out if he was in the present, past or future tense!

Let me give you a language lesson I learned from being in Limnos. In Greek, there are many words for the word 'the'. We call it the 'article' in English. If I was to say, 'the man', or 'the woman', or 'the child', each Greek word for 'the' is different. Like in English, Greek has words for he, his, she, hers, and its. But in Limnian Greek, it is very hard for an untrained ear like my classically trained one and having non-native Greek speaking parents, to recognise these words essential to knowing who they are talking about, and what!

Many occasions on that trip to and from the bath house, Petros would often chuckle at my accent, and he was very patient and helpful, correcting me on basic grammar and suggesting some of the Turkish words they had grown up with. Remember, the Turks had been on Limnos for over 450 years, so some of their ancient language had found its way into the vernacular!

I hesitantly asked Petros about Maroula and her family, saying that she was our donkey guide and vegetable seller a few years ago. He told me she was well, and now married with two kids. I don't know if I was shocked at this news, but it did not surprise me. Perhaps I didn't know what to expect, but I could not have been upset at someone I had met only a few times some years ago was now married.

If there was any good news, she now lived in the village of Pesperago. Petros told me of her home with her husband and family, and I realised we walked very close to it early on in the day on our way to Portianou. Her husband looked after a sheep flock just outside of the village, on the way to Sarpi.

All of our group loved their bath, by the way. I think they loved it so much, we had real trouble getting them to leave and proceed to our next destination. Both Georges regretted not having enough time to paint or photograph the establishment but promised to do so if they ever got a chance to return. Captain Bean even gave me a rare compliment.

"Nice one Angus. Nice one."

Given how frugal Captain Bean was with spoken words, I took this as a compliment. Years later, when I was fortunate to read his official history of the Gallipoli Campaign, he did mention these baths, so I guess he thought it important enough to warrant a line or two.

Our group returned the donkeys mid-afternoon, and then proceeded to walk to the other military cemetery, adjacent to the Portianou Orthodox church. The principal task here was the same as the day before, which was to attend to graves, and perform a general clean-up of that sacred ground. And like the day before, I came across men I knew, served with, and one who shared a hospital ward with me. Bean, Wilkins and Lambert could see that I was not in a good way and asked me if I wanted to leave.

"Not until I have visited every last one of them".

I think it was one of the Georges, but someone spotted the grave site of two Canadian nurses. During the campaign in 1915, there were two Canadian hospitals situated outside Portianou, and on land owned by Maroula's family. I remember her telling me this. I even remember one day meeting a nursing matron by the name of Jessie Jaggard, who was working at the Canadian hospital. I didn't talk with her for long, but I used my bargaining skills to help her buy some vegetables from a farmer.

Now, here she was lying in a cemetery in Portianou. All of us stood by her final resting place, along with Sister Mary Munro's grave, and said a few quiet words. Very sad. I also thought about Dorothy back in England, and the nursing friends she has lost. I told the others about Dorothy, and the train trip from Ely to London. I know cemeteries are a sacred place, but we did chuckle at the thought of Dorothy knocking back a rum in honour of her fallen comrades. Here's to you, Mary and Jessie!

I decided not to call in on Maroula and family, as that would have been totally inappropriate, considering we had just visited the cemetery, and we were all feeling like a stiff drink was in order. Once our work had concluded and we all agreed to walk back to Sarpi where we were to stay the night in what was the only fixed dwelling in the area. I was told that this particular home was used by officers during the Gallipoli campaign when they had soldiers resting at Sarpi. Whilst we spent time in tents on a slight hill, overlooking the hospital sites across at Pounda, this little room was sheer luxury. It had beds, a fireplace and the most important item — wine! I remember Bean had arranged in Moudros to bring some food for the evening, and all that I can remember of that night was a solemn discussion on how Limnos should be a place that Australians have to visit one day.

Next morning, Lambert went off to do some sketches, Bean and the others wandered around the rest camp area looking for artefacts, and I walked into Pesperago. Our boat back across the harbour was due to leave around midday, so I did not have much time.

At about the halfway point between Sarpi and Pesperago, I came across a shepherd tending his flock. I had the feeling that this might have been Maroula's husband, due to where Petros told me their flock might be located. As I was talking to him, and you guessed it, we were talking about the very animals I too loved, I saw Maroula carrying a child on her hips walking in our direction. She had been told the previous day there were some Australians visiting again, and I was amongst them. When she saw that I was talking to her husband, she smiled at me.

I was so happy at that moment. Seeing her again, knowing that she was happily married and with a child or two, I suddenly felt like I wanted to do the same. Get married that is, have kids and raise more sheep back home!

She formally introduced me to Haralambous, or 'Barbie' as everyone called him. Don't ask me how they get Barbie out of Haralambous, but they do.

"Maroula has told me so much about you. Welcome back to our island, and let me introduce you to our daughter, Maria."

"It is good to see you again Angus."

As we stood watching the sheep, we talked for about half an hour, I made some terrible grammatical mistakes, which is easy to do, especially when it comes to personal pronouns, and they politely corrected me. I told them we were going to Gallipoli later on that night, and the reason for the visit here and over on the Peninsula. They understood and asked me to come back to visit them and perhaps stay a little longer. I promised to do so but did not at the time realise that it would be another decade before I returned to this place.

Parting as friends, and walking back to Sarpi, I took one final glance over my shoulder and saw Maroula smiling and waving in my direction. Haralambous was swearing at his sheep and belting a metal bucket with a stick, but still Maroula smiled. I had never been so jealous and in love at the same time in my life.

Meanwhile, Bean and the others had finished the rest camp search, and were disappointingly unsuccessful, but they did find some intact British Rum ceramic jugs with the letters 'SRD' on them. I laughed, and Captain Bean asked me why I was laughing.

"We used to steal these jugs of rum from the British ration depot when I was in hospital over there, and in the rest camp here. We'd smuggle the rum jugs into the hospital tents and the patients would hide them from nurses and medical staff. We Aussies, and the New Zealanders were pretty good at pinching these."

I also told them about having a drink of rum from a similar jug on the train from Ely only a few months prior to being here. Sadly, my rum smuggling operation did not quite make it into Bean's official history. I wonder why!

The rest of that afternoon was taken up with a short boat ride back to Moudros, where Lambert started another sketch, and we packed our things onto a steamboat that would take us over to Chanak. I sat with Lambert as he sketched what he saw and imagined. We didn't talk. I let him do what he did best, and it was fascinating to see what became of the image created on his sketchpad, and what I was looking at. While my eyes were seeing boats on the water, my thoughts were elsewhere.

I was in many minds. Lots of thoughts buzzing around like honeybees on a hive. I'd just seen Maroula after just over three years, and I was so jealous of her husband. I don't know if I wanted to be with Maroula, but I wanted to be back on the farm soon, with a wife and children, and forgetting about war. I had made up my mind to be a farmer on my own, not with my parents.

But the thought of going over to Gallipoli again was foremost in my current thinking. What would we find? How different would it be to when we were fighting there? I also wondered for a moment thinking about Mustafa and what may have happened to him.

CHAPTER 14

GALLIPOLI REVISITED

(1919)

Captain Bean was pleased with what we had achieved on Limnos, but there were bigger tasks ahead. Returning to Gallipoli was the principal reason for this mission, and Bean was strangely silent on the boat trip across the Aegean. Equally quiet was Howie, because the last time he undertook this journey, was the afternoon and evening of April 24, 1915.

The mountainous volcanic hills of Imbros island emerged on our right. On any normal day, this would have been an amazing sight, but all eyes were focussed squarely on the left, to the mainland of Turkey, about 10 miles distant. Here was a coastline we knew so well, and within 30 minutes, a small patch of familiar sand and hills soon appeared in our vision. Even travelling at this safe distance off shore gave us all a disconcerting feeling. Little or no words were spoken by any one onboard as we slowly drifted by. Soon enough, the little patch of dirt we called 'home' four years ago, faded from view and we continued our journey along the coast.

I had never seen Howie so emotional as he was now. He was one of those soldiers who landed on the shores of Gallipoli on what we now know as ANZAC Day. He survived, but many of his cobbers did not even make it ashore that fateful morning. Even though we were not due on Gallipoli for at least a week, he was still a nervous wreck. None of us were there that day, and we did not know how he felt. We left him alone with his thoughts and his ghosts. Later, he confided in me that he felt deeply ashamed he had survived not just the landing, not just the whole Gallipoli campaign, but the entire war while many of his friends and comrades did not. His greatest fear was how he could return home alive and face the families of his departed mates. I understood his feelings totally. It was many years before I marched in an ANZAC Day parade back home.

Rounding the peninsula at Cape Helles, we saw the French and British ships that were sunk to provide breakwaters at landing sites. Bean recognised the collier ship *River Clyde* as one of the sunken vessels. To me it simply looked like it had run aground and was waiting for the tide to come and re-float it, but I guess it is still there today. We saw French trenches and the century old fortresses built to guard the Straits. Travelling with Captain Bean was a history lesson for all of us, and he kept a running commentary on what we were seeing. He seemed to know who built each of the trenches, castles, fortresses and when. Over time, it is now difficult to remember exactly what he told us that day, but some things will always stay with me. He was a marvellous teacher with an encyclopaedic brain.

Fortunately, Howie was feeling much better now, and quite excited at seeing life from an alternative viewpoint. Wilkins took several photographs of the massive guns inside the fortresses while we marvelled at the whole idea that we were now sailing through perhaps the most famous narrow water entrance in the world. Bean and I talked about the mythical Trojan war and wondered what it would be like to visit Troy. But, like I said, we had other plans. That little visit would have to wait.

We arrived at our destination mid-morning. The village of

Chanak was the German headquarters where General Otto Liman von Sanders commanded the Turkish army. Again, Bean knew many things about the General, but there was one thing he could not have known. At about the time we landed in Chanak, the General was arrested in Malta, a place we had been only days before. He must have been there when we were. That would have been a coincidence to trump them all! Anyway, we were now standing in the seaside town where Von Sanders once had command.

Bean had hoped to find the 7th Light Horse Regiment and Canterbury Mounted Rifles in Chanak but was disappointed to find them gone. Apparently after fighting in the heat of Palestine, they were re-deployed to remain on the Gallipoli Peninsula, but alas, the men did not possess any warm clothing and were officially withdrawn.

Bean did find help from the British who had taken over a lovely little villa in town as their headquarters. Being British, they put up a sign outside, and renamed the villa the 'Red Lion'. We were left at the 'pub' to fend for ourselves, while Bean and Wilkins continued to Constantinople. Our accommodation was unfortunately not at the Red Lion, but a much sadder excuse for a villa nearby. The weather turned nasty, which at that time of the year, meant it was bitterly cold, and we had no heating at all. No coal to burn, no wood, and no heater of any kind. The only way to stay warm was to wear everything we had!

Most of the mission members simply waited patiently that week for Bean and Wilkins to return, but Lambert immediately commenced work on several new paintings. His method was to make oil sketches on prepared wood panels and often started by making soft pencil marks as a guide, followed by larger background painted areas, or at least that was what I called them. His finer detail would come much later. Sometimes, he would leave the woodgrain of the board in the final piece, without any pencil or paint covering it. He had to work particularly quick that week as the weather, as I said, was lousy and he only had a few hours each day to make the most of his work.

Bean and Wilkins arrive a week later after their trip to the big city. The Captain managed to secure approval for a Turkish military person to join us for a few days to assist with better understanding the entire Gallipoli campaign. We would meet this person soon enough, but now we helped load up a boat with equipment necessary for our work on the Peninsula. This boatload of supplies included ample painting material needed for Lambert's work, camera gear for Wilkin's efforts, horses, mules and boxes of 'stuff'. In addition, eight British lads from the 28th Infantry Division based in Chanak joined our party to help with any jobs needed, and to cook for us.

Our landing place was a rather inconspicuous enough area, but to Howie, Johnny, and I, it was behind enemy lines. The feeling for us was difficult to put into words, but I'll try. For months on Gallipoli, we were relatively comfortable in our own spaces, trenches, beaches, tunnels, and huts tucked up against sand dunes. I know it sounds funny saying that we were comfortable, since we still were being shot at and explosions could be heard daily, so it wasn't really that enjoyable. Our only direct experience with the enemy was when the burial armistice happened, but even then, we didn't venture too far from No-Man's-Land. We now found ourselves walking along enemy tracks towards an old military hospital surrounded by thousands of Turkish graves. It was here we camped for that first night.

Next day saw our party make its way to Legge Valley behind Lone Pine where we established a base camp, for want of a better name. At least here, we would be protected from the wind and continual miserable weather. Other groups of Aussies nearby were the Graves Registration Unit and the Australian War Records Section. Over the next few weeks, we often helped each other because our duties overlapped.

To the Australian and British soldiers, this land was a former battleground, where thousands of men lay dead in graves and, sadly, some still where they were killed. But to the local Turkish people, this land was also their homeland. Hundreds of displaced former soldiers were returning home to damaged villages, farmlands, and buildings. If that wasn't enough, they were trying to plant spring crops. Severe poverty and starvation were real for them, and we were often approached for food, clothing, and anything else we could spare. The sight of dishevelled women dressed in tattered rags carrying crying babies asking us to spare some food would be an image that haunts me right up until the present day. We did manage to slip them some food, and at times, helped them with land clearing, but there was not much else we could do for them. They were grateful for any support we could give.

It was about this time that some returning Turkish soldiers appeared. If the women with babies looked terrible, these men were far worse. Battered and beaten, they came back home with no support from their government and abandoned by their officers. We did give several of them some work, and I am sure this helped them in more ways than we could possibly imagine.

Here is the problem for these soldiers. They scored a victory at Gallipoli. They fought off the aggressors and won the battle. From their point of view, they were victorious. But with little or no time to celebrate this win over the British Empire, they were immediately sent to other battles in Sinai, Mesopotamia and Palestine, and by October 1918, they were a severely depleted and beaten army. Now some of them returned home to find us digging around in their farms and villages. We were kind to them, offering work, clothing, and food where we could. What did they think of we Aussies? I had respect for these fighters back in May 1915, and I'm sure they had the same respect for us. Afterall, we did not start the war — our stupid governments did.

I don't know where they came from, but we also seemed to

inherit some of the 7th Light Horse who remained behind on the Peninsula. Maybe they were the only ones who had warm clothing! Anyway, we were happy to have them join the team, which by now was numbering over 20. Captain Bean had his daily plans well prepared in advance. Let me tell you what a typical day looked like. Breakfast at 8am, and off to work by 9am. Work involved visiting a site, criss-crossing all over it, Bean asking questions of those men who served there, note taking, photographs taken, artefacts located and tagged, and after lunch, more of the same. Bean instructed Wilkins on what photographs to produce, and from where they should be taken, and Lambert wandered off to paint. He would return to his tent before dark to make further use of what light remained, and we returned to base camp in time for dinner. Over dinner, we'd recount the day while Bean cross-referenced and asked even more questions. He was the epitome of meticulousness. Wilkins even found time to convert a ship's tank to use as a darkroom for developing his glass-plate negatives. Ingenious!

Perhaps the most important part of this mission was to accurately map, trace, walk and note the original landing sites from that memorable day four years ago. February 17th was the day we commenced this most important task. Bean had witnessed the landing from a distance in boats offshore, but Howie's platoon was amongst the first to land here. His memories and thoughts were vital to Bean gaining an accurate, eyewitness account.

Howie's story of the landing, recounting what he did, felt, thought, and saw, were invaluable as we were now walking over the very ground. Given that the original landing occurred in the wee hours of morning, no Turks could be seen. We climbed a ridge, and Howie remembered that they came across a Turkish soldier asleep in the bottom of a shallow trench. It would have been good to record his name, as he was the Australian's first Turkish prisoner.

We spent the rest of the day criss-crossing this ridge from the beach towards the heights of Plugge's Plateau. Howie's memories were vivid. He showed us the spot where they found their first Turkish casualties, who had apparently run into allied soldiers unexpectedly, and died of serious head wounds.

"I saw my first exploding artillery shell from here. It burst in a fleecy white puff. I'll never forget that."

On the night of February 20, I went to bed like I had done each night since we arrived. I was absolutely buggered! I felt as though I had earned a good sleep, and considering the cold, we were warm enough. The British boys turned out to be good cooks. Just before we all retired, skipper Bean said that tomorrow would bring some new people to help us. He wasn't sure who, but he told us a Turkish military official would join our team. I was too tired to even notice this comment and fell asleep before my head hit the straw.

When Bean was in Constantinople with Wilkins a few weeks ago, they had arranged with the military brass at British Headquarters to have a Turkish army officer join the mission. Bean wanted to gain a full perspective of the conflict and thought it could only be achieved with the assistance of the very people we were fighting. In his thorough fashion, he had already prepared a list of questions he needed help in answering, such as Turkish troop deployment and tactics. The list was formally passed onto Turkish officials, but Bean also wanted someone who was not only an officer, but someone who had served on Gallipoli, not some back-room General who hadn't fired a weapon in anger. This person would also have to be comfortable in staying with the mission and go over the battlefield with us.

One thing I neglected to mention was that while Bean was organising this, he was told how proud the Turkish military officials were in the whole campaign, and if you really think about it, they won! But what surprised Bean more than anything, was the level of survey detail in their historical maps made after the conflict. To his surprise, he was furnished with a set of magnificent cartographical charts made by the Turkish survey corps.

Friday morning, February 21 started like any other day on the mission. Up at 7am, breakfast by 8 am, and ready to work at 9 am. However, I was in for a surprise. The special guest sent by Turkish officials arrived by boat where Bean and a 28th Division staff officer were waiting for him at the pier in Chanak. After a shorter boat trip across to Kilid Bahr, Bean and the Turkish official immediately set out for ANZAC Cove on a pair of horses.

Captain Bean introduced us to a rather dapper looking, young Turkish officer named Zeki Bey, who at the time was around 30 years old. I don't know what I expected to see in him, but he looked just like us. Only he was Turkish, the former enemy. Zeki did not speak any English, and Bean did not know any Turkish, but their common language for communication was in French. Zeki's French was much better that Bean's, but it was good enough to have a proper conversation on the matters of importance to the mission.

At Kilid Bahr, two Turkish soldiers were still guarding a very large cannon, and were waiting to be relieved of this rather monotonous duty when Zeki Bey asked Bean if he could employ them to wander the battlefields with the mission and talk of their experiences only if they had battle knowledge in the area. When these soldiers were approached, Zeki Bey asked them a few questions, and within a heartbeat, the mission grew by another two mouths to feed. They were very happy to be relieved of their post as they had almost exhausted their meagre rations. Bean accepted Zeki's proposal and the party of four rode into our camp around 9am in the morning.

I did not hear them approach, but Wilkins, Lambert and Howie watched this strange group of men dismount and almost immediately, an Australian billy-made cup of tea was on offer. Bean introduced Zeki Bey to the group, and then asked him to introduce his two soldiers. He did so in French, but I heard the names Yusuf and Mustafa, and thought that they must be common names here in Turkey — much like John or William back home. I turned around to meet these new mission members, and bugger me, I was looking directly at the very man I met on the battlefield just over three years ago. Mustafa saw me, and gave me a cheeky wry smile, and we kept our obvious knowledge of each other quiet for the time being. I too was smiling.

Howie saw that I was smiling at Mustafa and Yusuf, and asked me why I was smiling at them. I had to tell him.

"Howie — remember when I told you about the unofficial burial truce I experienced in November of '15?"

"Yes, I remember you saying that a while ago."

"Well, I met that soldier standing right there, and his name is Mustafa. He and I helped each other bury a few of our comrades, and we swapped some items. We met under very strange circumstances, and something else he told me at the time was most interesting."

"Angus. I know you speak a few languages, but I didn't know you spoke Turkish."

"I don't speak any Turkish Howie, but Mustafa speaks Greek fluently, because he was born and grew up on Limnos until 1912. He knows Maroula because they only lived a mile apart, and his family and her family were friends, for a very long time."

"Why did he leave Limnos?"

"I don't know the full political story, but the Greeks had been occupied by the Ottoman empire for hundreds of years. In October 1912, it all came to an end and the Turks had to leave Limnos."

"I don't want Bean to know this yet. Can you keep this between you and me?"

"No worries Angus."

I went over to Mustafa and Yusuf and said in English, "Welcome to the mission." Obviously, they didn't know what I said, but Bean translated in French, and Zeki and his soldiers were officially welcomed by the rest of our group with handshakes all around.

Howie had experienced the friendliness of Turkish soldiers

in the official burial armistice at the same time I arrived on the Peninsula back in May 1915, but none of the others with us had that level of understanding. It would not be long before they all realised that Turkish soldiers and their officers were no different to us in any way.

I managed to talk to Mustafa later that first morning and told him why we were here, and he said that he knew of our purpose. We couldn't talk much because I was concerned that we did not have proper authority to talk, only Bean and Zeki were cleared to communicate. When the time was right, I walked over to Captain Bean and told him that Mustafa had a little knowledge of Greek but left out the bit of him living on Limnos. He said that was great news and gave me permission to ask him the same questions as he would ask Zeki. At the end of each day, we debriefed each evening, and I'm sure Bean was pleased at having not only Zeki to learn from, but also from two soldiers. I say two soldiers, because Mustafa and Yusuf never left each other's side and Yusuf too became a sort of friend of mine and Howie's.

Over the next week, I had many opportunities to talk with Mustafa and Yusuf. What I learned from them is that after Gallipoli, they both were sent to battles in Palestine and the Caucuses but returned to Constantinople soon after the Armistice at Moudros was signed. Somehow, they both gained minor jobs on the Gallipoli Peninsula with Turkish military officials doing odd jobs and trying desperately to survive.

Captain Bean and Zeki Bey were constantly talking throughout the week. Or should I say, Bean was asking questions and Zeki was doing his best to respond. Gaining the Turkish perspective was vital for Bean in his total understanding of the battles, tactics, and outcomes for his full and frank account.

Up until the three Turkish soldiers joined us, Wilkins and Lambert had been hard at work taking photos and painting scenes, with the say-so of Bean at all times. Even though Bean wanted to

control everything, he did let these two artists have some input —
but not much! I have seen Lambert's paintings made during this
time on the Peninsula many years later, and they are an accurate
representation of what happened. The only person who controlled
these two other than Bean was Howie's recollections of the landing.
As Bean was not present on the ground, he allowed Howie's judge-
ment when directing Wilkins and Lambert, and more importantly,
giving them his perspective.

I'll try to give you an example of what we did in walking over
the ground where the landing took place. As we walked, Howie
would say things like "I saw men dig into the soil here using the
end of their rifles to gain foothold so they could creep forward",
or "over there were the dense prickly scrub we had to crawl under",
and "I saw my first Turkish trench here". A moment I remember
was when he said that "here was where I captured my first Turk
and sent him down to the beach as a prisoner."

Howie once described coming across two Turks, one who had
died, and the other with a severe head wound grasping for our
water bottles.

"I wanted to stop and give him a drink, but I couldn't. If you
stopped, you never knew when a bullet with your name on it would
come fizzing out of nowhere."

Of the many events he described that occurred on that day, one
in particular which shocked the non-combat soldiers amongst us,
but not me. About half a mile from the landing site, Howie and
Private Frank Batt were scrambling their way across Plugge's
Plateau jumping in and out of trenches when two Turks jumped
up from behind bushes and shot at them, killing Frank instantly.
Howie doesn't know how the bullets missed him, but they did.
Howie had not been back to this spot since that moment, and
when he was telling us this story, he was visibly upset. Incidents
just like this happened to almost every soldier who survived the
war. Two of you are running along, your mate cops a bullet, and

you don't. Ten of you are in a trench, nine of you look up to see what is happening, and the tenth time someone tries it, he gets his face blown off. And believe me, you never forget those moments, ever.

Howie put it best when he said, "that could have been me, and you might have been talking to Frank today."

"He and I met on the *Ascanius* on our way over here in 1914. Of all the men on that ship, I had to meet the very one who would die next to me six months later."

I'm not going to re-live all that Captain Bean and the mission did or discussed during our time walking over that land again, but no story is truly correct, or cannot be close to being correct unless you hear from the other side.

For a number of years, Australians were told that the Allies landed on the wrong beach at Gallipoli, the wrong landing site, and that the British military brass were incompetent. They almost have never heard of any alternate views. Many Australians had no idea that French, British and Indian soldiers were fighting with us. There are even some who forget the letters NZ in ANZAC refer to our New Zealand brothers. Some are convinced that the evacuation of the Gallipoli peninsula went ahead without Turkish knowledge. Like all stories, there is always another opinion and perspective.

The Turkish military knew we were coming. They had aeroplanes in the air. They had fishing boats travelling between the Aegean islands and mainland, and remember, there must have been Turkish sympathisers living on Limnos during the weeks and months before April 25, 1915.

We learned from Zeki Bey that they were expecting us to land at a different spot, but in the end, it was not far from the actual landing site. They were due to conduct exercises near Hill 971 on the morning of the landing, so to receive news that a landing had occurred at Ari Burnu was not a huge surprise for them. The reason Zeki thought that they did not expect a landing at Ari Burnu was that he said it was "too precipitous"!

Apart from Bean's team, there was another group of Australians on the Peninsula at this time whose role needs a greater mention. While we had the two George's, the Australian War Records Section had the William's. The AWRS were on Gallipoli to also collect relics and take photographs so that scale models could be made for a proposed museum. William James and William Swanston were not official war photographers, but their brief was similar to Wilkins' work, and our paths crossed on many occasions. They were on the Peninsula for a lot longer than we were, and they were taking many more landscape photographs to assist in a topographical understanding of the ANZAC positions.

The key differences between Wilkins' work and both the William's work was that Wilkins wanted to show the human side of the conflict, and often inserted people into his photographs. James and Swanston's photographs showed the overall scene of principal battles showing the totality of the battlefield. They rarely if at all, inserted the human element into their work.

I liked these two a lot. William James was a member of the 1st Light Horse and served on Gallipoli from May through to December 1915. His knowledge of the area was excellent, and his first comment to me on his return to the scene of battle was one of deep sadness. On his first visit to the trenches around Lone Pine in early January 1919, he found the identity disk of a good friend, Charles Gibson, who was killed on August 7. William arranged for the disk to be sent home via the AWRS to Charles' family. We visited Charles' final burial place at Pope's Hill Cemetery and shed a tear together.

William Swanston was a photographer on loan from the Royal Air Force, and a completely different person to William James. He was kind of aloof, but his knowledge of photography was exceptional given his family had been pioneers in the photography business in the UK well before the war. Even Wilkins learned a lot from listening to him explain how he would set up his shots, and how he used the light in different circumstances. I loved listening to these two older men talk about their experiences and enjoyed it when our paths crossed. Lambert's discussions with Swanston about the artistic side of their work gave us all a very different perspective on war. As strange as it seems, when you hear artists discuss their trade, it was easy to forget that we were on Gallipoli at all.

Our mission work on Gallipoli wound up on March 10. Hughes' work with the War Graves Commission continued, the AWRS team continued on for a while longer, but our adventure had not quite ended. Our destination was Cairo, and Captain Bean wanted to take the sea route, but somehow, Wilkins persuaded Bean to take a slow train through the Taurus mountains from Constantinople. The train line was controlled by the British, so we were in no danger at all. We were allocated two empty livestock wagons for the trip, and before departure, some necessary improvements and renovations took place. With our own supplies and fresh produce purchased along the way, we were not short of ingredients for our nightly 'stew'.

At Cairo, we once again met up with Artie, who by now had recovered from his bout of influenza. Bean, Wilkins and Lambert had much work to do, and I was keen to find a vessel back home to Australia. Lambert succumbed to his persistent malaria and dysentery problems and was sent to hospital to recuperate, but he somehow managed to complete some interesting sketches of hospital life.

I bid farewell to the group in Cairo and found a berth on the troopship *HMT Port Hacking* and was bound for Australia thanks to Captain Bean stepping in to help me. The trip was completely uneventful, and I think I slept for most of it. One strange thing I do remember from that trip was a journal printed by soldiers, called the *"Port Hacking Cough"*. This rather witty publication had stories, anecdotes, drawings, poems, and advertisements on what daily events were scheduled for the voyage back home. Some of the more bizarre activities were blindfold boxing matches, water pillow fights, and of course the normal ones such as concerts by a brass band, choirs, deck quoits and various church services in all denominations. These were all nice, but there was one thing this boat had that I didn't realise I had sorely missed. It had a library! While my cabin cobbers were busy partaking in pillow fights on a log perched over a tub of water, I was enjoying the sweet delights of reading a book. After not being in a position for the past four years to safely find time and space for this leisure activity, I vowed never again to take the simple joys of reading for granted.

Before too long, we docked at Port Melbourne in late May. Home at last!

CHAPTER 15

MUSTAFA

(1916 – 1930)

Since the Allied Forces finally departed the Gallipoli Peninsula in early 1916, and right up to the end of the war, my life had been *'merde'*. As a snapshot of what happened, it reads something like this. We won at Gallipoli, and our country was happy. Those of us who fought there were treated like heroes, and we even had some time off, if you count two weeks as time off. But we really did not have a collective moment as a nation to celebrate. Eight infantry divisions were formed into the 2nd Army and we were hurriedly sent to the Caucasus Campaign. Although we had been moderately successful in that campaign, we were not in a good way. Many soldiers died, many starved, and our weapons were badly in need of replacement.

The Caucasus battles were going our way for a while with Kamal in charge of the 2nd Army, but in the summer of 1916, we started to fade militarily. Although the Russians were most likely winning these battles, it was a stalemate until the middle of 1917. Our forces were severely depleted, and so were the Russians. It appeared that nobody wanted to put any effort into one last push.

With the British exerting more pressure in Palestine, Enver Pasha moved five divisions away from the Caucasus down to Palestine and the Middle East.

Once again, I found myself facing off against Australians, but we were not doing well at all. Somehow, I managed to stay alive during the rest of 1917 right up until September 1918. We were beaten, and a decision was made to flee north from Maan to Amman, ultimately trying to get back home in one piece if we could.

The fight in us had left, and late September, we found ourselves bunkering down in open fields near the Hejaz railway station. We were in fear of an aerial British attack, and our leaders were urged to surrender to Australian and New Zealand horsemen at Amman. But it wasn't the British we were in fear of, but a force of over 10,000 Arabs who were taking particular delight in picking off our stragglers with pillage and murder. The alternatives were to surrender to the Australians, even though there were so few of them, or to attempt to face the Arabs.

In the end, and not being privy to decision making, we joined forces one night with these Australians, and fought side by side, against the Arabs, forcing them to flee. In the morning, we gladly surrendered to the Aussies, and once again, found myself in a burial truce with the same soldiers from nearly three years before! We proceeded to bivouac together with the Australians, share tea, make food together, and even swap trinkets.

It wasn't until much later that I learned of the atrocities committed against my people as we were fleeing from a defeat at the end of the war near the village of Tafas. An entire brigade of Ottoman, German and Austrian troops were wiped from the face of the earth by a band of marauding Arabs. Their excuse was that we Ottomans had done the same to many villagers earlier in the war. I am not trying to blame anyone, but quite often, these atrocities are committed on all sides during war. I have seen it too often, and no one is blameless.

Like I said, we were defeated, and news reached us that an armistice was signed to end the Ottoman's part in this horrible conflict. When I heard this, I remember asking an officer where this event occurred. His shoulders lifted and fell as he spoke with a heavy sigh.

"Of all places, this armistice was signed on a boat in the harbour at Moudros in Limnos. Do you know where that is Mustafa?"

"Yes, I do. I was born on that island many years ago, so I know the area well."

I thought the officer would chastise me for the country of my birth, but he turned away from me, and simply stared into the one cloud above us. I have never seen a man more comprehensively deflated than this moment.

After the Armistice signing, what was left of our division were simply told to go home. Our officers quickly abandoned us and vanished. We were alone, completely broken and dirt poor. I had only the clothes I was wearing, worn out boots, my broken rifle, a rusty knife and some less than appealing food scraps when I entered the door of my parents' home in Madytos. Luckily, the war had hardly affected this town after all Greeks were expelled. I was severely conflicted about this. On the one hand, my parents and siblings were safe, yet the innocent Greek population who had been there for hundreds of years were forced out, and some of their properties destroyed. Any destruction was done by our side, and not the enemy, although it made no difference in the end to the town.

The recently planted winter crops had barely enough food to sustain us, and work was impossible to find. Not long after arriving home, I left for the familiar battlefields of three years ago to see if the British military stationed there could offer me any work. Fortuitously for me, they did. It was this work that enabled me to be in the right place at the right time to accept a week of work with Zeki Bey, and my fortunate meeting again with Angus. Could the circumstances of this war give me any stranger coincidences?

Angus appeared to be shocked at my condition when we met for the second time. In 1915, during the burials, we were both very strong and healthy. I was in reasonable condition, but Angus looked much stronger. It was then that he told me he had a six-week break from the war on Limnos. No wonder he appeared refreshed.

We talked a lot. At first, we recounted our various battles, places, and strange events, and even the burial again with Australians near Amman. He laughed! But I really wanted to know about his time on Limnos. I asked him many questions. What did he eat? Drink? Where did he go? What did he see? Did he see the old Turkish taps? Which villages did he go to? Could he remember any names of people he met? I even asked him about some of the older people I remembered from Pesperago and Portianou, and to my surprise, he knew some of them.

But when he told me he had just been to Limnos with this current group of soldiers and friends, I was so surprised. Especially when he told me that he spoke to some of my old friends and neighbours, and he had told them about meeting me. I cried. He cried. We embraced. What a true friend.

The week with Zeki and Angus was perhaps the weirdest week I can ever remember. Here we were walking over the very ground where we fought off a determined enemy, killed thousands of them, lost many thousands ourselves, suffered irreparable damage to the landscape and crops, saw villages destroyed, and we were now happily answering questions about it all from a group of inquisitive Australians who wanted to know every minute detail from our perspective.

Not only were we answering questions and remembering our motives, actions, thoughts and the like, they had an artist/illustrator making wonderful paintings of the scenes he saw, photographers taking pictures of battlegrounds, cartographers constructing maps and diagrams of what they think happened, and a group of men finding the remains of their fallen comrades and giving them a proper burial, or at least, re-burying them in cemeteries that would be visited for years to come. But all I could think of was that they lost the battle! Imagine what they would have done had they won and been successful. What a truly strange bunch of people. I was beginning to like them enormously.

In that week, Angus and I became very close friends. We had much in common. We walked and talked every day, appearing to be serious with the work his Captain Bean required, but we found ourselves talking about sheep, milk, cheese, planting food and growing all kinds of fruit trees. We were both the same age, and both agreed to make something of our lives. I helped him with his Greek language, because his accent was very strange, and I was attempting to get him to speak like a Greek, and not an Australian who had never really listened to locals speak. He managed to teach me some English words and phrases, and then it was his turn to correct my pronunciation.

Zeki and Captain Bean spent many hours each day together, discussing past events, and gathering information the Australians needed. Zeki also had time to return the compliment with Bean and asked his thoughts on various battles and events. Even though Captain Bean was not a military officer, he appeared to know and understand more of what occurred and why, more so than the officers in charge. I spent time with Angus, George the photographer and George the painter, explaining our point of view, while Angus translated for me. I know our side used photographers, but it was the artist that intrigued me. Lambert spoke some French due to his time in Paris in the early 1900s, so I could talk to him as well as Angus without the need for an interpreter. He made me appreciate light and shade, colours, and textures of the land I now called home. It was a completely different perspective for me to consider. His insights were like a breath of fresh air to me after four years of war. He could see past the absolute carnage and find wonderous beauty.

I remember one time we happened across an apricot tree, sprouting out of sand discarded from tunnels dug by Australians. It had no fruit of its own, but being late winter, the tree was beginning to blossom. Wilkins the photographer asked one of the Australians to stand next to the tree, and we were all positioned behind the camera, looking past the tree out to sea. I queried Angus on how this could be, and he mentioned they had tins of fruit jam sent to the soldiers from time to time. He thought that the tree must have sprouted out of a stone in the jam.

"We gave you many of these tins Mustafa. Don't you remember?"

"I would have remembered tinned jam Angus."

"Maybe you missed these particular tins. They were packed with explosives."

"Well, my friend. You were obviously a woeful bomb maker. I'm still here!"

Later on, after my week of work with these Australians had finished, I suggested to some of the locals with artistic ability that they should go out and paint some scenes from the battlefields. I know they did, and some of their work is hanging in galleries today.

When I discovered that Lambert had been to Palestine in 1917 and created paintings of those battles where Australian soldiers were key players, I offered him my perspective, because I was a participant on the other side! Wilkins, the photographer, also used my stories to gain an alternative understanding for some of the locations he chose to take his photographs. He would find a place to set up his tripod and ask me for my recollections of the situation. On a number of occasions, I would give him a response, and he'd change the position of the camera shot, based on what I said.

On the day of the invasion of our land in April 1915, there may have been photographs taken looking up at the cliff faces. The perspective here is from the British and ANZACs view of what they faced. Equally, there is a completely different view of the same situation. All you need to do is to climb to the top of these cliffs and take a photograph down to the sea, so that our perspective is revealed. Same situation, two very different visions.

The day Angus and his colleagues left for the second time, was a sad day for me. I suddenly had no work again, and my prospects were not at all promising. To my surprise, Zeki Bey also became a close friend, and he promised to mention me to his friend, Mustafa Kamal. While my life did not suddenly become one of high politics, knowing Zeki and having Mustafa Kamal know me certainly did help.

During the time Captain Bean and Angus were on the battle-fields conducting their mission work, so too was another group of Australians. I met Lieutenant Hughes and Sergeant Arthur Wooley whose job was to coordinate the Graves Registration Unit. They had the task of locating all the known graves of Australian soldiers and give them a proper burial plot. Following the departure of Bean and Angus, I joined Hughes and Wooley as a labourer with the Graves unit. Lieutenant Hughes was easy to talk to as he spoke very good Turkish. He also spoke Arabic, and with my knowledge of Greek and some French, we spent a lot of the next year working at our primary role of locating missing soldiers, and also our language skills. After one year, he was becoming extremely proficient at Turkish, and the other local members of the Graves unit respected him for being able to communicate directly, and not rely on an interpreter.

The two years I spent working with Hughes were physically demanding, but it was honest, hard work, and I was gaining back much needed health, strength and self-respect. One day, Hughes noticed an Australian man approaching us from a beach. He walked up to us and asked something of Hughes that I did not understand. Apparently, this man had lost his son in the fighting and was looking for his grave. He must have been a very brave man to travel all this way, to a country he knew nothing about, and to attempt to find his missing son. However, we could not help him, but he did stay with us for a week searching and asking questions. He left us knowing that although we weren't successful, he was at least happy that there were people looking for his son on his behalf. To this day, I am not sure if we ever did find his son's body, but I hope he was eventually found.

Before we encountered this Australian man looking for his lost son, another Australian man arrived on the Peninsula to begin work for the War Graves Commission. Tasman Millington arrived in November 1919 direct from England, and at first, we didn't know what to make of him. Working alongside Hughes, with all the work he was doing finding missing soldiers, Millington had the new task of creating and looking after the military cemeteries all over Gallipoli. I only worked with him for a few months, but my association with Millington and his work lasted many years, and I met him on numerous occasions later when I would return home to visit my family.

I helped Millington learn Turkish, and within about two years he became quite proficient. I can't take all the credit for that. He was helped for many years by Pasha Ismail, a veteran of the trenches of Gallipoli, like me. Ismail worked alongside Millington for many years, and we too became good friends. By now, Hughes had departed for Egypt, and Millington and Ismail oversaw the cemeteries, alongside a workforce of Turkish and later, Russian workers.

Not long after leaving employment with Millington, I met a woman called Zehra in Madytos and we fell in love. She and her family moved into the village after the war ended, and one thing led to another, and we were married at a time when our country was at the beginning of a tremendous political and economic upheaval. There are many books written about this period in our history, so I won't go into all that again.

Zehra and I moved to Constantinople soon after we were married and have lived there ever since. Fortunately for me, being on the right side of the political fence, or at least giving the impression I was, after Mustafa Kamal became Ataturk, our lives as a family seemed to prosper. When I say prosper, I really mean we were largely left alone. We rented a modest home, I worked as a language teacher because my French was becoming quite proficient, and we started a family. In my spare time, I became heavily involved with the sport of wrestling.

The saddest period of this time of my life was between 1920 and 1923. During this time, we managed to have three children, which was the source of so much happiness. But all over the western borders of Turkey, the Greeks who had lived on the mainland were being driven out. Just like we were expelled from Greece in 1912, now many thousands of Greeks were being expelled from Turkey. Great swathes of populations were exchanged, cities destroyed, and atrocities committed. I am sure many people lost their lives and my country was doing its best to destroy the very thing I treasured most — that it was a cosmopolitan country accepting of migrants and other religions. While on Limnos, my family kept the Muslim faith, but I was really not that interested in any religion. Now, if you were not a Muslim in Turkey, you were considered evil and a foreigner, and your life was made extremely difficult. Zehra and I kept our heads down, and survived these early, troubling years. After all, we now had three hungry mouths to feed, and that was life enough for us.

My interest in wrestling came about quite by accident. Many returned soldiers like me were looking for an activity to help regain our fitness and for us to be together to share stories and support each other. One former soldier started a wrestling gymnasium near our house, and I joined in 1920. By 1930, I had won a national title and helped form a new wrestling academy in the recently renamed city of Istanbul. I enjoyed my teaching, my children, my wife and my sport.

Life was now complete. Being a teacher gave me a sense of purpose. I had many reasons to get up each day. I genuinely loved my work. My children were my future. In them I saw enormous possibilities for a new Turkey. My sport gave me salvation and a chance to heal mental wounds with my war comrades. My wife was simply my angel.

Life could not have been more comfortable, but there was one thing missing. What had become of my friends, Maroula and Angus?

CHAPTER 16

AN INTERESTING CHAP

The years immediately after arriving back home in Ballarat from the war were the hardest, not only for me, but more specifically, for my new and ever-expanding family. Let me unravel that for a moment.

First, my family. In the time I was away, both sisters had found husbands, and mum and dad were slipping towards a comfortable retirement, but still very active each day on the farm. I found a wife, and before I knew it, I was a father of three by the time I was 30 years old!

On my return, one of my first orders of business was to attempt to catch up with any old war buddies. Sadly, these rather joyous events were interspersed with discoveries of friends and acquaintances who enlisted, served and either had died, or who had returned as merely shells of their former selves. I made it a point of visiting the family of everyone I knew who had died and to pay my respects. Some of my mate's parents were most grateful when I told them the circumstances of their son's death. No matter how traumatic this must have been for them, I think they appreciated the truth, instead of the telegram regretting the news of their son's death. For some of the 8th Battalion boys, I could share moments with their parents and siblings of the time I had with their son and brother.

I have been visiting my wounded cobbers ever since the war ended, and right up until this day, I don't think I have ever gone a week without seeing at least one of them. We may not have even been in the same unit, but we all shared the same experiences. Even those who had been given a land grant instead of a pension — I have visited many of them over the years. I also made it a purpose in my life to catch up with all my friends from school days, whenever possible.

When we were living near Lake Wendouree, my sister Daphne had a friend, Rema Gilbert, and the two of them were best friends for a number of years. Rema often visited our house, and I have fond memories of playing with Daphne, Rema, and our older sister Rosie in the streets and on the lake's edge.

Rema remained a friend of Daphne's, and before the war started, moved to Melbourne to find work. Her quest for work was successful, but more importantly, found a husband in John Garner. They married, but being late 1914, John made the decision to enlist and was one of the first Australians off the boats and ashore at Gallipoli. Rema and John were due to have a baby, and a baby girl was born in August 1915. Sadly, John was killed in the war, and never did meet his daughter. Rema was completely devastated at the news and returned immediately to Ballarat to live with her parents.

She was living near one of my naval cadet friends in 1919 who also died at Gallipoli, and we met up by chance at the local church memorial service, lighting candles for the recently departed. Rema and I started to see a lot of each other, and although I didn't know her late husband John, I really began to like him. I think Rema could talk to me easily, because she understood that I knew how she felt, even though I could never know how she really felt. What made it OK for Rema was the fact that her parents knew me when I was younger, and her daughter laughed at my jokes.

Before too long, we were an item, and we married in 1921. She came with an instant family, and as far as my inherited daughter Amy was concerned, I was her father. Rema and I didn't muck around, and by 1925, my lovely wife had given birth to a little girl who we named Alice, and a son who we named James.

By the time I was 30, I had three children and a new job. With my language skills, I too moved into teaching, and was doing just as my father had done, although I was principally teaching English whilst dabbling in foreign languages. Schools gave a lot of us returning soldiers the chance to teach, and I actually enjoyed it. I still lived on the farm just out of town, and to make it to work in the city, I purchased a motorcycle. I loved my Australian-made Lewis motorcycle. Amy loved riding in the sidecar, and I only wish now that I had kept it. So many nice memories of riding with Amy, and later with Alice and James.

Life for other returned soldiers was less than ideal. Some were given land to resettle on, some gained a life pension that was not quite enough to live on, and some disappeared from public view, not being able to handle civilian life anymore. There was a noticeable difference in the community regarding how returned service men and women were treated. Men with a visible injury such as a missing limb, scars, and even men limping who were obviously injured, didn't attract criticism. But the ones I really felt for, were those who did not have a visible injury. It was those who had mental demons from years of military service, found that public sympathy soon evaporated. We would hear things like "just get over it", or "man up". We all had these mental problems, but Mr and Mrs John Public didn't think those injuries were real. One of my mates returned home with what we called 'shell shock' and could not tolerate the presence of people who were not veterans.

I lost a lot of friends to suicide, grog, gambling, violence, or some other nasty affliction that only people like me understood. Don't get me wrong, there was sympathy there for some of us returned boys, but not for all. It broke my heart to see my mates suffer. We didn't talk about it publicly, and we didn't share our feelings when we possibly should have. We most certainly didn't try to explain our position to people who weren't there to understand what we experienced. It just wasn't done.

Indeed, how can one possibly explain this situation to those who haven't experienced war? Every time I went over the trenches, there was always some fellow who went nuts. Men were being pulled away from the front line in every attack I was involved with. There was quite often no warning of who or when it would strike next. One of my mates, who I won't name, came back with 'shell shock' and was completely unable to speak to anyone unfamiliar for months. The only people who could talk to him were us returnees. It was just as bad for the nurses too. A Ballarat family friend who served in France and Egypt in hospitals survived a bomb blast in France, yards from her hospital ward minutes before going on duty. She and her fellow nurses were walking to the ward to commence their rounds when a massive bomb landed, killing one of the nurses and wounding half a dozen others. One of the male orderlies was also killed. When she came back to Ballarat, she found it impossible to re-enter the work force, and had to retire from a promising career in nursing. But she did not have any visible injuries, so most people thought she was just a 'woman' and should never have been there in the first place, so her injuries and condition were not recognised as being real.

One 'shell shock' cobber was called a coward by an old lady in Sturt Street one day soon after he came back. Instead of saying anything to her, he just burst into tears and went home. I saw him later and he told me what happened. If I was there with him, I would have told her that no one who was at the front was a coward. If they were cowards, they would not have gone. Simple. I often had the feeling of saying to these people this:

"How about I put you in a muddy trench, in the dark, with

bullets whizzing overhead, and bombs going off nearby where you see bodies flying through the air. You don't see all of the body land either. I leave you there for 24 hours with no one to talk to, but your dead best mate who is next to you missing both legs."

Most of these people like the lady in the street had lost sons, and were unable to express their feelings of overwhelming sadness and loss, so they took it out on the ones who returned and had no physical signs of injury. In a way, I felt so sorry for these mothers. I couldn't bring their boys home even if I wanted to. I didn't know what to say to those people.

If someone had called me a coward in those first few years, I'd probably have punched them in the nose. Thankfully, it never came to that. But there were times I would simply want to be alone for a day out on the farm. Just me and my sheep. Thank God for those bloody sheep. I talked to them a lot. Most of them were new, but some of them remembered me. Until I became a father, those sheep were my children. They were my responsibility, and they were a big part of how I survived the first few years. My family, my work and my desire to help others meant that I had some way of getting through the challenging times of a post-war Australia.

Back in Ballarat, and I suppose like many towns and cities all over this country of ours, there were mothers, fathers, brothers and sisters who had lost a son or brother to the war, and were now buried in a far-off land. Sure, they had been sent a photo of a known grave, but for many, this was not the case, and still some boys' bodies had not been found. These people were grieving, and taking it out on the returned lads was not the right way to grieve. I became obsessed in trying to help them, both the suffering families and the returned lads.

One day in about late 1924, I heard of a story that had me thinking that perhaps I could do the same.

The story went something like this: A New Zealand grandmother, about 56 at the time, wanted to visit her two sons and one son-in-law in Europe. When I say visit, she wanted to see their graves. One son died on April 25, 1915 on the day of the first landing at Gallipoli, one died of wounds in Belgium in 1917 at *Bailleul*, and her daughter's husband died in *Le Quesnoy* one week before the Armistice was signed. Even though I had been there as a soldier during the war, and seen these places, the sad part of the story was trying to understand the impact these tragedies had on this wonderful lady from New Zealand. I learned soon after that this particular story had a huge impact on many mothers and fathers in our part of the world, as they also wanted to visit their dear sons' graves.

When I was part of Captain Bean's mission in 1919, I remember meeting Lieutenant Cyril Hughes, a 30-year-old Tasmanian who joined the Graves Registration Unit, and was given the task of finding the bodies of missing soldiers on Gallipoli, and constructing proper cemeteries and monuments on the Peninsula.

The work of finding bodies after four years was extremely difficult. His team had to probe the ground, locate, identify, and find the remains of Australian soldiers, then re-bury them. On a number of occasions while working with Bean, we were in the same area as Hughes and his team, and I was often lent out as an extra hand. Cyril was a Gallipoli veteran like me, but what made me instantly like him was not an interest in sheep, but he had language skills that made mine perfectly second rate. If my memory is right, he was fluent in Middle Eastern languages, and had no trouble in picking up Turkish. He and Mustafa met on a few occasions and were conversing quite comfortably in Turkish. While I suddenly felt left out, I was really proud of them both.

The New Zealand mother did end up visiting her boys' final resting places, and also spent time visiting other cemeteries, about thirty in all, to pay her respects on behalf of all grieving mothers. In Gallipoli, she almost didn't get a chance to disembark from her boat at Chanak, as Turkish authorities would not allow anyone who had transited through the Athenian port to enter Turkish land. But when she showed her wreath to an irate and obstinate official, he immediately knew what she wanted to do, and allowed her to set foot on land.

Cyril Hughes was not on hand to meet her, as his work had been concluded, but another Australian, or should I say, another Tasmanian by the name of Tasman Millington, was on hand to show her the graves and cemeteries. Cyril had been promoted to running the whole of the Graves Commission and worked out of Egypt.

Eliza O'Donnell became the first woman to visit the Peninsula after the war from either Australia or New Zealand, and within a few days, had laid her wreath at the grave site of her son, Jack. Tasman Millington at the time was the caretaker of all cemeteries on Gallipoli and had been there since 1919. He arrived just after I left in that year. While Cyril Hughes established the cemeteries and memorials, people like Tasman have been looking after them ever since.

Tasman and Eliza spent almost a week visiting the important sites. He took her to the almost completed New Zealand memorial at Chunuk Bair where Eliza was permitted to place a brick in the monument. I can just imagine her bending down with a newly cut stone, mixing some mortar, and placing it in position on the monument. How proud must she have felt?

Reading her story made me think that we could undertake such an odyssey from Ballarat, so I began to ponder and plan. I'd been looking for a way to help the grieving families, and now I had found a way forward. It is not that easy to simply take a wonderful story of visiting a cemetery on the other side of the earth and leave in a few weeks. All up, the planning took me nearly five years! In the end, a group of about a dozen from the district left the port of Melbourne *en-route* for Athens via the Suez Canal, where we would board a smaller vessel bound for Chanak. I was the only returning soldier on the trip, accompanied by five mothers and six fathers, all of whom had lost a son, and one man who had lost two sons in Gallipoli.

For many parents who could not make the journey, they gave us objects to place on their son's grave, wrote some personal words to be spoken over their final resting places and wished us a safe trip. We all felt the heavy weight of their expectations, but I believe we were ready for it.

I had been given time away from my teaching job in Ballarat, and I departed with the full cooperation of my supportive wife. She could see that I was becoming more and more withdrawn and frustrated in the months leading up to our departure, and I could not begin to explain my feelings to her. I was ever grateful to her for understanding my feelings on this deeply personal matter.

About six months prior to our leaving, I wrote to the Imperial War Graves Commission in Turkey seeking approval for our visit. I did not have a name to send our request to, so it was addressed as generically as possible. A reply came three months later from Tasman Millington, and he said that he would be pleased to sponsor our visit and looked forward to meeting all of our group.

Since the 8th Battalion 4th Reinforcements left from Melbourne in 1915 on the *Wiltshire*, this trip 15 years later was a joy. I had lost my fear of sea travel, well, largely anyway, and thoroughly enjoyed the company of these people.

The entire boat trip from Melbourne to Chanak via the Suez took one month from start to finish. On leaving Cairo, bound for Turkey, I became nervous and unsure what to experience. Even though I had spent considerable time with Bean, Wilkins and Lambert over ten years ago as a part of the Mission, now I was an older, wiser, family man, travelling with people who had suffered extreme grief at the loss of their precious boys. My emotions were running in all directions. Landing at the wharf in Chanak could not come quickly enough, which it did only two days after leaving Cairo.

Standing on the bow of our little boat gliding into Chanak, I could see some westerners standing on the wharf. It was Tasman Millington, his wife and 6-year-old son. They seemed like a typical family simply waiting for their relatives to visit. They even had small hand sized Australian flags to wave at us.

It had been 11 years since I was last here, and time had been good to the little village. It had grown and absent were all the British military personnel. The township was looking much better than it did in 1919, and our group was transported in two carriages to our hotel. One thing I will say — our accommodation was a lot better than in 1919! It was July 1930, and the weather was beautiful. Tasman gave us a little time to settle in and agreed to meet us in two hours' time.

At the appointed *rendezvous* point, a small café overlooking the Dardanelles, I arrived an hour early to see Tasman sitting alone, waiting with a coffee and glass of water. I joined him. We talked.

I told him I had been part of Bean's mission in early 1919 and knew Cyril Hughes. At that mention, his eyes lit up.

"You met Captain Hughes?"

"Captain? When I knew him, he was Lieutenant Hughes."

"He is Captain Hughes now, and living in Cairo."

"Oh no. We were just in Cairo. Not long enough to meet up with anyone, but I'll try to see him on our way home."

"I was part of Bean's Historical Mission, here with Lambert and Wilkins too. We stayed here in Chanak, but our digs were not as nice as these you have arranged for us. We also worked from time to time for Cyril Hughes, finding bones, identifying lost soldiers, and re-burying them. I fought at Gallipoli and found the mission work very rewarding. I'm looking forward to seeing what it is like now."

"It will be an honour to show you Angus. Indeed, it will be an honour to show all your group, and to find their sons. Many people over the past 10 years have come here to do just that, but sadly, not many from Australia. It is a long way, and it is expensive, but I understand."

We could have talked all day, and at times over the next week, we did talk a lot. We had so much in common, I liked him immediately. I talked about being shot and ending up in hospital on Limnos, and he said, "Me too".

"I was on Limnos — managed to get a bad case of diarrhoea in October 1915. Then shipped out to Malta, and back to Limnos before returning to ANZAC Cove. The day before we came back over here, a few mates and I took a donkey ride to the beautiful thermal springs on the island."

"Do you remember where you left from, and who took you?"

"As a matter of fact, I do. It was from a little village called Port something, and a beautiful angel of a woman and her friends took us on four donkeys. Later on, we came back to her village and had a coffee in a café there."

I let him talk. I couldn't help but smile at his story. So much like mine.

"Why are you smiling Angus?"

"I know exactly where you went Tasman. Did the beautiful Aphrodite have a name?"

"I think it was Mary or something."

"Was it Maroula?"

"Yeah. That was it. Gorgeous lady. So too were her friends."

"The village was Portianou, and the coffee shop was run by a man called George."

"How did you know that?"

"I did the same. During 1915 when I too was in hospital there, and later in 1919, when we visited on our way here. I took Bean and the others on the same donkey trip you did. On that return visit, I met Maroula, her husband and one of her children. I hope to see them again soon."

"How did you get on with the language divide Angus?"

That is when I told him a little more about my background. "That explains everything" said Tasman.

"How do you get on with the language here, Tasman?"

"Aah. That is a story on its own, but here is the short version. When I was sent here from the War Graves Commission, they gave me a small house to use. I had no additional help and found it difficult to hire Turkish workers to dig graves. To them, they simply dug huge holes and shovelled the dead into large, unmarked pits."

"Every time we found a new body, I would stop work, attempt to discover the poor bugger's identity, and inter them with proper dignity and respect. I insisted the Turkish workers remove their personal headgear, but most importantly, not to touch the bones of anyone we discovered. They didn't understand our methods and reasons, and simply walked off, never to return. I got so angry, I mentioned this to the Commission's visiting caretaker, and within no time, I was appointed a Turkish go-between."

"The Commission arranged for a Turkish man to help me, and he arrived a day later. His name was Pasha Ismail and was himself a veteran of the Gallipoli conflict. He probably tried to shoot you and I many times."

"Must have been a lousy shot. We're still here."

"Ismail spoke very good English, and finally I had someone to explain what it was we were doing, and he was able then to pass that on to the hired workers. That completely changed our working arrangements and work commenced at a pace."

"But you wanted to know about my language acquisition?"

"Yes. If he spoke English, why did you want to learn Turkish?"

"As you would know, as a linguist Angus, it helps when you know the language of the country you are in. Just common sense and demonstrates respect. I asked Ismail to help me, and to this day, I am still learning, but at least I can hold a conversation with any of the Turkish workers, thanks to Ismail."

"My wife and son speak Turkish better than I do. My son has no accent because he was born and raised here. He often corrects me when I make grammatical mistakes."

Tasman and I could have spent the rest of the day talking in that café, but we did have much more important objectives. The rest of my tour group arrived soon after, and we all sat at the café to discuss the next few days' schedule. Tasman told us about the work he does over the other side of the Dardanelles for the cemeteries and mentioned some of the people who had made pilgrimages here just like us. Because it was late in the afternoon, after Tasman left us to return to his family, I took it upon myself to act as the village tour guide.

That night, the heightened level of anxiety of the group was palpable. So near to their ultimate destination, the nerves were kicking in. We bid each other good night and agreed to meet back at this café the next morning at 8 o'clock where Tasman was to join us to take a short boat ride to Madytos.

CHAPTER 17

GALLIPOLI PILGRIMAGE

(1930)

This trip across the Dardanelles was to be no picnic with sandwiches, a beach swim and a game of cricket. Tasman had organised some of his employees to assist with our visit, and they were waiting in Madytos with donkeys and four horses to help carry supplies. All members of our touring party had brought with them items to leave behind, such as wooden signs, wreathes, personal trinkets and framed photographs. Both Tasman and I had experience in fighting here, so questions were coming thick and fast.

"What were the conditions like?"

"Did you get shot?"

"Did you shoot anyone?"

"How bad were the British generals?"

"What did you eat and drink?"

"Tell us about the enemy."

The questions brought a quick response from Tasman. "You see these four men walking with us? They are all Turkish soldiers who fought against us during the campaign."

A collective gasp went up amongst the group.

"These other three men are Russian, and they now live here since leaving Russia 10 years ago to avoid a civil war where they were on the wrong side of the Government. We are a mixed bunch, and it doesn't matter anymore that we may have been enemies in the past. We are just men trying to get on with our lives."

"For the Turkish men, you have to remember one thing about them above all else, they were defending their homeland. They saw us as the aggressors. The average Turkish soldier was a farmer who was doing his national duty to defend his home."

"After the burial armistice on May 24, 1915, Australian soldiers helped Turkish soldiers bury their dead, and they did the same for us."

"Maybe I can help here Tasman. I was there the day of the armistice for burying our dead. In fact, it was our first day here on Gallipoli. We gained a lot of respect for each other after that day. We didn't know why we were fighting and neither did they. I have respected the Turkish soldier ever since."

After those brief words, I could see a different attitude towards our additional guides. Tasman helped translate for us. To me he didn't have an accent, but then again, I probably couldn't tell if he did!

Each of the five days at Gallipoli started the same. From Madytos, it was to leave with the horses and donkeys, visit cemeteries, perform our duties, and cry a lot. There were many tears, and offerings and prayers were quietly spoken for many lost men. If it wasn't for the help of our Turkish and Russian assistants, some of the older group members would not have been as comfortable as they were. They were all most grateful for the experience, and each night at our hotel in Chanak, the debriefing sessions lasted for hours. Each person who laid wreaths for their dearly beloved were given the time to talk about their lost sons and tell us all about who they were. I felt as if I knew them all as brothers.

On the last day, I asked Tasman why he stayed with Cyril

Hughes' team. He said that he felt like he was doing important work for the first time in his life, and after all, he had his wife and son with him, plenty of work, and a deep respect for the Turkish people, who respected him.

I told him about Mustafa, and how he and I met on the day of the burial armistice, later in that year again when we once more buried our dead, and then after the war ended, here on the Peninsula where he was employed by Bean as a helper.

"Did you say Mustafa?"

"Yes, I did."

"How did you speak with him? Do you speak French?"

"You are not going to believe this, but Mustafa spoke Greek. I found out that he was born in Limnos, but was forced to leave in 1912, and came to live in Madytos."

"You are kidding me Angus. I met him in 1919 when I first arrived to work here. He also helped me to learn some basic Turkish. I think he might even be a teacher now."

At that moment, I became very emotional. For the first time since arriving back in Turkey, I cried openly. My tour group must have thought I was some tough soldier man who never showed any emotion, but that is as far from the truth as you can get. One of our group, a man called Greg, offered me a handkerchief to wipe away tears. I explained to the group how I met Mustafa, how he and I conversed, and where he was born. I explained to Tasman that Mustafa was a good friend of Maroula and the team of donkey leaders in Limnos. He smiled at that thought.

Here was a Turkish man I was talking about with these grieving people, and I was talking about a man I knew who was as familiar as their sons. To them, I gave 'Johnny Turk' a name, a face, and a back story. I think I helped them understand that the enemy was in fact, another version of ourselves. He was no different. He had parents. Brothers and sisters. Family grieving for them too. He was not to be feared, but respected.

Mustafa was the first Turkish person I ever met, and I liked him immediately. That brief moment in May 1915 meant so much to me, I didn't even realise it at the time. Now, I do. We had so much in common, and we probably still do. This was the message I tried to convey to my visiting party.

Two days before, we had found the grave site of Greg's son. When he saw where his boy was buried, he knelt on the ground, rubbed his hands in the dirt and cried. I offered him my handkerchief, and now, it was his turn to acknowledge the gesture. No words were spoken. They were not necessary.

Tasman told me that he hadn't seen Mustafa now for many years, but he would often see him in Madytos visiting family when he came from Constantinople. We didn't have any spare time on this trip for me to try to find him in the city, so I asked Tasman to pass on a personal message if they were to meet again soon.

"Please tell Mustafa that I was here again, and that I still think of him every day."

"I will do that Angus."

Our visit to Gallipoli had sadly come to an end all too soon. All members of the tour group were satisfied they had done what they set out to do. They had become much more knowledgeable about the whole Gallipoli conflict, and although upset still that their sons could not be buried closer to home, they understood that their memories would never be forgotten, and as long as men like Tasman Millington were around, their graves would be lovingly tendered.

Tasman informed us that a new memorial was planned soon for ANZAC Cove with an inscription by Ataturk himself, and the words would be carefully chosen. He didn't give too much away, but Tasman wanted the words to ensure any potential visitors that their sons, who were now lying here, would never be forgotten.

"Tomorrow morning, we leave for Greece, but I have a surprise for you. We will not be going to Athens as planned, but instead, we will do the reverse trip our boys made on April 24 1915, the day before landing at ANZAC Cove. We are going to the Greek island of Limnos where the Allied forces practiced landings, where they left from to come here, and where the hospitals were located for the sick and wounded. It is also the place where Turkey formally signed their Armistice to end hostilities in October 1918."

"I also promise you a donkey trip like you cannot possibly imagine!"

Greg asked me "what is it about you and donkeys Angus? I thought you were a sheep man?"

"Wait until you see where I am taking you tomorrow. I promise you some sheep."

Next morning, our boat arrived and we made our way out of the Narrows, down the southern coast of the Peninsula, around Cape Helles, turned right and travelled along the coast line to ANZAC Cove, then made a left turn to go close to the island of Imbros, and finally in a westerly direction to Limnos. The weather was beautiful, and the sea calm. All on board were like little children going for a tram ride around Lake Wendouree on their way to the gardens to play in the park. What I'm trying to say was that they were highly excitable!

Our boat took us directly into Moudros Harbour, and we docked at the port in the township of Moudros. It looked as though time had stood still here. Nothing seemed to have changed all that much. Arriving at the port, the Church on the hill was still the most striking landmark to be seen in the village, but there appeared to be some additional permanent establishments between the wharf and Church.

After all customs formalities were completed, we unloaded our belongings and met on the wharf for a briefing. I gave a little speech and outlined what I knew of the contribution Limnos played in the Gallipoli campaign.

"Today, we find ourselves in a part of the world not many

Australians, apart from the nurses and soldiers of the AIF that is, have ever visited. As far as I know, this is the first large group from Australia ever to visit the cemeteries here in 11 years. Some individuals have obviously made the pilgrimage, but we are the first group." I can't really remember what I said next, but we put our sun hats on and headed out of town towards the first of our stops — the military cemetery of Moudros.

Walking past the Church, an old lady wearing a head scarf tied under her chin, a long skirt down to the ground just covering her shoes, a dark blouse and an apron with two pockets, was sweeping the steps outside with a homemade straw broom. Appearing to be sweeping the ground to within an inch of its life, she stopped for a moment, rested her hands on the broom handle, wiped her brow and mumbled something.

"*Good morning Auntie,*" I said to the toothless dirt sweeper.

That startled her. Not that someone said good morning, but that an obviously foreign looking group of tourists were speaking in her language.

"*Good morning to you all. Where are you from and why are you here?*"

I told her who we were, and when she heard 'Australians', she smiled to show us her bare gums, but the smile was genuine.

"*One of your dentists took out all my teeth, and I have no more pain. Thank him for me, will you?*"

"What did she say? Who is she? Why does she like Australians?"

There were lots of questions, but I did my best to answer them. After a brief conversation, where we learned that she had lived there all her life, and all about her family, she told us that she remembered the Australians above all else, because they were kind and helpful, and did not show any disrespect at all to the locals all those years ago. She explained to us that many people who had medical issues were given free treatment for a number of years, until the last of the doctors left. She was most thankful for that. But she also did say that the French soldiers had some very nice wine!

Leaving the dentally challenged sweeper alone with her well-swept steps, we walked through town and made our way to the military cemetery. After visiting many such places like this over on Gallipoli, I did not expect any surprises, but was I wrong.

Walking through the gravestones and reading the names, we found a few 8th Battalion names. These were my friends. These were my cobbers. One of our group found the name of a soldier who was the best friend of her son, now buried at Quinn's Post. I wouldn't call this an unexpected surprise, but you know what I mean. All of us stood back and gave her the space to grieve once more. We stopped at the grave of Colonel Linton, who was the Commanding Officer aboard the *Southland*. Although he never set foot on Limnian earth, he was now buried here. I was surprised to learn the level of understanding among the group in relation to this little part of our history. The *Southland* did not end up sinking after copping a German torpedo, but about 30 men had died that day in September 1915. The story made many local papers back home, and one of the tour group knew some of the boys on that vessel who had survived.

Our next stop was once again in the port of Moudros to board a caique for the short journey across the harbour to Sarpi. Or so I thought. Once on board, I was told by the boat's captain that Sarpi was now renamed Kallithea, and where the tent village used to be, is now Nea Koutali, a migrant village built for Asia Minor refugees in 1923. So much progress!

The new village of Nea Koutali was built in the area around the pier constructed during the war for the Allied supplies bound for the rest camp. Since those days, this new village was now pre-dominantly dependent on fishing, and the pier was bigger than I remember. It was good to know that the small engineering feat of a pier could have such a lasting and unplanned benefit for the locals. I felt proud.

Before we journeyed into Portianou, we had lunch at the one and only café in Nea Koutali, where 11 years before, I stayed with the Mission team. Sitting in the café, I could make out the hospital sites across the water, or rather, where the hospital sites were. I took the role of tour guide very seriously and tried to point out any major places of interest.

We were not the only people in the café, and I approached the owner and asked what he had to eat. My Ballarat tour group had never been to this part of the world, apart from our week in Turkey, but I was sure they were in for a gastronomic treat.

"We have stuffed tomatoes, fresh bread, wine, goats and sheep cheese, olives, cucumber and dips of all kinds."

After translating, all I could hear was 'yes please'. Of course, I struck up a conversation with the owner, and he told me all the food came from around here. He made his own cheese from the milk supplied from a farmer in the next village. *"Which village?"* I asked him.

"From Pesperago."

I thought better than to push this any further, imagining that Haralambous and Maroula had personally milked the animals to help with the production of this magnificent cheese.

During lunch, I asked the owner if he could help us locate any donkeys so that we could travel to Therma and Portianou.

"Hey Savva. This man wants 10 donkeys. How long before you can get them here?"

I didn't see Savva leave the café, but in no time, he produced 10 of the ugliest donkeys known, but promised us they were reliable. Some money changed hands, and I told the group we had secured our transport.

Lunch concluded, the donkeys were mounted and we were ready for the next part of our journey. Greg laughed at me, and now the rest of the group were also laughing. The owner asked me if I knew the way, and told him I certainly did.

I thought the best thing to do would be to visit the cemetery first, then on to Therma for a bath, back to Portianou for a coffee at George's café, and then return to our boat to take us over the water to Moudros.

Well, that was the plan. To a large extent, it went off without a hitch. We visited the cemetery, placed flowers on graves, quietly said some words to the two Canadian nurses, and left. It was nonetheless sad to be in that place, especially for me as I could remember seeing funeral processions coming past me, and hearing the bugle echoing across the fields.

The group loved Therma, and asked me why we didn't stay in the newly built resort next to the baths. I told them that on my last visit, this hadn't been built.

I don't know what the locals of Portianou thought as we ambled through the village on our donkeys, but as soon as George saw me, he came running out of his coffee shop and dragged me off my mount. The same two old codgers were sitting at their table, sucking on the same shisha pipe, and mumbling the same words to each other, but this time, one of them also remembered me.

"Weren't you just here Aussie?"

"That was 11 years ago Uncle."

"Really? I thought it was only yesterday."

I am sure if I had visited again in another decade or so, they would still be there, and doing the same things.

George and I spoke while he refreshed my tour group with coffees, cakes, and a quick shot of his finest rot gut clear liquid. He looked much older, and I discovered he had not been well. We talked of our families, and this time, I could tell him about mine. He was so happy, and I said, *"that makes two of us George."*

I asked George if Maroula and Barbie were still living nearby, and he said that they were. *"Would you like to see them again Angus?"*

George sent a village boy to fetch Maroula and Barbie from Pesperago. He always seemed to have a village urchin on hand to run errands for him. I never did ask how this could possibly be, but the young lad returned with two dear friends and three children in about 30 minutes.

My group were enjoying the shade of a huge, ancient mulberry tree in the village square where George served fresh bread, olives, cheese, watermelon and wine. After sitting on donkeys for some, and walking for others, the shade of this tree with the hospitality shown us was a delight. A local mandolin player serenaded us while we ate and drank. We still had a few hours before the return boat trip to Moudros, so camping under this tree, with refreshments, music and great company, no one was complaining.

Maroula, Barbie and the children had been resting at their home, and when they knew we were in Portianou, they dropped everything and came over immediately. Maroula helped George in the café, the children ran off to play with friends in the village, and Barbie and I talked about family, sheep, and life since we last saw each other. Even though I desperately wanted to talk to his wife, I was loving the chat with Barbie.

Life had been difficult for them, but they were happy. Barbie explained the two lots of refugees to arrive on Limnos over the past decade, being first the Russians, and then from Asia Minor. Although the Russians left an impact on them, it was the arrivals from Asia Minor that had the greatest effect on everyday life. The mixing of cultures had created some tension and hostility amongst some of the older Greek people, but Barbie and Maroula and their friends welcomed the new people with open arms. He told me about their children, and I told him about mine. We talked about our wives, sheep and everyday things. It was good to hear about his family and normal life for once.

For our group, seeing them enjoy the afternoon under the beautiful tree, experiencing life in a quiet, rural village on an island in the north east Aegean, with none of the trappings of our life in Australia, was also good to see. Just good friends, good food, and conversation. Even the two old shepherds joined our table and were loving the free wine shouted by some very thirsty Ballarat drinkers.

It was almost time to leave, and I finally savoured a minute to talk with Maroula. Given the limited time available for any meaningful conversation, and given my limited conversational ability in Greek, she seemed happy enough with her life and enjoyed me talking about my family. Nonetheless, it was still a wonderfully short, yet memorable moment in my life. While Maroula and I were chatting, Barbie had wandered off to find his children, and Greg rounded up the tour group in preparation for the walk back to the waiting boat.

Given the amount of food and drink we had consumed, the walk back to the boat was slow. Maroula, Barbie and their children joined us, and I had one last question for Barbie as we left Portianou.

"Where are your sheep right now?"

"They will all be home and resting in the shade."

"Why don't they wander off?"

"Not during this heat. At this time of year, they will come home on their own, and I'll take them back out in a few hours after milking. My son is helping me now."

"My sheep would never do that. I have to show them everything."

"Not here Angus, we train them from a young age to do this in summer. It saves us a lot of unnecessary work in the heat."

Our boat was waiting for us at the pier. Travelling over the bay to Moudros, each of the group thanked me for the experience of seeing how life on the island was during a normal day. While it doesn't make the loss of their sons any easier, I think they all gained something special from visiting Gallipoli, but also here, where some of the boys recovered from wounds, spent time practicing the landings, and for some, where they eventually died. For me,

I had mixed feelings. I was glad to have been the group leader but was feeling sad that I most probably would never see my Limnian friends again.

CHAPTER 18

RUSSIANS, REFUGEES AND ANGUS

(1920-30)

Our life returned to normal on Limnos after the end of the big war. However, we still had French and British soldiers stationed on the island. The French took over a building in Portianou, and we hardly ever saw any of the British. What I am trying to say is this — they did not interfere in our daily lives!

Towards the end of winter, and early in 1920, some Russians arrived in boats and made camp in the surviving remnants of the hospital sites at Pounda. We watched as boatload after boatload of these poor souls landed on our cold, windy shores. We were not told who they were, or why they were here, other than they had escaped a civil war in Russia. We did eventually discover that many of the men were military, and had wives and children with them.

Conditions must have been terrible. We wanted to help in some way, but the French officials, warned us to stay away, due to any diseases the refugees may have. So, we stayed away.

Thankfully, the water purification plant was still in existence on Pounda, so they had access to drinkable water, and some of the remaining wooden huts were used to house the hundreds of additional mouths to feed. A hospital was quickly constructed and for some months, we did not see any of them in our villages. From a distance, we could see an increase in the number of tents each day, but being winter, the tents would not keep out much cold. French officials found the refugees additional blankets, beds and some other basic items from their stores left over after the big war.

For many months, they stayed away from us, building up their camp sites with more canvas tents, building kitchens, food storage facilities and schools for children. We kept our distance, not wanting to catch any diseases they might have had. Some French officials notified us that the Russians would have to remain in quarantine for a while until it was safe to begin trading. The Russians kept to their camps until the sickness was under control.

As soon as it was safe to do so, some of them ventured away from their camp and managed to walk to Portianou, Pesperago, Kontias and Tsimandria. They were looking to buy food, and desperately needed work. Some villagers employed them on the land, and soon enough, they were drinking, dancing, and singing in our taverns and attending church.

The Russians loved their dancing and singing as much as we did. They also loved their drinking as much as our men did too. Their church was Orthodox, so instantly, many villagers welcomed them with open arms. I was always wary of them at first, because no sooner had they commenced leaving their camp in search of food and work, some small and unexplained thefts occurred. Some of our sheep went missing, and we were not the only shepherds to lose animals. One Russian man was trying to buy military guns in Kontias but was arrested by French police on his way back to the camp. Some Russians approached boat owners to either buy boats, or to take them to Constantinople. We could see they were desperate to either return home, or to find a better place to live than here on Limnos.

The French police told us not to take any of them off the island, but I know of some desperate boat owners who did exactly what they were warned not to do. I heard there may have been over 10,000 Russian refugees on Limnos, but we did not feel it was that many, probably because they kept to their own, newly established community out on the site near the water purification plant, with their wooden huts and sprawling tent village.

Some of Barbies' friends with boats managed to smuggle food to them, mostly at nights, when the patrols were less active. On one occasion, a woman told one of the food smugglers that what they really needed were clothes and shoes.

I grew to like the Russians. They were just like us. They were refugees, and not here by choice. They were grateful to be given the chance to live away from war. They made the most of their time here, but really only wanted to be able to return home safely.

Some of our people learned enough of their language, and some of them learned enough of ours to communicate. At first, it was considerable grunting and a lot of finger pointing, but over the course of their time on our island, we grew to understand them a little better. On some occasions during summer, we were invited to their camp site to witness musical events and theatre. I had never been to the theatre before, and my first experience of a play was performed entirely in Russian. None of my friends and family could understand a word of it, but we loved it all the same. They provided the entertainment, and we provided fresh food and, of course, wine.

Towards the end of 1920, many more Russians arrived and set up their camps in Pounda and Moudros. An abandoned church in Moudros was given to the Russians to clean, and to use as their place of worship, so that they could conduct services in their own language. This small token of appreciation endeared us to the Russians in ways that are difficult to explain. To be so far from home, in a strange and inhospitable land, but to experience just this small piece of normality must have been wonderful for them.

Perhaps my everlasting memory of these people was their singing. They sang about everything and anything. They even made-up songs about life on Limnos! Their souls may have been badly beaten, but they were not destroyed. By the summer of 1921, most Russian refugees had been moved away from Limnos to other parts of Greece and to other countries. I often thought of what became of those wonderful people. From time to time, Barbie and I would take our sheep out to the end of Pounda, near where the Russians constructed a cemetery, and remember the people who had lived and died here while our sheep munched on grass nearby. We also took our flock further out to where the Russians had built a stone monument on the spot where the English navy had built a wooden shipping beacon during the big war.

Once again, life returned to normal with the departure of all Russians, but normality only lasted for a few years. In 1923, refugees again sailed into our shores, and this time, like the last time, these new arrivals were also Orthodox. Like the Russians, these new people were refugees, but there was one big difference. They were refugees from Turkey. According to the Turks, these people were not Muslim, so they had to leave. Regardless of their religion, they were Turkish, but because the new country of Turkey wanted to have only one religion, people who were Christian were forced out. Greece willingly agreed to take nearly one million people, and Limnos took its share.

The families arrived with suitcases of memories, and little else. They had very few possessions, and all over Limnos, new villages were created, or parts of existing villages expanded.

Nea Koutali had been only a small fishing village, but in 1923, it gradually grew in size. Kontias and nearby villages added to their neighbourhoods with the construction of new houses. About an hour's donkey ride from our house, a new village of Agios Dimitrios was built especially for the newly arrived refugees. We were told that these refugees were Greeks from Asia Minor, but very few of them spoke much of our language as they had lived in Turkey for hundreds of years. I now wondered what had happened to Mustafa and his family, who were ordered out of our country. These refugees were not here by choice, and I and many of my friends were determined to welcome them.

There were some of us that did not welcome these new people to our island. It didn't matter what we said to them, they were determined never to fully accept the new arrivals into our community. In church, they would not stand next to them, on the streets, they would walk on the opposite side, and in cafés, they would not sit at the same table.

Gradually, over the next five to ten years, these new Limnian refugees became part of our community. We only really differed in language spoken at first. Our music, culture, food, dance, clothing, and many words were the same. Because many of us still spoke Turkish, we could make them feel welcome almost immediately, but housing construction took its time, and soon, these new villages gained a life of their own. Vacant land was given to them to establish farms, and gradually, the new arrivals settled into a new life.

Our children found many more friends to play with and schools were overflowing. The new people improved their spoken Greek, and for me, it was nice to speak again in Turkish, although many others in our village refused to speak to these people at all. Within 10 years, the first mixed marriages were celebrated, and gradually, our two cultures became one — well almost. Many of the older houses vacated by the departing Turks in 1912 were renovated and life returned to our villages. Some older people took many years to accept these new people. Some never did.

In Pesperago, the house vacated by Mustafa's family now had a new family living in it. Barbie and I lived nearby, and every day I walked past my friend's old house, I thought of him and his family. I also thought of a funny Greek-speaking Australian man and wondered if he had found a wife and was blessed with children.

It wasn't long before this thought of mine was resolved. I'll never forget the day a boy came running to our house just as we were preparing for a rest after a morning on the farm. He came running up to the house and said that there was a group of Australians in Portianou and they wanted to see us. Angus? It couldn't be!

Sure enough. It was. Angus and a group of people from his Australian village were here on the island.

"Come on kids. We are going to visit Uncle George."

The kids loved vising uncle George. Every time we went to his café, George would give the kids some bread and in summertime, a piece of watermelon. It didn't matter how many kids came past the café, as George always managed to find something for them to eat. For many kids, this might have been the only thing they had eaten all morning, because life was still a struggle for many of us. We saw Angus and he introduced us to his friends. George asked me to help in the kitchen, the kids found friends to play with, and Barbie sat with Angus and talked about sheep.

It was lovely seeing Angus again. He had not been here for nearly 10 years, and he looked older. I loved hearing about his family, and he had plenty of questions for us. He explained why they were here, and I understood. One of my other uncles Dimitri, came to the café with his mandolin, and played songs while we sang. Angus' friends loved it, and for a short while, I did too. I know my husband was now a friend of Angus, and that made me very happy.

In no time, the afternoon was over, and Angus needed to return to Moudros. I was sad seeing him leave because I truly believed that we would never meet again. Barbie took the kids home, and I walked to Nea Koutali with Angus and his group to catch the boat. Standing at the pier, waving goodbye, I had a tear in my eyes. Angus stood on the boat, facing me, and didn't turn around until I could hardly see him anymore.

CHAPTER 19

TASMAN, ISMAIL AND 'SMITH'
(1935 – 1941)

Many years ago, a strange Australian man and a Turkish man came to Portianou. At the time, I was visiting Uncle George in his café performing my normal delivery of milk and some vegetables from our farm. I even remember having a bottle of wine Barbie made from his grapes to give George to see if he liked it. I was not a fan of Barbie's wine, but he loved it, and we always gave Uncle George a bottle as soon as the new vintage was ready. When I look back at it now, Uncle George never did say he didn't like the wine.

The Australian man looked familiar to me, but I could not remember where I may have met him. It could only have been here, but I had difficulty in remembering each of the people I met all those years ago.

The Australian man was sitting at the café drinking one of George's famous coffees, and his Turkish friend was talking quietly to him. I came out of the café and noticed them at the table closest to the front door. I could hear them speaking Turkish, so I said *"hello"* to them.

Taken aback at this, the Australian man asked me how I knew the language, and I immediately asked him the same question. Uncle George could hear this conversation and he asked me if I had time for a coffee.

"Only if you join us."

I told them both that we had Turkish people living amongst us for 450 years, so learning the language was not a problem.

"My best friend growing up lived in the village not far from here where I live now."

I explained to them how Mustafa and his family were forced to leave this island over 15 years ago, but that I considered them all to be as Greek as I was.

"The only difference is that his ancestors were considered Turkish, and as our occupiers, we also called them Turkish, but they were as Greek as a bouzouki and sheep's milk."

The Turkish man was still quiet, and not saying much. The Australian was doing all the talking. But I couldn't help myself.

"If you don't mind me asking, but you speak very good Turkish, although your accent is not very good. Are you Australian by any chance?"

"How could you have possibly known that?

"I knew an Australian man many years ago, and he spoke Greek with the same bad accent as your Turkish."

I asked them why they were here, and the Australian man said that he and his friend worked for the Imperial War Graves Commission on the Gallipoli Peninsula and they were here visiting the cemeteries in Portianou and Moudros.

The Australian man said his name was Tasman, and his co-worker was Ismail, and I told them that I was Maroula and that the old man who brought them a coffee was George.

"I was here many years ago too. During the war, I was very sick with diarrhoea, and after I had some rest over in the hospital, some other patients and I came by here to see if we could get to the thermal springs for a hot bath."

"I used to take people on donkey rides to the springs. Did you come with me Tasman?"

"I think I did. It was nearly 15 years ago. If I remember, you had two other young men with you, and we travelled for about an hour — or maybe two. The springs bath was delightful. I had never had a bath like it, and I probably never will."

"Did you know the Turkish discovered the hot springs and constructed the buildings?"

Ismail was very pleased when he heard this. He said that he can't wait to see what his cousins had built!

"Can we go to the baths tomorrow, Maroula?"

I told George that he had to find me three donkeys for the next day, and if he could, I would take Tasman and Ismail to Therma. George agreed, and the two Cemetery employees agreed.

"Were you working in Gallipoli in about 1930, Tasman?" I asked.

"Yes, we both were. We have been working together since about 1919. Is that right Ismail?"

"Yes, I think so Millington."

"Why do you ask, Maroula?"

"My Australian friend visited Gallipoli again in about 1930 with a group from Australia, and they came here directly afterwards to visit these cemeteries. Do you ever remember a man by the name of Angus? He was here many times during the Gallipoli conflict in 1915, after the war in 1919, and the last time I saw him was 1930."

It was highly unlikely that he knew of Angus, but it was worth a try.

"I remember Angus well. We were both soldiers who fought against Ismail in Gallipoli, but Angus and I were not part of the same battalion. He told me he came back here after the war with Captain Bean and a few other Australians."

"Did the Captain have bright red hair? Did they call him Carrot?"

"Yes. How do you know that?"

"I took them to Therma, where we are going tomorrow."

"Maroula. You said that you had a friend who lived in your village who was Turkish by ancestry. Can you remember his name?"

"Yes, sure. Mustafa was his Turkish name, but we all called him Michali."

At the sound of Mustafa, Tasman turned to Ismail and gave the biggest smile.

"Why are you smiling?"

"You are not going to believe this, but we both remember Mustafa very well. He worked for me in 1919 for a year or two. He taught me Turkish! Or to put it more accurately, I learned some very simple Turkish words and phrases from him."

"I remember him Millington. He talked about Limnos from time to time as being his place of birth. He was a good worker. Very good at stonework if my memory hasn't failed me. Remember, he helped build that first memorial near Alcitepe?"

"He also told us of an Australian man he met during the war, when they both were part of an unofficial burial armistice."

"Mustafa did mention that he lived not far from here."

"I can show you the house he lived in. It's near here. Can you tell me anything about him now? What is he doing? Where is he living?"

"All I remember is that he returned to live in Madytos after working for us, and he was possibly a teacher now. It makes sense that he lived in Madytos. There was a big Greek population there at the end of the war. Not many now, but big back then."

"I think he was also involved in wrestling, and he was very good. Won some big national event I think."

Tasman said that he had not heard anything from Mustafa for about 10 years now, and neither had Ismail. I wished them a good night, and helped George clean the café in readiness for the next day. But before they left, we agreed to meet at about 9.00 am after a good night's sleep.

The next morning, I took them both to the thermal springs, stopping off at an old Turkish tap at the base of Mt Elias along the way for a drink, like thousands of people had done for hundreds of years. Ismail was very keen to study this particular tap and he noted its construction. *"Nice stonework."*

The remainder of that journey was the same as I had undertaken on many occasions. Nothing different. They had a hot bath, towelled themselves dry while I waited outside, and afterwards we immediately returned to the village.

That was how I met Tasman and Ismail. The next time we were to meet would be under very different circumstances. I didn't know it at the time, but their trip to Limnos was not only to visit the cemeteries. I was to learn years later that they were conducting a reconnaissance mission to see where they were to meet a British agent who was to sell them a boat, or something like that.

A month or two before the Germans arrived in 1941, another strange man was having a coffee in the plateia outside Uncle George's café. As well as ordering a coffee and some cakes, he gave George a verbal instruction and some money to find the lady who had taken British soldiers to the thermal springs during the first world war. George sent for me, and I arrived within the hour.

He said his name was '*Smith*' and he wanted someone to take him to the thermal springs, but he also said that I had been recommended to him. What struck me as odd was not that he asked for me, but his Greek was flawless. Much better than Angus, and better than many local people.

'*Smith*' and I mounted our donkeys and headed off in the direction of Therma. There was still no direct path, but rather a collection of goat tracks made over the years from sheep, donkeys, people and of course goats. I decided to ride to the left of Mt Elias, past one of the many old Turkish taps built a long time ago, which was the same one I showed Tasman and Ismail. The tap in question was constantly dripping water into a series of hollowed, carved stones, and gave our farm animals a much-needed drink of clean, clear water all year round. 'Smith' wasn't all that interested in Turkish taps, but he did stop for a drink.

Attached to a rusty chain was a metal cup, used by thirsty farmers for as long as I can remember. 'Smith' dismounted, took the cup, filled it with water and took a long slow drink, appearing to be lost in his thoughts. Placing the cup down at the tap's base, he walked to the rear of the little Turkish stone monument admiring its age.

"This must have been here for hundreds of years, Maroula. Isn't it wonderful how we can harness underground water, bring it to the surface, through a pipe, and have it constantly flowing for us to quench our thirst? Amazing."

He walked around the tap, carefully caressing the old stones, studying it like he knew something about its construction. He asked me what I thought about Limnos, and why I liked living here. I think I simply told him that it was my home, my parents' home, and all of my ancestors were buried here. I knew nothing else. He listened intently to what I was saying, not saying a word. Just nodding.

We mounted our donkeys and made our way to the thermal spring bath house. When he spoke, I was not ready for what came out of his mouth.

"Maroula. I don't know how to put this, but we need your help."

I thought what an odd thing for him to say. I didn't have any idea who 'we' were, and what kind of help he needed from someone like me. Instead of taking the track around the mountain where we would have ended up in Therma, he changed direction and turned to the right, on his way to the church at the top of Mt Elias.

"Why are we changing course?" I asked him.

"I want to see the island."

"Ok, but who is we? You said we need your help."

He didn't respond immediately, preferring to climb with our donkeys to the top of the island.

Once at the summit, he dismounted, stood and studied the

horizon like he was committing it to memory. Carefully turning to face all directions, he asked me "Is there a hidden bay anywhere around here that can land a small boat without being seen?"

Stunned at this question, I answered "Of course. We have many. Why do you want to know?"

"Maroula. I work for the British Secret Service, MI6, and we need someone here on Limnos to help us. The Germans will be here any day now, and we need to get messages to your resistance fighters. Can you help us?"

"Yes, of course, but what can I possibly do?"

"Just be willing to take a few Turkish 'fishermen' on a trip to Therma on your donkeys. They will find you in Portianou at George's café from time to time."

'*Smith*' was speaking in riddles, but I think I understood him. Turkey was neutral during the second world war, and therefore fishermen could travel to Limnos freely for 'fishing'. There might be a time when a fisherman would come to the café and ask for me to take them to visit the 'Turkish' baths house at Therma. All I had to do was live my normal life and wait. I must say, I felt anxious, nervous, terrified, but excited at the same time after '*Smith*' and I came back down Mt Elias, never even going to the springs. I kept on talking, and he seemed to be a good listener. But maybe he wasn't really listening. He was just scanning the area to see where the Germans might potentially set up their camps and observation lookouts.

Then he said something to me that proved he was taking notice.

"That old Turkish tap at the base of Mt Elias has a number of loose stones at the rear where we could hide messages without being seen by the Germans prying eyes. It appears the tap was designed for this very purpose. The stones give the impression of being fixed in position, but they are not. When the fishermen come for a bath, take them past that tap and they will stop for a drink. The tap will act as a sort of post office if you like. The Germans won't suspect anything."

'Smith' explained my role in some detail, but really, it was very simple. Turkish 'fishermen' would come to Limnos and moor their boat in plain sight of the Germans. After passing initial inspection, slipping some of their best fish to the soldiers, they would proceed to Uncle George's café, and ask for me. They would pay me of course, and then I would take them via donkey to Therma under the guise of wanting a bath, stopping off along the way at the Turkish tap. It was there they would leave messages for the resistance, who 'Smith' had already contacted. How he had done that, I still to this day do not know how, or indeed why, but he did.

The weather started to turn bad, with a strong wind blowing and some light rain falling. My donkey seemed keen to return home, so I suggested to 'Smith' that we should hurry and make our way back as a storm was approaching. I asked him how he knew of the Turkish tap, and he told me that he had studied a map drawn by someone who once worked with the Australian man working on Gallipoli as a gardener. This piece of rare news from 'Smith' caused me to probe a little deeper.

"You wouldn't happen to have the map with you?"

"Actually, I do. Would you like to see it?"

"Yes please."

His map was stunningly beautiful. I had never seen such a visual representation of our wonderful island before. It contained every village with its population, bays and inlets, whether the landing spots were sandy or contained rocks, all tracks, hills, churches, but the thing that was blindingly obvious to me was the location of every Turkish tap on the island. There were hundreds. Almost all of them were unknown to me, but the map looked like it was drawn to highlight their existence.

The map had distinctly Turkish place names, but as I knew the language, they seemed perfectly normal to me. It was clearly made by someone who was Turkish, and who had a solid understanding of every part of the island.

We arrived just in time at the village before a deluge swamped us. I barely made it home, and I never saw '*Smith*' again. I didn't get a chance to ask him more questions about the origins of the map. That night, I remember lying in bed wondering about the map, who may have drawn it, and why. By morning, I had many more questions for the mystery man '*Smith*', but like a puff of smoke on a windy day, he simply disappeared.

Within a week, another mystery man wandered into George's Café asking for me. In Turkish, with some broken Greek, he asked for a coffee and sour cherries, a local delicacy served on a small glass plate, about the size of a child's hand. Every woman in Portianou made these sweets with the abundance of sour cherries available. George served the 'fisherman' and the visitor took a seat outside the front door on his own, keeping well away from any local men.

George immediately thought of me and sent a boy off to my home to inform me of his arrival. I had only recently returned home after milking sheep, and was due to take a small rest, but the insistence of this boy was impressive.

"George wants you to come right away to the café Aunty."

"Ok Stavros. Tell him I'll be there soon."

Quickly washing my face and changing into some of my cleaner clothes, I walked gingerly to the plateia. I say gingerly, because these days, sitting on a wooden stool to milk one hundred sheep was starting to get much harder for me. Normally my son Niko would help me, but this day, he was helping someone else on their farm. My usual routine after milking was to return home, lie down for about half an hour, and then I would feel much better.

On this day the sun was shining brightly, and the village was full of children running in and out of houses, down and along alley ways, up and behind trees, and playing all sorts of hide and seek games. Rounding the corner to George's café, I saw the 'fisherman' sitting alone by the entrance to the café, sipping his coffee, and reading a book.

I initially thought it was another '*Smith*' character, but closer inspection told me he was an older man, about my age, and obviously educated, or at least he could read. As I came closer, I noticed the book was Greek, a collection of poetry by Γεώργιος Σεφεριάδης.

The poetry book reader had a Turkish fisherman's cap on his head covering his eyes, and he could not have noticed me approaching his table. I was within one step of him when he put the book down, looked up at me, and said in perfect local Limnian Greek "Good morning Maroula. It has been a long time."

"Mustafa. Is that you?"

"Yes, my old friend, it is, but can you please keep my identity quiet."

I didn't know what to say, think or do. I stood in front of his table and looked into the eyes of my best friend from over 30 years ago. He was obviously older, but to me, we were both 15 years old again, and innocently naïve on the ways of the world.

"Sit down before you attract too much attention."

There was no one else at the café, apart from the children running around our tables. George served me a coffee with a glass of water and looked at the man sitting down at my table. He knew it was Mustafa but didn't let on.

"What are you doing here? Why are you here? But it is so nice to see you. Tell me, what have you been doing for the past 30 years? Are you married? Do you have any children? How is your family?" Where are you living now?"

"Maroula, slow down. I only have one mouth and one brain. All in good time. I could ask you all the same questions. Where do we start?"

Mustafa told me as much as he could about his life after leaving Limnos in 1912. He was married with three children and working as a teacher. I told him of my life, married, but now widowed, four children and still helping with sheep.

We skipped over the children conversations and went directly to what he was doing here.

"You met my friend Mr Smith recently, and he asked you if you could help him."

"How could you possibly know that?"

"I met Mr Millington in Madytos, who you also know, many years ago after the war. I was working for him for nearly two years, and I taught him Turkish. He was a very good student, and I enjoyed teaching him. After the war ended in defeat, we returned home, and I desperately needed work. Mr Millington and Ismail gave me the opportunity to work for them, save some money, and before I really knew, I had a new life."

"Not only Millington, but I also managed to teach Turkish to about a dozen Russian men working with Mr Millington. I have never forgotten those days, and every time I returned to see my parents, I would visit Millington and Ismail to say hello."

"I could see a new war coming to Europe, and once again, I visited my parents and of course Millington and Ismail. They knew of my background here growing up on Limnos and asked me to help them. They needed a map of the island, showing many different things."

"So, it was you? You drew that map."

"Not quite. They already had a good one but needed someone with local knowledge to show them where there might be secret locations to land a boat, out of sight of the Germans, and somewhere to leave messages for the Greek resistance. I knew a place to land boats, but I recommended my father suggest a message hiding place. Remember, my father and his father were stonemasons, and he helped keep and repair many of the fountains and taps all over the island for many years. The tap at the base of Mt Elias was used as a secret hiding place for many years by my grandfather to hide money, gold and documents. My father didn't say why, but just that it existed. Millington, Ismail and 'Smith' were most interested in the location of this Turkish tap."

"Mr 'Smith' helped convince me to complete this task for him. He will be picking me up later on tonight from that cove we used to visit when we were kids. Remember where that was? Just over in Fakos, near where your uncle had his farm down on the water. Remember?"

"I do remember. So, you have a few hours."

"I would like to see what became of my old house, if that is OK with you."

Mustafa and I walked the two miles to Pesperago, as if we were still a pair of 12-year olds strolling with our friends around the villages without a care in the world. No one who saw us on that afternoon, apart from Uncle George, knew who he was. I don't know what they would have done if they recognised him, but that didn't happen. He asked me a lot of questions about the houses, farms, people, families, our old friends who had died, new members of families, and anything else he could think of. For a time, I forgot my own aching body, and was oblivious to the world around us. I was so happy to be seeing and talking with my old friend. He asked me about Barbie, and how he died. I was very sad telling him this, as I remember they did know each other when they were children.

Entering the village of Pesperago, Mustafa approached his old family home with trepidation, which had been abandoned for a number of years since an Asia Minor refugee family moved away to a different village. He wasn't sure what he'd find there. I remember the day well. There was the typical sound of cicadas echoing off stone buildings all around us, and little or no wind. Near the water tap in the plateia was a young girl playing on her own, while her grandmother filled a jug with water. This older neighbour lived next door to where Mustafa once lived. We were asked by the neighbour what we were doing in the garden, and I just told her that this was Michali, and he was from a village I knew she would never have visited, far away on the island.

That is a strange thing about our island. You can meet a person from a village only 10 miles away and know nothing about them. I told the neighbour that Michali was from the village of Plaka, in the far north-east of the island. When he spoke to her, the neighbour didn't suspect that it was Mustafa, and she was now talking to a neighbour from 30 years before!

"Was that Aunty Eleni? The years have not been kind to her," Mustafa said as we forced open the front door. Entering the house, it was as if time had stood still. While the exterior of the 100-year-old stone house was in need of repair, the roof tiles and interior were largely intact. Mustafa seemed to have an urgency about visiting the house. Memories for me also came flooding back. I had not been inside this house for many years. Walking along past two doors leading into rooms on the right, Mustafa ignored them and went directly to a cupboard under the stairs at the end of the short corridor. He opened the broken hinged door and peered inside. Surprisingly, it still contained some of his family's objects. He wasn't interested in them but took everything out of the cupboard anyway.

"Found it."

"Found what?" I asked hesitantly.

"My father's secret hiding place, here behind this stone."

"My father re-built this part of the house. He and his father designed a secret space in the wall where they would hide our valuable items, like gold coins and jewellery. The last occupiers it seems, did not even open this cupboard door."

With two knives, Mustafa gently eased a stone from the wall and carefully placed it on the floor. He then reached into the wall cavity, fumbled around a little while and cautiously withdrew a small metal box, with a rusted image of birds and feathers on the front. He handed it to me.

"This is what I was after."

"What is inside it?"

"Open it."

"No Mustafa. This looks like it could be important, and it is for your family."

"No, Maroula. Well, not entirely. It is ours, but if what is inside is what I think it is, my father said I should give it to you. And before you say anything, I won't hear a word of your refusal. The contents are yours now."

He opened the tin and gathered a handful of gold coins in the palm of his right hand. I was stunned. I didn't know what it was, but it sure looked valuable. Showing them to me, they were very old Turkish gold coins, and according to Mustafa, were more valuable here in Greece than in Turkey, where this currency was now outlawed.

"Maroula. I cannot take these coins back home. My father wants you to have them and do with it what you want."

I was so emotional; I didn't know what to think.

"I can't accept this Mustafa. It is not mine. They belong to your family."

"My family had a number of these boxes of old coins. When we left, my father took enough for us to build a new house. Most of the coins gathered over the years have been distributed to different people, like your Uncle George. How do you think he raised the money necessary to buy that café? This money represents taxes not paid to Turkey, raised from the sweat and tears of you and your people Maroula. Like I said, most of it has been given away in secret to people over many years who needed it."

"He told me that he always wanted to give it to your family when we left, but the forced nature of our departure, meant that he completely forgot about it. You see, my old friend, this tin box and all its contents are now yours. But please share some of it with George. He'll know what to do with it."

"My father also told me where you should now store this box. Especially now that the Germans are only a matter of weeks away from occupation. They will confiscate all your coins, guns, and anything of value you may have that is not nailed down or concealed in a secret hiding place."

Mustafa's father and his father before him had apparently been syphoning money from the Ottoman authorities for many years, using the proceeds to help people in need when necessary. To keep the money safe from prying eyes and thieving fingers, they had built many secret locations in plain sight, in such places as houses, stone walls and of course, Turkish taps.

We Greeks normally keep valuables in wine amphorae buried in gardens. Most people did this, and most people knew others did it, which made it a stupid place to hide things of value.

To prove his point, Mustafa showed me a safe hiding place in my own village of Portianou. He pointed to a stone wall near our old house that had such a compartment, unable to be found by any searching eyes. He was aware of its existence because his father built the wall! When he showed me the wall, he asked me to find the secret spot. Spending a few minutes, I gave up looking.

"I have no idea where it could be Mustafa."

He touched a particular stone, he asked me to remove it, I saw a gap in the wall behind big enough to fit something small, but a position that no one would ever find themselves. There was nothing there, but according to Mustafa, it was one of a number of them around my village. All I could think of was how clever these stone wall builders really were.

"I must go soon Maroula, but I have one more thing to ask you. Do you remember the Australian man, by the name of Angus?"

"I do. He was last here with a group of grieving families visiting the graves of their sons, lost in the war. I think it was about 10 years ago. Why do you ask?"

"He was responsible for me finding hope in my new country. During the war, we nearly shot each other, but ended up as friends. We met on the battlefield by chance when we stopped shooting each other to bury our dead. Discovering a connection to Limnos, we talked about you and your family, and he told me that you took him to Therma on a donkey. I know this might sound strange, but if you ever see him, please thank him for me. He may return one day to Gallipoli and here. Who knows? It was him that convinced Mr Millington to employ some hungry and depressed returned Turkish soldiers to help in the building of memorials to their dead, and to ours. If it wasn't for Angus, I wouldn't be here today. I owe everything I have achieved to him. And before you say anything else — he really liked you Maroula."

Our brief time together was at an end. Mustafa had to leave to travel by boat back across the seas to his home. His boat was moored at the new pier in Nea Koutali, where two other Turkish fishermen were conducting some simple repairs. When his family left the island all those years ago, this was not a village. I explained to him how the Allied armies used the area to make a camp for resting soldiers, and how later it became a village to house refugees from Asia Minor.

On our way to his boat, he spoke to one of the local people for a few minutes, a man of about his own age while I sat on a stone seat by the water's edge. I couldn't hear what they were saying, but Mustafa handed over some coins and thanked him for his work.

It was clear to me that Mustafa and this man, who I recognised later, knew each other. I couldn't help but think that Mustafa's family had actually been syphoning money from the Ottoman empire for many years, to be given to people in need! He may live many miles away in another country, but he still has connections to this place. And Uncle George was fully aware of this.

Mustafa had to leave before it was too dark, and we parted once more. It was lovely to talk with him again. I had a new and deeper appreciation of him, his family, and the good work some of my fellow Limnians were doing to help those people who desperately needed help.

CHAPTER 20

GERMANS

(1941)

Over the centuries, Limnos has existed as an island where people from other places come for a short time, stay a while and then leave almost without a trace. Take the Turkish people for example. They came in 1478 and stayed until 1912!

The British came in 1915 and stayed until the end of that war. The Australians, New Zealanders and French were also here, and I met some wonderful people. But after 1919, they were all gone and we were left alone again. In 1920, the Russians came and stayed for almost two years. I felt so sorry for them, as they had fled from persecution in their own country and landed here on Limnos. The American Red Cross were here to help them, but many Russians died from starvation and the cold weather because they had no shelter and no food. We did our best to help, but we too had very little.

Then in 1923, our island was flooded with refugees from Asia Minor, who had been forcefully flung out of their country, much like the Turkish who were forced to leave here 11 years prior. New villages were planned and established overnight, and we suddenly had many more mouths to feed. These people were Greeks by historical ancestral birth but were Turkish to most Limnians. While they spoke our language, many preferred to speak in the language they were comfortable in, which was Turkish.

Some of us still spoke their language well enough to make them at least feel at home, but it was difficult. Most of these refugees arrived with the clothes they were wearing and, if lucky, a suitcase with some mementos from their former life. A new village sprang up next to ours, in a place where only eight or so years before, many foreign soldiers had their rest camp. The big war tent rest camp became the village Nea Koutali, and the actual village of Sarpi grew to become Kallithea. In fact, many of the existing villages added some more dwellings in order to house the new arrivals.

Life for the next 18 years was not easy for any of us. But we found a way to integrate and the new Limnians became part of us. They brought with them a culture as old as ours, and with it, many customs and ways of doing things that we still use to this day. Perhaps the one thing they shared freely with us was their music. Their songs, their music and their dances blended with ours and life in the villages was richer for the additional culture. Music was everywhere, and I loved it. Don't get me wrong, there were still some here who looked at these people as foreigners and kept their distance. I saw them as long-lost Greeks returning to their ancestral home and welcomed them accordingly.

I remember seeing my old friend Angus from Australia here with some people from his country visiting their sons buried in our soil. It was so nice to see him again. I remember him telling me about his wife and children, and I introduced him to my husband and children. I often wondered how he was and wished to see him again one day. I think he reminded me of a life of joy when we were young and full of energy. Of all the Australians I met during the big war, he was the only one who attempted to speak our language, and I respected him for that. Many of his countrymen attempted some words here and there, like νερό (water), ψωμί (bread) and κρασί (wine), but not like Angus. He wanted to understand us and converse with us.

Does he think of me from time to time? If I saw him now, I would say that my life has not been all that good. Just five years after he visited with his group, my husband Barbie died quite suddenly. It was the saddest day of my life. He was out with our sheep one summer's morning, bathing them in the saltwater close to our village. This was something he did regularly in the summertime. Apparently, he had almost finished his sheep dipping when he fell over in the water and hit his head on a submerged rock. My son found him lying face down in the water a few minutes later when some of the sheep made their way back to our home without him. We rushed out to see why he was yelling and found Barbie motionless in the water. The doctor said he drowned, but the water was only up to his knees I said. Apparently, he fell on a rock and knocked himself out, and while face down and unconscious, he drowned. It was a freak accident, and I cried for a week.

Every morning, at about the time he died, I visit him in the cemetery next to our village church and talk to him. I light a candle, tell him about the kids, the sheep, and who is doing what to whom in the village. It is my way of coping being a single parent, and it certainly helps me unburden myself every day. I still cry from time to time, but not as much these days. I can't be that upset with him. What good will it do. My biggest problem was slowly removing my black clothes and gradually introducing colour once again. You should have heard the comments from other women when I first wore a dark blue head scarf! You would think I had committed a murder. The more these women criticised me, the more determined I was to try other colours, like dark grey and brown. I ignored them all, and within a year of the headscarf incident, I burned all my black mourning clothes. Time to move on, one garment at a time.

Just when I thought we had settled down into a routine of our seasonal farming and family life, war was once again on our doorstep. The British were back on the island but not for long, and this time, the principal enemy was not the Turkish, but Germans. For some years, we were kept isolated from the horrors of war, but that changed in early 1941. The British only managed to stay a week or two, and then disappeared as quickly as they came. In the skies above we could hear and finally see aeroplanes. Soon enough, the engine noises overhead were joined by humans on the ground in grey-green uniforms with backpacks and rifles. The Germans were here to stay! Some of our local garrison attempted to shoot at the invading army, but it was completely useless. Much like putting your palms up towards a howling wind and expecting it to die down. The army shot back, and our once-brave fighters escaped in civilian clothing, hiding in areas like Fakos and at Cape Agia Irini. Some policemen joined the local resistance fighters, but they soon realised it was futile. I heard that one policeman was too infirm to escape to Fakos, so he was hidden in Tsimandria. The Germans knew he was there, and when he was not given up, all the old men were rounded up and marched away. These men were only released once the injured resistance fighter surrendered. Then he was marched away!

It seemed as if there were Germans in every village. They marched into ours, and demanded to speak to the mayor, or someone in charge. Our mayor was hastily sent for, and a meeting was held in the plateia. One of the German soldiers spoke some Greek, and he asked the mayor to provide a list of all unoccupied and occupied houses in the village, highlighting all those who had married couples and families and single, widowed women. We were not sure why this was asked for, but the mayor obliged. Not that he had any choice with a gun pointing at his head, but a list was soon drawn up of all houses, and those with single or widowed women marked with a red square. I was frightened when I knew that our house was such a property, and it was not long before I was informed that I was to house four German soldiers. One of them seemed to be more important than the others, and his uniform was slightly different too.

As simply as that, our house grew in size by four more people. At that time, my home had two upstairs bedrooms, while downstairs was a kitchen and sitting room. Immediately next to and attached to the house was our barn with a solid roof, housing another kitchen for outside cooking during the warmer months, and a straw-filled floor space for any animals that needed somewhere dry to keep away from the cold or if they were sick in any way. We always had chickens to feed, cats to keep the mice, snakes and rats away, and quite often, a sick sheep or two.

Without any say in the matter, the upstairs bedrooms were to be occupied by these soldiers. My bedroom was taken over by the important looking one, and the smaller bedroom was to be inhabited by the other three.

Using sign language, I asked where they thought we should sleep, and they pointed directly at the barn. We had one afternoon to make ourselves comfortable in that space, but thankfully, our animals didn't seem to mind their new sleeping arrangements away in the family mandra. The only animals that remained were the cats. They still had an important job to perform.

I thought we would have these men with us all the time, every day, and all day, but as it turned out, they only used our house for sleeping. By around 7.00 am each morning, they would leave to have breakfast with all other soldiers in a tent city established outside of the village, and were gone for most of the day. They returned at night around 9.00 pm and immediately retired to their bedrooms. They never ate with us, and apart from taking over our bedrooms, they did not occupy any other part of the house or barn.

There were some abandoned houses in the village, and those were also assigned some soldiers. Because our home was established, and some of the village houses were empty, the soldiers spent any free time they had trying to make these abandoned buildings liveable. It was a strange sight indeed seeing German soldiers, some of them no older than boys, labouring away repairing walls, roofs, windows and doors. Some of these old houses were gradually brought back to life again, and silently, we appreciated it.

The day before the Germans arrived in our village, all local men were warned to hide any weapons they might have in their possession. That warning proved to be accurate, because one of the things our new visitors would not tolerate was any local person in possession of a gun of any description. Within only a few days, one farmer from Tsimandria was found to have a rifle, and when caught, he was taken away and no one ever saw him again. Rifles and handguns were hidden in all sorts of places, but never hidden inside our homes. Some of the more inventive places were ones buried in plain sight of German officers, such as in the plateia around the communal water fountain. A stonemason removed large rocks from stone walls around the church, placed any contraband guns inside the walls, and re-laid the stones. One of my neighbours buried his weapons underneath the large stone directly in the middle of his entrance gate. It was good to see these burial places follow the secret location ideas created by Mustafa's family.

Nobody was stupid enough to try to hide guns in their houses or mandres. A week after the soldiers arrived, every property was searched, and throughout the next few years, random searches took place weekly, but each time they occurred, the soldiers conducting the searches took less and less time to carry out their duties. They were masters at appearing to be busy, so that if any senior officers were around, they could easily fool them that they were very thorough. On one occasion, an officer accompanied one of our young, billeted house guests to conduct a weapons search in our home, but he only looked in the same places as he had always done. While the two Germans were doing this, I couldn't help but quietly giggle at the acting ability of the younger man attempting to look at different places, only to search the same ones. His superior officer was very happy with the younger man's actions and we never saw that officer again. I found out many years later that these young soldiers were petrified at the possibility of finding any weapons, knowing what would happen to us. As strange as it might seem now, the Germans became very respectful of us, and even started to learn some of our language.

I was fortunate enough to be offered work at their campsite as a cook for lunches. I say fortunate because I didn't want to get up early to help in any breakfast preparation, so lunch time suited me. Besides, we still had our sheep to milk. I was paid for this work, and indeed any of us that were conscripted into working for the Germans were paid. Many young boys from ours and neighbouring villages were sent to work in a factory near Kontias making bricks. Again, they were paid, but in the early months of occupation, there was nothing we could spend our wages on.

My work in their canteen allowed me to learn some of their language. I was a very good listener and playing the grieving widow at times allowed me to convince them to speak slower so that I could master their accent as well as learning some key phrases. I had to borrow some black grieving widow clothing to play the part perfectly, and I became excellent at looking sad the whole time working in their lunch kitchen. The canteen workers were a mixture of some of the village women, and some very young soldiers, who probably preferred to be working with us instead of patrolling.

Food preparation was confined to things like making sure bread was in good supply, along with cheese, dried or fresh figs, eggs, honey and wine. Any butchering of meat was done by the German boys. I don't think their officers wanted us to use large and sharp knives too much! One thing the Germans asked for in the early months was potatoes! Of course, we didn't grow many, so my daughters along with other local people planted lots of potatoes on land between Tsimandria and Portianou. I don't know why, but the Germans loved their potatoes.

In these early months, right through the summer period of 1941, I heard of many examples of Germans taking ripe vegetables from farms and confiscating most if not all of the grape harvest in September. Many villagers went hungry in that first summer, but things slowly improved later with more winter and summer vegetables planted.

Although I heard stories of some local people being killed, I did not have any first-hand experience with this. But a problem was bound to occur with our Jewish neighbours who had come to Limnos from Asia Minor in the 1920s. Towards the end of the war, many of them were rounded up and taken away. To save as many of our friends as possible, I became part of the resistance movement, and secretly plotted to rescue as many of these migrants as we could.

CHAPTER 21

THE TURKISH 'FISHERMEN'

(1941)

Life under German occupation as I have said was difficult, and extremely stressful for my family. Food was in short supply, and we never knew what was coming next. Rumours of atrocities committed by soldiers against village people were rife, yet uncorroborated, and people kept to themselves. The worst thing for me was not just knowing these terrible things were happening, but that they could happen to anyone at any time. Our house guests also kept to themselves, my children had their duties to perform, and I was working at the soldier's kitchen for a few hours in the middle of each day.

Late in the summer of 1941, the first of the Turkish 'fishermen' arrived at George's café asking for me. It was Ismail, and he was with another Turkish man. Ismail told me that they had landed their boat on one of the English piers from the first war and walked overland to Portianou. Before they even set foot on land, they had been approached by a German patrol of two soldiers, who apparently bought their story of being fishermen. The boat they had come over on did have nets and fishing equipment, and stunk of fish, so Ismail said. The Germans checked their documentation and let them walk to the village, not suspecting a thing, convinced they were simply selling fish. Just to make sure of the ruse, Ismail gave the German soldiers some fish to take back with them. He had learned enough German in the first war to speak a few phrases with these soldiers, and they were very happy to have some fresh fish for their evening meal.

I took Ismail and his friend to the tap where we paused for our usual drink. Germans were watching from high above on Mt Elias, but they would have been very lucky to see the second 'fisherman' leaving a message in the rocks behind the tap. Before the message was comfortably placed in the correct spot, our donkeys were also strategically placed in front of the tap so that the spying Germans could not see what was taking place. In no time, we were gone, on our way to Therma.

I never asked what was in the messages, nor did I ask who was to retrieve them. I didn't want the risk of having that knowledge, as Ismail said it was for my protection not to know these details. Many people came past that tap on their way through on any given day. Farmers with goats and sheep, old men on donkeys heading to and from their farms, and people like me, middle aged women taking some 'fishermen' through to Therma for a good bath, to wash away the fish smell, and many German soldiers in need of having their thirst quenched.

One particular day at the tap with some other 'fishermen', a German patrol came past to see why we had stopped. They had been in their lookout and noticed us approaching the tap, so out of boredom, they decided to check us out. One of the soldiers was my house guest, Klaus. When he saw that it was me, he put his rifle away and joined us in a cool drink from the now well-dented tin cup attached by chain to a metal ring drilled firmly in a large rock. Luckily, the message had been secreted safely behind the stone structure before Klaus arrived with his patrol. Klaus had managed to pick up some Greek language, and he asked me who these fishermen were, and I said they were Turkish, and they were going to Therma to have a bath.

"Why you here with them Maroula?"

My answer seemed to satisfy him.

"Klaus, I don't want any Turkish fishermen getting lost on their way to the bath house, so I take them to and from with our donkeys. It could be very dangerous for them to be wandering alone through these farms, don't you think?"

"I see. But don't be long."

Klaus was a good boy. I say good boy because he was only about 22 years old, the same age as one of my children. I don't ever think he had fired his rifle at anybody, and he probably never did throughout the whole war. He always seemed slightly on edge. He was very respectful, and as I mentioned, took time to learn some of our language. He didn't fit the typical German soldier type to me at all. He actually looked at and saw us, not like some of his comrades who looked at us as though we were a speck of dust on their uniforms.

Klaus and another soldier sometimes went searching for turtles in a stream near our village. After rain, the stream would flow quite quickly, and turtles seemed to love the faster flowing current. The first time Klaus went in search of turtle food, he returned with about six of the slimy animals and asked me if I knew how to cook them into a thick soup. When I said yes, he gave them to me and told me to prepare them here at the house. He didn't want to share them with anyone else apart from our family. If we had been caught, I don't know what may have happened, but Klaus made sure that we were never caught. He loved his turtle soup!

As for Tasman, the only time I saw him again was in early 1944, when the war was not going very well for Germany. There was a general feeling of unease in the villages, from the soldiers, and especially from some of my Jewish friends who had come from Asia Minor over twenty years ago.

Tasman and a 'fisherman' were sitting in the plateia with George, sharing a coffee when I arrived late one afternoon. He appeared a little stressed this time, and I asked him what was wrong.

"Fishing is getting very difficult these days Maroula. It is a dangerous job. Do you mind if we go to Therma for a bath? My friend Yusuf here stinks, and I can't quite remember the way. Do you mind taking us?"

"Sure. You are right. He does stink."

Yusuf looked Turkish, but he certainly didn't speak any Turkish. I'm sure he was British, but I didn't ask. I knew not to. Tasman and I were speaking Turkish, and Yusuf didn't appear to understand any of what we said. Even when we talked about how much he smelled like fish guts and rotting seaweed.

On our way to the tap, Klaus met us coming the other way. He appeared nervous this time. He wasn't alone, but the soldier he was with looked as young as him, and equally nervous.

While I said that Yusuf appeared to be Turkish, he could say a few words, with little or no trace of an accent. To Klaus, he must certainly have appeared to be Turkish. But what happened next surprised me even more.

Klaus and his friend Wolfgang sat down with us and brought out a metal canteen to fill up with water. In perfect German, Yusuf asked Wolfgang and Klaus if they were sure. Klaus said *"Yes. We are sure."*

"You can't come with us, but can you help them reach the rendezvous point at 1.00 am tomorrow morning, and we'll do the rest?"

Tasman could see that I was thoroughly confused by this turn of events. Before I even opened my mouth, Tasman tried to explain what was happening.

"You have probably figured out by now, Yusuf is not Turkish. He is a British agent, working for the Greek resistance, and we are here to arrange safe passage off the island of 20 Jewish people tomorrow morning. I am well aware that you know Klaus. His friend Wolfgang and he

are preparing to desert the German army and cross over to the Greek Resistance very soon, although we have to complete this mission first."

Wolfgang, Klaus and Tasman then started to speak in English together, but I could not understand any of it, so I suggested that we continue speaking Turkish or German, which I was starting to understand a lot more of.

Klaus said that the German high command has requested they round up all Jewish people on the island ready to take to camps in Germany within the next 10 days.

"They are to be taken away and killed, Maroula. This is now very serious. Germany is losing the war, and we are soon to be re-deployed to the Russian Front, and as you can probably see now, Wolfgang and I are not too keen on doing that."

I was very happy knowing this secret regarding Klaus and his friend Wolfgang, who I had seen many times before at the canteen where I still worked. I knew we couldn't happily sit down at my uncle's café in Portianou and have a genteel discussion over a cup of coffee and some biscuits discussing desertion and the possibility of being found out, so I resigned myself to the fact that this would have to remain a secret until the end of the war, or even later if necessary.

I also could not trust anyone in Portianou or any village as we never knew who potential traitors might be. By traitors, I mean local people, my so-called friends, and maybe even family, who had sold information to the Germans on who they thought was suspected as being a Greek resistance member. Equally, I am convinced no one suspected me as being with the Greek resistance.

From that moment on, until the last of the Germans had left our island, I had a new respect for some of the German soldiers. Many of them did not want to be here. Many were forced into the war. Wolfgang was once convicted of treason in Germany before the war, and some others were former political prisoners due to their vocal opposition to Hitler. Some were activists and some were homosexuals, and all of them wound up on Limnos in a probation battalion for discipline and training!

A story I will always remember was from one of my friends, who like me, was a widow living with her children in Portianou in a house not dissimilar to mine. When war came, so too did six Germans, who occupied her upstairs bedrooms, leaving her and the children to sleep in the barn with the animals.

My friend Maria had a daughter and three sons. The boys were all very young, but her daughter Katerina was about 20 years old when the new house guests arrived. The boys did not really appreciate the delicate situation of having uninvited Germans living upstairs, but Katerina most certainly did.

The young German soldiers were very respectful to Maria, Katerina and the boys. On their first Christmas in Limnos, one of the soldiers shared his care package sent by his family back home with his new family in Portianou. The officer, a man by the name of Andreas, also shared whatever he could with Maria and family. But perhaps the greatest gift came in early 1944, when Katerina was to be married to her sweetheart, a young man from Kontias. Andreas had become such good friends with the family, Katerina asked him if he would walk her into the church in place of her long-departed father. Andreas agreed, and we were all invited to attend the wedding feast in the plateia outside Uncle George's café. I have never seen so much wine drunk in one night as I witnessed on that occasion. Andreas managed to acquire, or perhaps steal a lot of German wine and presented it as a wedding gift the happy couple. For one night, we completely forgot we were being occupied by a foreign army, and sung, danced, drank and ate our way through a very special wedding feast.

However, there were still many people extremely resentful of the German presence, and rightly so. Their lives had been a misery during the occupation. I can fully understand those who had lost family members to the German executions that took place in

Myrina. They would never forget, nor should they. I have mixed emotions even thinking about these stories now. To me and my family, I periodically saw the good in these soldiers, but there are those who saw nothing but evil. Yes, our lives were severely disrupted, some of us starved, but we did not die of starvation. Mass killings on Limnos did not occur, and the Greek resistance was alive and well during the entire occupation.

The 'Turkish' fishermen managed to safely remove about 20 or so of our Jewish neighbours to wait out the war in Turkey. As soon as the last German soldier had departed Limnos with a hefty boot up their collective bums from us, these old Jewish neighbours of ours began to return home. What always seemed strange to me was that the country that expelled these refugees 20 or more years ago, gladly took them back in order to escape German punishment.

CHAPTER 22

A YEAR TO FORGET

(1949)

You would think that a person who had gone through the first big war as a participant would be used to death. If you thought that, you would be wrong.

It is true that a soldier can, at the time, put the death of his mates in battle to the back of his mind for a time, but then, uncalled for, memories rears their ugly head. You don't expect your mate who was standing, sitting, lying, running, or hiding next to you to die, but it happened. It was over in a flash with no time to mourn or think. You just don't have that opportunity. But in civilian life, when you watch the slow then rapid deterioration of loved ones, it is heartbreaking.

Many more families in Ballarat lost their sons during the second world war. I knew many of the lads who did not come back and added an entire list of families to visit and offer whatever comfort I could. Even some of the boys I taught in school paid the ultimate sacrifice. I couldn't enlist again because I was too old, and even if I could make the age grade, my own physical disabilities, thanks to Turkish and German soldiers just like me, made me ineligible health-wise.

But nothing could prepare me for the death of my beloved wife and both parents in the space of one year. Rema developed a rare form of cancer and passed away in the short space of only three months. Our daughter Amy, who had trained as a nurse, became Rema's fulltime nurse and carer. She moved back home to live with us and never left her mother's side. All any of us could do was to make her as comfortable as possible, but the cancer ate away her insides so rapidly, it was both a blessing and a curse. We shared 28 marvellous years together, but if you count the years as children, it was much, much more. We produced fine children and wonderful grandchildren, and looking at each of them, reminds me of Rema. Her life and spirit still live in each of us to this day.

Mum and Dad still lived with me, and at the time of Rema's funeral, were 84 and 88 years old. Even though we all shared a house together, they were independent enough, but were obviously slowing down after more than 35 years living and working on a farm. Rema loved them both, and I could tell that they were going to miss her in a different way to me.

I noticed a rapid decline in their health when they almost ceased to cross-examine each other in multiple languages. Friends of ours loved it when mum and dad 'put on a show' in ancient Greek, Latin or German. Rema couldn't understand a word of it, but would often just stare in wonder at these two linguists battling out over quite mundane or normal topics. Now that Rema had gone, they lost their audience.

On a normal workday, I would leave for school early, and not see my parents. James lived near us and he was always the first at work on the farm, followed by mum and dad after breakfast. On this particularly unspectacular day, I left for work at the usual time, James arrived at his usual time, but mum and dad did not surface for their usual pot of English tea. James didn't think anything of it until he noticed that by lunchtime, they still hadn't made an entrance. He gently called out to them but received no answer. He called more loudly, but still no response.

Thinking they had gone off early for a walk, which they sometimes would do, he went back to his daily tasks. I arrived home at around the same time Amy did. She had now started to make a habit of visiting every day, just to see Violet and Charles and share afternoon tea with them.

Amy and I found James and asked him where the grandparents were. He thought they had maybe gone for a walk and assumed they might have walked over to see Alice, which is again something they did from time to time. Alice by now had two children of her own, and her kids loved playing with my mum and dad.

I asked if anyone had gone to their bedroom, and when James said he hadn't, I thought I'd go in to see what they may have taken. Their door was shut, and I gently opened it. There were Violet and Charles. Lying together on their bed, holding hands. They most certainly had taken something together — their last breath!

CHAPTER 23

NEW SOUTH WALES – VICTORIA
(1951 – 1955)

After the German army evacuated Limnos in 1944, life attempted to revert to whatever normal was. In other words, life was still difficult.

I was sad to see Klaus and Wolfgang leave. That might sound strange, but to me and my family, they were respectful and courteous to us. They did not want to be in the army and did everything they could to appear to be on the German side, but all the while working feverishly against them. I was actually sad to lose my kitchen job. But, overall, we were glad to see the end of the occupiers. There are times when I sit at night and wonder what might have happened to those young men after they left us.

I also wondered what happened to the Australian from Gallipoli who risked his life to rescue those poor Jewish neighbours of ours. But after the war ended, they all did return. One day, over the hills near Tsimandria, Tasman Millington visited us with his Turkish friend. They had berthed their vessel in their usual spot, hidden from anyone, and walked into Portianou to sit once again at George's café. I was home looking after my grandchildren when

218

George, who by this time was an old man, came knocking and told me I had some visitors.

Mr Millington and Ismail had taken a seat at the café and ordered coffee and sweets. George and I walked towards them, smiling as we took our seats. By now, George had passed on the running of the café to a number of family members, but as long as he was breathing, it was obvious who remained in charge. He barked an order to one of my nephews inside to get drinks and some sweets ready. Millington and Ismail thanked us both for the help we had given them, saying that the people we saved would be coming back soon to resume their lives. It was wonderful to see them, and good to know that the people we helped were safe and well.

I asked them if they had any idea what happened to Klaus or Wolfgang after the war, and they said that they both eventually made it back to Germany after spending time as British prisoners of war. I did not fully appreciate how much Klaus and his German friends did for us during the war, especially towards the end. When the German authorities realised that the war wasn't going very well for them, an order came through to blow up all bridges, and all infrastructure built by them on Limnos, including the German-built electricity system. Klaus and Wolfgang had managed to steal the demolition orders and pass them on to resistance fighters, thus undermining some of the plans. Luckily, not all demolition activities were carried out. The Turkish tap was certainly put to very good use.

Mr Millington told me that Wolfgang, Klaus and several others from the 'Limnos Unit' were held in British captivity for two years after the war and permitted to return home to assist with their country's rebuilding. During his time in a British prisoner of war internment camp, Wolfgang even managed to set up a 'university' where he lectured to German captives on matters of economics and politics.

By 1949, I was living on my own in Pesperago, and my children were all living close by in Portianou and Tsimandria. My son Panayioti helped me with the sheep, and together, we managed to retain our little vegetable garden on the land once used in WW1 by the Canadian hospitals. We had enough to feed ourselves, sold most of our milk to the local cooperative and kept just enough to make cheese. I worked in the garden, and Panayioti tended the sheep. Although we were largely untouched directly by the civil war, life was becoming more and more difficult. There was no future for our children here anymore, and I felt sad for their children. My second son Niko, who, at only 25 years of age, was already considering leaving the island to seek life and a future elsewhere.

He was a self-taught mechanic, and ever since he was a young man, he helped older men repair farm machinery. During the war, Niko was employed by the Germans to fix and repair any machinery they had. He soon learned as much as he could from their mechanics and engineers, and it wasn't long before he was teaching them how to repair some rather tricky mechanical problems. Instead of working in the brick-making business near Kontias, Niko was clearly much happier fixing mechanical things.

He was an expert also at stealing spare and reconditioned parts from the Germans, and developed a stash of inventory items that, if he was caught with, would have resulted in a bullet to the head. But, and I only found this out later, Wolfgang was helping him steal these things! He had a real passion for motor vehicle repair and would work on old German motor bikes left behind after the war.

Niko somehow managed to earn a small amount of money from his mechanical repair work, but if it wasn't for our farm, he would not have been able to do many of the things he wanted. After the war, he found a nice girl to marry, and continued to help me on the land.

He married in 1950, and soon after, he and his wife gave birth to a healthy baby girl. Life was changing for him, and for me, yet another grandchild had entered the world. The population of each village suffered after the big war, and gradually, we faced the problems of another disruption to our lives with the civil war. If the island wasn't in enough trouble, it wasn't getting any better either. Many villages suffered significant drops in their population due to migration to the mainland and other countries. I could see that Niko was getting rather itchy feet and began searching for a place for his own family, away from the island.

One day in the summer of 1951, he visited me early one morning with a tattered newspaper article explaining the possibility of working in Australia, in a very large construction program called the 'Snowy Mountain Scheme'. Apparently, since the war ended, many young men from all over Europe had migrated to Australia to help build this massively big electricity project. I laughed at it at first, because we still didn't have basic electricity on Limnos, and here were the Australians building an electricity system created with water! I had trouble getting my brain around the concept, but Niko was convinced he could secure a job with his skills.

"But Niko, this says they want qualified mechanics and engineers."

"Mum, I'll just say I am qualified, but unable to find my papers due to the war. I'll tell them the Germans stole my papers. All I have to do is be able to fix stuff and show them. It will be alright Mum, I promise."

His plan was to apply for a job and gain employment, work for a year, save money, then have his wife and child join him later. If he could earn enough money in Australia, he would then return to Limnos with money in the bank! Easy.

Niko applied to the Australian Government for a visa that would allow him to work in a place called Cooma. Soon after applying, he was asked to visit Athens to undergo a health and security check. Passing these checks, he returned home to await the final decision.

Barely two months had gone by, and Niko was accepted as a migrant worker in Australia for two years, with an option to extend. He was also allowed to bring his family, thus by Christmas of 1951, Niko, his wife and darling child, packed their clothes and necessities into three suitcases preparing for life in Australia.

Soon after they departed for Athens on the first leg of their journey, I began to think of Angus, the nice young man who came here during the first war several times and once again about 10 years later. I wondered what he was now doing. I hadn't spent much time thinking about him, but now that my youngest son and his family were headed to the country where Angus lived, I was suddenly very interested.

People were leaving the island, not only for the mainland, but for a range of other countries. There were even some men who had left for Germany to find work and Niko was not the first Limnian with his family to travel to Australia in search of work and a better life. Indeed, I had heard of some who left before World War 2 and have not returned.

Niko was my baby. He was my youngest, and the child who most reminded me of my dear departed husband, Barbie. As Niko grew, he looked more and more like his father every day. His facial expressions, bodily mannerisms, the sound of his voice, and the way he walked were almost identical. Once he was gone, I desperately missed them all. Yes, I know I had three other children and their families close by, but I felt lonely again. And yes, my daughters often visited me, and Panayioti was still working with the sheep, but life for me was becoming increasingly lonely.

Niko wrote to me every month for two years, telling me about his work, where they lived, the cold of the Australian high-country climate where it snowed quite a lot, and most of all, the sheer size of the bush. He told me of the flowing streams, mountains, dirt tracks, strange animals, bushfires, and meeting hundreds of people just like him. He was friends with Germans, Italians, Slavs, Hungarians, Polish, English and even some Greeks. At nights, they learned English by what he called 'correspondence' and told me how happy he was when they moved into a proper house in Cooma.

He was loving his work as a mechanic, fixing four-wheel drive trucks, graders, cranes and even making saddles for horses. In the beginning, Niko helped build swing bridges over streams, and soon graduated to working on the machinery needed to transfer people between villages and to get supplies in from the main cities.

I tried to imagine a country where clean fresh drinking water was flowing above ground all the time, and even in big pools he called reservoirs. We did have flowing streams on Limnos during most months each year, but in summer, they had all dried up, and all drinking water had to be pumped or raised by buckets from the wells. Sometimes our water did not taste very nice, but Niko told me that in Australia, the water tasted fresh all year round.

His best news by far was the arrival of their second daughter, who they named Maroula! I was so happy. By the end of 1953, Niko wrote me a wonderful long letter explaining all the things they did that were different to being here. The letter went for about 10 pages! On the last page, he asked me if I wanted to come to live with them. They were moving to Melbourne soon, as he had secured a higher paying job at a motor vehicle manufacturing and assembly factory. I asked Panayioti, Vasiliki and Olga what they thought about me visiting Niko, and surprisingly, they all agreed I should go. Panayioti said that he could manage the sheep on his own, and his kids were now old enough to work on the farm.

I had never left Limnos, and early 1954, I found myself standing at the port of Piraeus, nursing a small brown suitcase, and feeling as excited as a teenager with my whole life in front of me. No one was there to wave me 'goodbye', but I didn't mind. I had no real concept of the country to where I was headed, or just what I would do when I got there, but Niko needed Γιαγιά, and I needed Niko. Walking up the gangplank was easy for me. I kept my eyes down and never looked back. It was more difficult for me leaving Limnos a few days earlier, but I knew my family supported me, and that was all that mattered.

The ship was an Italian vessel, with mostly an Italian crew, but some Greek sailors joined the staff from Athens. The food was slightly different to what we were used to, with an abundance of pasta and rather nice wine every day.

On the boat to Melbourne, were many young families from all over Greece, even some from Limnos. Once we overcame our seasickness, the voyage was passably bearable. There were very few women my age, and I instantly became γιαγιά to about 50 children. I loved it. One story these young families had in common was a desire to provide their children and any future children with a better life. We shared stories of the war, German occupation, but the saddest stories were from those families leaving a country they still loved, but had been ravaged by civil war. Whether by a world war or civil war, the loss of loved ones was something that no one ever truly emerged from unscathed.

Most passengers had someone to meet them at the end of this voyage. Someone who had left our homeland earlier and had made a life of sorts on the other side of the world. Someone to meet them and to share an embrace. But equally, there were single men and women, adventurers, wanderers, people wanting a better life and who were prepared to do anything to achieve it.

I shared a cabin with three other mature aged women, all like me, who were going to be with their family in Melbourne. Each of us were travelling alone, and I found it nice to have their company. We were each from very different parts of Greece, but the thing we had in common was that we were all widows. Apart from feeling sad, we were all excited, nervous, and a little apprehensive at first, but after two or three weeks at sea, we were all looking forward to the next part of our lives.

I remember a particular young Greek man, in his early 20s, who would eat with us for dinner. He had no family onboard and gravitated to we older woman for the first few weeks. He was very naïve in the world of drinking wine, and we managed to get him drunk every night. It made us laugh a lot, and after a while he found the courage to leave our dinner group to find some single women to dine with.

Some attempt was made by the ship's crew at teaching us a little English, but I don't think anyone was ready for that. We did learn some basic words, and I immediately thought of Angus and Tasman, the only two Australians I had ever spoken to at length. But I had spoken Greek to one and Turkish to the other, so that wasn't much help to me now. There was a daily English class held in the early afternoon by a Greek woman who was an English-speaking teacher from Athens, and she made some progress with us. It was a purely conversational class with no written work. I enjoyed it very much.

For the entire trip, there was very little need to spend any money. All food and drinks were catered for, but I did manage to buy a tablecloth for Niko and Fotoula from a man somewhere in the Suez Canal. Our boat did not stop along the canal, but we were moving at walking pace for a lot of the time. Street vendors would come to the boat with their wares, show us, and we'd point to what we wanted. I pointed to a beautiful hand stitched white with floral design tablecloth, and put money in a basket. After it was lowered, the vendor placed my item in the basket and with his simple, yet effective pulley system, my purchase rose to where I was standing. Many items were bought and sold this way.

The journey took around four weeks, and the first four were plain sailing on calm seas. To occupy our time, we walked around the boat, played games on deck, rested in our beds, ate three meals each day, learned some English, and talked and laughed with each other. However, for the final few days, from Perth to Melbourne, the seas became rough, and we were constantly sea sick. I couldn't eat much and spent a lot of time in our cabin. I never want to go through that nightmare again.

Eventually the seas were calm, and we very slowly drifted into

Station Pier, which is where all the boats like this one dock in Melbourne. The pier was full of people eager to embrace their loved ones. They had streamers, flowers, handwritten signs on cardboard, balloons and smiles as big as a sunset. It appeared to me that there were just as many people waiting to see us, as we were on the boat! I couldn't see Niko in the expectant crowd, but I knew he was down there somewhere.

CHAPTER 24

CARLTON

(1954–1955)

Niko, Fotoula and the girls lived in a two-bedroom cottage house in the Melbourne suburb of Carlton. The house had electricity, running water and a proper flushing toilet! Apart from my cabin on the boat, I had never been exposed to so much luxury. Although I shared a room with the girls, I had my own bed, with the girls in one bed and me in the other! To turn an electric light on or off, all I had to do was flick a brown switch on the wall, and not have to light a kerosene lamp.

There were some adjustments to make in my life. No longer going out into a paddock with a small shovel and paper for my ablutions; just walk out the back door, along a concrete path to a small room at the end of the garden, open a door, flick another light switch, and sit on a wooden seat. No digging a hole anymore. And, I could do all this with a door shut!

Niko travelled by tram and train to work each day, leaving around 6.30 am and returning at 6.00 pm. Fotoula and I looked after the girls, but I loved spending time with them on my own while Fotoula walked to the nearby shops for groceries, fruit and vegetables, meat and fish and practically anything else we needed. Each morning, I would wake early to meet a man delivering milk in glass bottles to our house. Given my life of milking sheep for the white liquid, it was nice having someone else do all the hard work now. It also gave me a chance to practice my newly learned English words.

"Good morning Maria. Same as usual today? See ya tomorrow."

The milkman had a big old horse that pulled a white milk truck. I learned the name of the horse before I learned the milkman's name. He called the horse 'Farlap', or something like that, and his name was Frank. It took Frank months before he got my name right. First, I was Maria, then Mary, and finally he got my name right.

"Good morning Maroula. Did I get it right this time missus?"

"Yes, Frank. My name Maroula. Today, same please."

"No worries. See ya tomorrow."

I loved my morning talks with Frank. His horse Farlap always managed to deposit a very large pile of manure either outside our door on the street, or very close. Because I was always outside early each morning, I would scoop up the horse poo before anyone else stole it, then carefully spread it over our small garden.

Apart from Frank the milkman, there were other men who delivered bread, ice and mail each day to our front door. I met other women and kids in our street and became friends with many of them. We had Italian families, Australians, some Greek, a German family two doors down and a Polish family across the road. Once a week, a man would run along our street and pick up our garbage tin, put it on his shoulders, then run after a truck slowly making its way along the street. In the back lane behind our house, once every week, another man would come along and remove our toilet waste. He always seemed to have a flat hat on his head, and when I saw him hoist the toilet pan up onto his head, I immediately knew why his hat was always flat!

Not long after I moved in with Niko and family, I remember saying to him how different the construction of houses looked to me here in Australia. I was used to stone houses, with terracotta roofs, but many homes in the area were made from horizontal wood panels with tin roofs. I was worried these homes would leak in the rain and blow away in a strong wind, like the μελτέμια winds back home in Pesperago. We Greeks used any type of material to construct our farm buildings, and often used various kinds of wood and metal, but not for our living and sleeping. Niko assured me that this style of housing construction was common in Carlton, and they did not leak or blow away. Our house was made from bricks with a metal roof, but the backyard toilet and outside bathroom and laundry had horizontal wooden panels. It was nice listening to the rain beating down on the corrugated iron roof, while I was safe inside doing my personal business. An Australian family living nearby told me that the correct name for this little building was the 'dunny', but nice people referred to it as the 'out house'. The only thing I had to worry about in the 'dunny' was when a heavy rain blew in from the west, as there was a six-inch gap above the wooden door to the top of the door jamb support beam. Luckily, rain from this direction was rare.

Niko didn't improve his English as well as I expected of him, because he said he worked with so many Greek men, they spoke together in the language they were comfortable in each day. One weekend, I suggested to him that both he and I should join a class held each Saturday afternoon at the nearby church hall, where a teacher was taking English classes for new arrivals like us. He agreed, and for the next 20 or so weeks, we attended these classes at 11.00 am each Saturday morning. We both became confident enough to try our newly found language skills at the corner milk bar at the end of our street. It was still difficult for us, but at least we were not alone in Carlton. On our first day attending the class, we walked in like two children attending school for the first time, but when I saw who the teacher was, I was immediately relaxed. It was the same Greek speaking English teacher from Athens who came over on our boat.

Once a week, Fotoula and I had some young mothers around to our house to learn how to make Greek food. Fotoula was becoming good friends with the Italian, German, Polish and Australian mothers in our street. There was an Italian grandmother, a nonna rather than a γιαγία, who came with her daughter, and she spent the mornings looking after about 10 kids while we cooked. From time to time, I would do the same whilst Margherita came inside to teach us how to make pasta. Levels of language varied, but we managed through our children, grandchildren and food to communicate comfortably with each other.

One evening in late 1954, Niko had invited some of his Limnian friends over to the house to talk, bring their wives and children, and share stories. He had planned this Friday evening for many weeks, and on the night agreed to, we had over 25 people in our house and backyard. Fotoula and I prepared food for two days, and Niko managed to buy a lamb and some chickens from the Victoria market. He and his friends killed them, butchered the meat and started the barbeque. That day, the ice man agreed to return late in the day for a special delivery, so we had ice for cool drinks that night.

It was so nice to see many people from our island in one place, so far from home. Even though we had people only from Limnos, they were from different villages, and we met many new friends for the first time that Friday. One of the men started to talk about a big village about two hours away from Melbourne, heading west along a train line. He said the name of the village was Ballarat and wondered if we all wanted to take the train one Saturday, for a 'picnic' at a lake.

When I heard the name of the village, I remembered Angus had told me something about it. Either he lived there, or he lived nearby. I didn't think much more of it, but Niko's friend organised a Limnian Community excursion to the town of Ballarat, set for mid-January 1955. Niko and Fotoula and all their young friends wanted to start visiting the countryside a lot more to see what this land was like. No one in the Limnian community had left Melbourne since arriving, so a trip to Ballarat on a train was to be a wonderful experience for all of us. A date was set, train tickets purchased, and closer to the day, food was prepared.

CHAPTER 25

FISHING 1
(1954–1955)

It had been nearly 25 years since I took a group of people from Ballarat to Gallipo'li to visit graves of their loved ones. I remember that first and only visit well. Coming up to the 40th anniversary of ANZAC Day, there was talk in town again of another visit to the sacred ground of the Gallipoli Peninsula for people who wanted to see the battlefields for themselves.

Most of the potential tourists, if that is what you could call them, were old veterans like me who had fought there, but unlike me, had never returned. Some of us were now grandfathers, with very comfortable lives. However, many of my old mates had died, and sadly, many succumbed to unseen illnesses even this late in their lives. There were some scars that never healed for these men, and I fully understood their feelings.

By the end of 1954, the potential group of Gallipoli veterans and others had grown to nearly 30, and as I had organised one visit all those years ago, I was quickly installed as the unofficial travel agent and tour organiser. I didn't mind this job so much, as I had time on my hands as a widower and living on my own meant that I had no children to fuss over. A reporter by the name of Jack from the local newspaper visited me in December to conduct an interview. We had arranged to meet in the Lake Gardens Tea Rooms to talk about the proposed Gallipoli trip.

Jack arrived on time, and after ordering two cups of tea and some cakes, proceeded to ask me questions regarding my service history in the first war, and places and battles I fought in. In other words, he was establishing my credentials. I told him as much as he needed to know, and he wrote unreadable shorthand hieroglyphics representing my responses to somewhat mundane questions. I had the feeling this story was not high on his list of major journalistic achievements, but we needed some publicity to gain some sponsorship money, so I gave the best answers as I possibly could.

Towards the end of the interview, which coincided with us running out of cakes to eat, I mentioned my usual jocular story of having a bath in the thermal springs of Limnos during my time recovering from a gunshot wound and having a coffee at George's Café. Suddenly, all his senses were tuned in, and he became much more interested in what I was saying.

"Angus, can you say that again please?"

"If you want. I met a young lady in the village of Portianou, who arranged for me and my hospital buddies to visit a thermal spring so that we could have a hot bath. We travelled to the baths on donkeys."

"Where was this?"

"I just said. It was the island of Limnos, 60 miles from Gallipoli. The place where the military hospitals were located, and the place where the ANZAC landings were practiced."

"Isn't that a coincidence. A group of people from Limnos are coming to Ballarat in a few weeks. I recently interviewed a spokesperson from the Limnian Community in Melbourne, who said that about 50 people are coming to Ballarat by train in mid-January, for a picnic here at the Lake. His English wasn't that good, but we managed to communicate well enough."

All of a sudden, I was now interested in what Jack was saying.

"How will they come from the station to here?"

"By tram."

"It has been many years since I was in Limnos, so the chances of anyone knowing me, or me knowing them is almost none."

Jack gave me the date of the picnic, and I agreed to meet him on the day in question at midday, but I thought I'd give him one more piece of information.

"I forgot to mention one minor detail Jack. I speak Greek!"

He now was flabbergasted and turning over a clean new page to scribble some of his shorthand symbols, fired a dozen or more excited questions at me on my proposed tour to Gallipoli, and was now a different interviewer. His change in attitude could not have been more pronounced. As far as I knew, Tasman Millington was still the caretaker of all cemeteries on Gallipoli, and he took copious notes when I mentioned his story and promised to conduct some more research into his life.

When the story appeared in the newspaper, we managed to secure a half page article with my ugly mug in a photo, and in the week following, enough funds had been promised to make sure the trip was now subsidised by some major local sponsors. I noted the date of the Limnian community's trip to Lake Wendouree and agreed to act as an interpreter if needed for a follow up story. Many of the Gallipoli touring party were busy themselves running various chook and meat-tray raffles to help in their own fund-raising.

In the meantime, our core group of veterans and various family members to travel to Gallipoli and Limnos for the 40th anniversary had settled on 25 people, with the dates set for July/August of 1955. This time, the group was going to fly to and from Athens, with a boat ride from Athens to Chanak, Limnos and back to Athens.

Much of my time was spent in planning this odyssey. Most of

the veterans had not left Australia since returning after the war, and of them, none had ever been in an aeroplane before — me included. This was to be a new experience. With our sponsorship and raffle money, it made the trip affordable for all, and we were counting down the days until departure. My role was to help everyone obtain passports, visas, travel tickets and accommodation.

I didn't give much thought to the Limnian Community visit to Ballarat due to my involvement with the upcoming Gallipoli visit, but the date came around very quickly. I had almost forgotten about it when a phone call from Jack reminded me of the day and my possible need to act as an interpreter for him. Another reason I had put this visit out of memory was that it was Christmas time, and I was busy with my own children and their families. Life as a widower was lonely, but when there are grandchildren around you, life is never dull.

On the third Saturday in 1955, the Melbourne to Ballarat passenger train left Spencer Street station on time at 8.30 am and arrived in Ballarat at approximately 11.00 am. Two special M-Class trams had been booked which took the 50 or so visitors from the train station directly to the Botanical Gardens at Lake Wendouree. Jack arrived at the rotunda next to the Tea Rooms where he arranged to meet his contact. By the time I turned up, a little after midday, the Limnian group had already taken over the rotunda with their picnic items and there were little children running in all directions. The women seemed to be preparing food, while the men were throwing perfectly good worms wound onto hooks into the lake in the hope of landing a juicy big fish. As I approached the rotunda, I noticed the strict division of male and female roles and chose to head straight to the fishing men.

"Does anyone here speak English?" I asked politely.

As I expected, deafening silence was the response, so I changed tack.

"Does anyone here know what type of fish are in this lake?"

Suddenly, the previously uninterested young men answered me without even noticing it was the same person who asked them if they spoke English. But one of them did.

"We do not really care what kind of fish there are in here, just as long as we can catch something."

He then looked at me and realised I was not one of their group and asked me a further question.

"Who are you? How come you can speak our language?"

I am sure many of these men had never talked to an Australian man before in Greek, and probably safely assumed there were no Greek speaking locals.

"Try casting your hook further out over those reeds. You might get a bite of a good-sized trout."

All of a sudden, the remaining half dozen men successfully cast their bated hand line hooks further out, and bugger me, if there was a bite almost immediately. The one young man who asked me the question continued.

"I will ask again. How do you come to be speaking Greek? Your accent is quite strange, and your words are very proper, but I can understand you fairly well. My name is Niko, what is yours?"

"I have visited your island a number of times, during and after the first big war. I was a soldier with the Australian Infantry Force."

"All of us had parents who remember you and your friends. They were very helpful to us. It is so good to meet one of you in person. My mother and father often talked of how kind and generous the Australians were. Especially the nurses and doctors. My father had a broken hand fixed by your doctors. Hey boys, this man here visited Limnos during the first war."

The man who had landed a small trout handed his fish over to his mate and came up to me to give me a big bear hug, much like the one my grandmother Mae did to me all those years ago. He kissed me on both cheeks and had genuine tears in his eyes. I started to feel like an important person!

At this time, Jack saw me from afar and called out my name. He had arrived late and noticed me down by the water's edge with a group of men.

"*Who is this?*" asked the bear hugger.

I replied that he was a journalist from the local paper, and when I said that, Niko spoke to him — in English.

"Hello Jack. It is good meet with you. You did not say this man speak Greek."

"Niko, I only met Angus a few weeks ago, soon after I spoke with you about coming here today. I didn't know he spoke your language."

"Did you say, Angus. My mother know Australian man many years back with name Angus. Is common name, no?"

"My name is not common, Niko. Not here in Australia, but maybe in Scotland. I have been told it is an ancient Greek name as well as Scottish. It means strong — 'δινατός'. Did you say your mother knew a man called Angus?"

"Yes."

"Niko — which village you from in Limnos? Maybe I have been there."

"I was born Pesperago, but I go Portianou when I marriage. My wife she has village in family. I sorry. Family in village. Do you know this village?"

When he told me that, I nearly fell into the lake. Could this be Maroula's son? I remembered speaking to her and meeting her four children nearly 25 years ago. Why is one of them now here, if it is him?

"Niko. Is your mother Maroula, and father Haralambous?"

"Yes Angus. What…are you…you have sheep? No?"

"I knew your mother and father a long time ago. I think I met you when you would have been only 5 or 6 years old. Yes, I still have sheep."

"My mother she will very happy I meet you here. She speak of you many times. My father he like you too."

"Next time you write to your mother and father, please say hello from Angus."

"My father has dead, now many years."

"I am so sorry to hear that Niko."

"But my mother is over there."

"Is she still living in the same house in Pesperago?"

"No Mister Angus. She is there. With children, feeding swans."

At this moment, Niko was pointing to a lady with long greying hair, standing by the lake about 25 yards away, feeding the swans with pieces of bread.

"*Γιαγιά! Γιαγιά, come over here. I think you know this man.*"

My heart was racing. Jack was stuck for words. Niko was asking his mother to come over, and I was stuck for words, as the beautiful looking vision of greying loveliness walked over to see why her son took her away from the all-important feeding of swans.

She was obviously enjoying feeding the big black water birds and looked a bit annoyed at having to come to where the young men were fishing. Then she saw me. She stopped. We were about only 15 feet from each other.

CHAPTER 26

FISHING 2
(1955)

Many Limnians came from all over Melbourne to Spencer Street station to catch the train to Ballarat. I spent two days preparing food for the picnic and was excited to be taking a train trip into the land where Angus was from. I didn't ever expect to see him, but thought it would be nice if I did.

Our little Limnian community had grown from about 20 people at the barbeque some weeks ago to now over 50. I didn't know at the time, but some people from our island had been living in Melbourne since before the war and were well and truly part of the new country now. My English was improving, but I still preferred to speak my own language.

The Saturday morning was a beautiful day. Fotoula and I asked a local baker if we could buy some bread sticks from his shop early on Saturday morning. He said *'of course'*, because bakers are usually up and baking well before any normal person is awake. Even earlier than a sheep farmer!

The first part of our journey began on the East Coburg to City tram, and we got off at Bourke street. Then onto another tram down to Spencer Street train station. We were early, and already, there were over 10 families nervously excited, waiting to depart. With so many happy Greeks in one place, the language of choice was only natural to us. But to the Australians standing nearby, we received some rather unpleasant looks, and a few of them shouted at us *'speak English, ya wogs. This is Australia. Go back to where you're from ya bloody dagos.'*

We just ignored them, but one of our boys, a man of 25, 6 feet tall and hands the size of dinner plates, had had enough of the lip and walked up to one of the most arrogant, foul-mouthed antagonists and suggested to him very politely that he should *'fuck off back to England yourself!'* That seemed to quell the anger immediately.

Niko and one of his friends Peter, had a list of all the travellers, and with 15 minutes before the train was due to leave, all were ready and keen to go. Then Niko and some of his work friends from the automobile manufacturers walked along the train platform to look at the big green and black steam engines. I could see one of the drivers standing on the side of his engine talking with Niko. After a minute of conversation, they came back to us very happy. He was explaining the size of the engine to me, and how it was powered by coal, but I was not interested in anything he said. As long as it worked!

Luckily, the train was not full, and we managed to obtain an entire carriage to ourselves. Once some of the 'Australians' saw a crowd of Greeks swarming onto the train carrying picnic baskets laden with food, and excited children in tow, they politely gave up their seats and moved carriages. How nice of them.

Our red carriage was the second last one on the train. Once inside, the kids and men opened windows so they could poke their heads out to see what was going on. The panicking mothers were inside, holding onto children so they wouldn't accidently fall out onto the tracks. Maybe they should have held onto their husbands, because they were the ones most likely to fall out a window.

For the entire train trip, I sat with my eyes glued to the view from my window, watching the passing scenery closely. This was my first trip on a train, and I was as thrilled as the children. Now I think of it, we were all delighted at being on this train.

Every time the engine driver pulled on the loud whistle to blast a deafening warning sound, the children tried to imitate the noise. This never ceased to amuse them, and each of us joined in eventually. I think we made as much noise as the driver did. The children were waving at anyone outside they could see at the stations and crossings along the way, and every now and then, they would wave back. From time to time, a child's head came back inside, and a mother had to rinse out soot from sore eyes. But they weren't deterred by a little inconvenience. Back to the window, head out, not missing anything. The scenery was totally different to anything I had seen. Grass, trees, birds, clouds, bushes and creeks — all different. One thing that still amuses me is that the sun travels a different path to back home in Limnos. The moon too.

Arriving in Ballarat, we were hurriedly rushed off to two waiting trams. These were slightly different to the ones we have in Melbourne, but to have the two all to ourselves was special. The trams took us through a maze of shady streets, and we ended up travelling around a big lake. Some of the fathers had packed hand fishing lines, and one even had a tin full of worms pulled from his garden. They were eager to try their hand at fishing for something to eat, but to me, it is always an excuse to be on their own and talk about 'men' things. I didn't mind that, because I liked doing the same with women.

On the lake, we saw people in thin boats, with oars, travelling backwards. I had never seen such a thing. They were going quite fast. But the thing that I liked were the big black birds sitting on the water like ducks, only these birds were much bigger. Someone said they were black swans, but I thought all swans were white.

The trams stopped briefly outside a big building where many trams were under a tin roof. Next to the building, a man was washing his big black car with a wet cloth and bucket of water by the side of the road. I remember him very well because he had circular glasses, and the sun shone off them. I had never seen glasses shaped like this. He waved at us as we rattled on past in our trams. Soon we arrived at a very beautiful place, surrounded by colourful flowers and trees of all kinds. The children were eager to get out and run, so we let them. We took our baskets of food, drinks, and blankets over to where Niko said we were to set up. A man was there to show us exactly the spot, and in no time, we women made a kitchen. The young mothers leapt immediately into food preparation, the fathers grabbed their fishing lines, and I somehow ended up with about six small children, a loaf of stale bread and found ourselves feeding the beautiful black swans.

Above the noise of children feeding these big black birds, pecking at our bread in the water, I heard Niko call out to me. At first, I ignored him, but he continued, and waved his arms wildly, beckoning me to where he was standing with his friends. One of the young mothers noticed Niko calling for me, and thankfully, she came to look after the children to allow me to see what the fuss was about. Maybe they had caught a fish, I thought!

"Γιαγιά! Γιαγιά, come over here. I think you know this man."

Leaving the swan feeding briefly, I wandered over to see why Niko was so animated.

"What man? Who are you talking about?"

That is when I saw my old friend Angus. He looked the same. Memories of my life as a young, single woman came flooding back. I knew this was where he lived, but I had not seen him for 25 years, and knew nothing of his life since then.

We stood still, looking at each other, not wanting to talk. We were smiling. Niko broke the ice.

"Mum. This man wants you to organise a donkey ride to the thermal springs. He says he stinks and needs a bath."

That was enough for us all to laugh uncontrollably.

"Hello Maroula. Welcome to my village."

"Hello Angus. It is good to see you."

I don't really remember what happened next, and in what order, because I was far too emotional. Since losing Niko's father many years ago, I had often thought of Angus, wondering what he was doing, and thinking about his family here in Australia.

Niko took the reporter aside and the two of them had a long talk. I asked Angus to join me in getting something to eat and to have a drink of water. We found a seat next to the lake, sat, and talked for what seemed like hours.

He told me about his wife and children and living alone now since she died. I told him about my children, and the same sad story unfolded. Although, it seemed that I was now no longer alone, and no longer sad.

CHAPTER 27

GALLIPOLI REVISITED

(1955)

Seeing Maroula again was a joy. To me she hadn't changed. Still that same determined fire in her eyes, and not afraid of telling me what she thought. But really, she had changed. I too had changed. We were now 60 years old, with 7 children between us, many grandchildren, and we were both widowed.

My days as a sheep farmer were coming to an end, as I had others in the family to take over the business. My son James was like me in that he loved animals, and had branched out into goats for milk, as well as obtaining some fine dairy cattle. Together with chickens, a large olive grove where olive oil was being made, a veggie patch big enough to feed an army, horses, a stable and a milking shed, the small farm my parents once owned had now turned into a much bigger enterprise. Not only bigger, but we now lived on a farm 15 or so miles from Ballarat in a place called Learmonth, right next to the lake. James not only loved the farming life, but he had plans to sell produce directly to the public from the farm. His business skills were far better than mine. I just loved being with my sheep!

James and his wife now ran the farm. Their children lived in the main house, and I was living on my own in a four-room cottage built at the entrance to the property. The house reminded me of my grandparents' home in Cambridge.

After Maroula, her family and the Limnians left Ballarat, I agreed to visit Melbourne one time before the end of summer. Luckily, Niko had a telephone installed in his house, so I could call them from the post office in Learmonth, as we did not have a telephone line at that time to our property. A day was agreed where I was to bring with me my daughter-in-law and one of her friends so they could do some Melbourne shopping in the city, while I spent the day with Maroula.

Arising early to drive my beautiful Ford Zephyr Six to Melbourne, we set off from Learmonth and drove to the suburb of Carlton in just on two and a half hours. I introduced my daughter-in-law and her friend to Maroula and her family, and in about 30 minutes, the two Ballarat women departed for a day of shopping in the city. Maroula and I spent our day walking, talking, and sitting in Princes Park, then wandering around the nearby University of Melbourne. We had never spent this much time together, and talked non-stop for many hours, in Greek, where she helped me with my words, and in English, where I could help her with many new words, her accent, and some quirky colloquialisms.

I told her that I was planning a trip in five months' time to Gallipoli and of course, to Limnos, to visit Military cemeteries and to see the battlefields of the conflict that had become a powerful cultural phenomenon in the story of Australia. Maroula still thought it strange that we celebrated a battle loss, and not a victory, and I had some difficulty explaining this to her. I said that we don't celebrate a loss, but rather that we commemorate the coming together of a new nation under a united federation. I think she understood.

While returning to her home in Carlton, I asked Maroula if she wanted to remain in Australia or go back to Limnos.

"I think I would like to return one day Angus, but not yet. I miss my other children and grandchildren, and miss my home. Even though this is very nice here, it is not my home. Does that make sense?"

It was then that I thought I would ask her something.

"Maroula. I have been thinking. Would you like to return for a visit to Limnos this year with me and my tour group? I could use your skills as a Turkish interpreter, and I would pay for all your expenses. What do you think?"

She did not give me an answer straight away, but wanted to talk to Niko about it first.

Before long, the girls returned with far too many bags of shopping, and it was time to travel along the Western Highway to home. We all said our farewells, and I asked Maroula when she might give me an answer.

The answer came in a week. No.

CHAPTER 28

GALLIPOLI TOUR
(1955)

I saw Maroula and her family one more time between their journey to Ballarat, and my trip to Gallipoli for the 40th ANZAC Day anniversary. I was mildly disappointed in her response to my request, but I fully understood her decision. If she was to return to her place of birth, it would need to be with family. I promised to take gifts and messages to her loved ones on Limnos when we travelled to the island at the end of our duties.

The final count of people in my group was 24. That consisted of 10 veterans, six wives and seven adult children of veterans. None of us had ever flown in a commercial aeroplane before, so the thought of flying such a long way were a mixture of excitement and sheer terror.

In a pre-departure meeting at the Ballarat Returned and Services League hall, we agreed not to wear any medals on the trip, and to leave them at home. There was some dissent, but in the end, we all agreed. It was possible that we would meet Turkish soldiers, and as a show of brotherhood, we would go as friends. Of the other 10 veterans, some were three-figured numbered former

AIF members, and the rest of us were four-figured. All of us had been on Gallipoli at some point in time, whether at the landing, evacuation, or some time in-between. Of the others, none had ever made a return visit to the battlefields. I was the only one who had, and as a result, was proud to be the unofficial tour leader.

The four-day trip to Athens was undertaken via a number of cities. First stop was Sydney, then Darwin for our first overnight stop. Day two took us to Columbo in Ceylon. Day three went via Bombay and Tehran, and day four took us to Athens via a stopover in Beirut. We only flew in daylight and slept in hotels near the airports. Arriving in Athens, we were all visibly and physically tired. Luckily, we had a few of the veterans' children with us, as they were not as tired, and could assist in much of the luggage carrying.

We stayed in a hotel in Athens for two days, taking in many of the city's tourist locations, including museums, the Acropolis and lots of walking. The final leg of the first half of our journey was from the port of Piraeus to Chanak with a Turkish passenger ferry.

I had not been to Chanak in nearly 25 years, but it looked eerily similar. Arrival at Chanak saw us clear Turkish customs with little or no fuss, and as I expected, we were met at the end of the wharf by Tasman Millington and his wife Ruth. We had been accompanied by several Turkish customs officials, and after speaking quietly with Tasman, we were permitted to continue. Tasman said to me that I looked older. I said the same about him. I introduced each of our group to them both, and after about 15 minutes of idle chit-chat, we were taken to our hotel, which fortunately, had a view of the Dardanelles.

As each of the group settled into their hotel rooms, Tasman, Ruth and I sat in the front café and had a long talk. We spoke of our families, life since we last met all those years ago, and a host of other things. Ruth remembered that I spent some time with George Lambert on the mission in 1919, and she mentioned to me that she now dabbled in water colour painting. Her love of painting came from her first passion, which was botany, and now she paints the beautiful wildflowers of the Gallipoli Peninsula.

One by one, each of the veterans came to join us at the café tables. Tasman spoke to the waiters and told them that the group had come from Australia and were going to visit the battlefield cemeteries tomorrow. One waiter told Tasman that his father was a Turkish veteran of the war and always spoke highly of the enemy. The waiter made a point of shaking every man's hand and mumbling something in his language. I think he was happy to meet these former enemy soldiers of his father.

Within an hour, the café was full of chatter and questions and comments were flying around like paper confetti at a windy wedding. Some of the veterans wanted to see the landing beach where it all began, and some wanted to see if they could find lost mates. Because I served with some of these men, I too wanted to visit the places so dear to our hearts.

We spent the rest of the day, or what was left of it, walking around the city and taking in the sights. Not much to look at, but the anticipation was high for what was to come on the next day. Later that night, Ismail joined us for a short while, and welcomed each of the veterans to his country again, together with each family member who had come to the country for the first time.

As usual, it was a bright and early start to the morning. Up at 6.00 am, breakfast at 7.00 am and waiting at the pier to take us across the water at 8.00 am. The weather was perfect for a short trip, and the group sat nervously on wooden seats aboard Tasman's boat. Each man clenched the rails as tightly as holding the reins of a runaway horse, knuckles turning white with their grip.

Even though we were not going to land at ANZAC Cove, for the men who were present at the initial landing, their minds were taken back to that moment. It was Friday morning on August 5, and the weather was beautiful. Sunny and quite warm, with little or no wind.

"Last time we did this, we were 20 years old and shitting ourselves."

"All I can remember was how quiet it was. We could only hear the oars dipping into the water."

"Then the shooting started."

One veteran stood up and said "I remember my mate just falling down over the oar. I told him to sit up. He didn't respond. I asked him one more time to sit up. Then I noticed the blood ..."

He sat down as his voice trailed off to barely a whisper. Then one by one, memories flooded in, and each former digger spoke to the group.

"I remember him. I think his name was Dougie Miller. Wasn't he from Gippsland? Farm boy if I remember. Real funny bloke."

"I remember one bloke who jumped out of the landing boat with his pack loaded up like the rest of us, and he never surfaced. Poor bugger couldn't swim."

"Paddy, Jacko and I made it to land, crawled along the beach on our guts, then I remember coming down a slope. We hadn't eaten for a day, and we were starving. We found two Turkish tents, no one home thankfully, and found two loaves of bread, and I think there was a tin of sauerkraut."

"I made it to a ridge near a cliff. Couldn't see Turks at all, but they could see us. I can remember the sound of bullets fizzing past. Got to another cliff, and I saw what looked like a cricket ball coming my way. A bloody fuse on a bomb. Without even thinkin', I had my rifle in front of me, and I slogged it away. Bloody good hook shot I reckon. No explosion, but I definitely shat myself."

"I was with five mates when we found ourselves under heavy fire on that first night, about two miles inland. We were lying in a trench, with gunfire and shrapnel all around, unable to put a little finger above the trench without it being blown off. Suddenly, the noise died down, and I looked up to see a man carrying a wounded officer on his back. We pulled them both inside and gave what help we could, before sending them off to the beach hospital, if you could call it that. I learned that the man carrying the wounded officer was aptly named Private Martyr. I kid you not. We recommended that the courageous Private receive a bravery award. Heard later that both did OK, and both survived the war."

"Steppin' over dead mates on our way back to the beach in the dark. Never forget that."

"Boer war bully beef tins from 1901, bullet-proof biscuits, dysentery, flies, and pinching rations from our dead mates."

It was a sobering experience for the diggers families to hear these recollections now, given where we were. I'm sure they have heard these stories many times over many years, but hopefully, the old narratives will now be contextualised. Tasman and Ismail had heard many old diggers like these men returning to this sacred ground reminiscing, remembering, and replaying moments locked away in the endless corridor of their distant memories. I could see that even for our two guides, hearing stories like these was always deeply emotional.

We arrived at the beach and put down anchor about 30 yards offshore. To set foot on solid ground, first we had to climb down and step into a smaller wooden boat following along on a rope behind us. This proved difficult, but with enough help at hand, and it being summertime, the water was warm and some of the younger group members didn't mind helping. After all, they were now standing in shallow water on hallowed ground.

Once we were all safely on the beach at ANZAC Cove, Tasman gave a short talk on what his work involved, and responded if the men had any questions about places, cemeteries, or battles. He had walked the land so many times, he could take us to exactly where they wanted to go and answer any questions. The problem for us was going to be this: over the years, the land had changed substantially, and what you can remember 40 years go will not be the same today, so it was important not to be disappointed.

After Tasman's talk, we were left alone for 10 minutes to soak in the emotional atmosphere, be at one with our thoughts, remember fallen mates, and reflect on the reasons we had come so far to be in this place. Each man wandered thoughtfully on his own, looking up into the distant hills, out to sea, left and right along the beach, and into the misty eyes of his mates. I was no different.

Tasman wasn't wrong. Over the next few days, we visited almost all of the cemeteries, battlegrounds, trenches, beaches, hills, tunnels, gullies and even the trees that have remained. Each of us had different memories, and before too long, disagreements arose regarding memories of particular events.

At the end of each day, safely back at the café in Chanak, discussions continued, and memories were tested, usually fuelled by a few beers. There is nothing more opiniated than a WW1 digger's remembrances of events from 40 or so years prior, gently massaged by a couple of pints of lager. Being cut from the same cloth, I have participated in many of these events, so I was completely prepared for it again. I had a copy of Bean's history, and at the appropriate moment, I would refer to the agreed historical record, hoping to settle any of the disagreements. I had told them, and they did agree, that if Bean said it took place at X and not Y, then X was correct.

"Remember. I was here when Bean carried out his groundwork for this history."

I had to use this line on many occasions to let them know that Bean was meticulous, thorough, thoughtful, and truthful. Thankfully, the misunderstandings between veterans evaporated, and having Tasman and Ismail there to add any recent discoveries not evident in Bean's work, was very useful to us.

Using Tasman as an interpreter, each of the veterans took turns asking Ismail questions about the Turkish perspective, and he was very forthright and candid in his responses. For the first time, my fellow comrades had a chance to put questions to the very person they were trying to kill 40 years ago. Not only that, Ismail was doing the same thing to us.

"Why did you attack here?"

"Why didn't you push on at this spot when you had the momentum?"

"Couldn't you see that we had an advantage over you, and attack was foolish?"

"Did you know that we were thoroughly defeated here, and you didn't know?"

I took them all to the spot where Mustafa and I participated in the 'unofficial' burial and showed them where I helped bury some Turkish soldiers. We all stood silently at that sacred ground to me and I broke the silence by saying that it was here that I truly learned we were fighting a foe as humane as we were, and where I learned that the Turkish soldier was just like us.

"I saw one of our boys sitting with his back to a Turkish parapet, and he was obviously injured. We kept calling to him to try to come back to us, but he couldn't move. Then, the most extraordinary thing happened. A Turkish rifle appeared over his head, and we thought he was going to get shot. Instead, it had a water bottle hanging from it."

Each of the veterans at different stages had similar stories of instances where they could have quite easily killed defenceless Turks, and where the Turks could have done the same to us, but nothing happened. Ismail was present at the evacuation and told us that he and his mates were laughing at our game of 'cricket', the rice on the ground, and the self-firing guns we left behind. He also said thank you for leaving some cans of food and blankets, as he was cold and hungry! "You're welcome", and we laughed.

The wives and children had the rare opportunity to see, at first-hand, the land where their husbands and fathers fought. They began to understand the source of their persistent nightmares, and why some returned with shellshock, or worse, those that couldn't bear it anymore and took their own lives.

Even after all this time, there were still objects from the battles lying just under the surface in many places. Tasman told us that it was forbidden to dig, and we couldn't legally dig anywhere to find these artefacts, but nothing stopped us from using what he called 'toe-kicking archaeology'. Rusty metal objects were everywhere. Nothing of value was found, but many bullets, buckles and even some rifle parts were 'kicked'. Everyone found at least something to take back home, in addition to some well-washed pebbles from ANZAC Cove. Tasman and Ismail had found many deeply personal objects over the past 35 years. Apart from uncovering skeletons of soldiers from both sides where they would be re-interred with the due considerations, Tasman and Ismail donated any objects to a variety of museums around the world. That depended on what was found and what could be identified.

The normally chatty group were always quiet and solemn at the cemeteries. Many graves of former friends and cobbers were found, and personal space was given to each and every man to mourn at the final burial place of a mate. Tasman and Ismail told stories of how the places of burial were established, how in some cases, bodies were located in No-Man's-Land and moved to a proper cemetery, and how over the years, more bodies and items had been located, re-buried and for some unknown soldiers, finally named.

On the last day of our short visit, Tasman spoke to the group.

"I have received many letters over the years of sincere thanks from family members back in Australia and New Zealand when dog tags and other personal items located have finally changed a soldier's status from missing to found. This is but one reason Ismail and I do what we do."

One of our group asked a final question as we were walking the long trip back to our boat to take us for the last time across to Chanak.

"Tasman. Why have you stayed here for so long?"

He thought long and hard and had a short conversation in Turkish with Ismail.

"That is a very good question, and very easy to answer. Firstly, I have stayed because of this man here. He's taught me that war is such a waste of life. Secondly, I feel a responsibility to the future generations of visitors who make a pilgrimage to this sacred land."

A week after arriving at Chanak, it was time for the next leg of our own odyssey — the reverse journey from ANZAC to Limnos. Travelling down the Dardanelles in our little Turkish boat, we turned right at Cape Helles, up past ANZAC Cove to Suvla Bay, where we swung right. We passed Imbros, where many of the diggers remembered spending some time resting there. We continued on to Limnos and proceeded directly to Moudros Bay where we had a hotel booked for two nights.

This time, memories from practically all the diggers were ones of good times. The hotel at the port looked as though it had not changed in 25 years, and I think some of the staff working there were the same. The hotel also doubled as customs clearance for us, and after all the group settled into their rooms, we met on the wharf across from the hotel.

I arrived at the rendezvous point early, and looking back to the town, I couldn't help but notice a larger stone building to the left, of our hotel. I asked a fisherman about it, and he told me that the Germans used in during WW2 as their headquarters. It was a most impressive structure.

The port area looked bigger, with more boats than I recalled from 25 years ago. Some of the diggers made their way down to where I was standing, and I asked one of them who was a 'three figured' man what it was like here on April 24.

"All you could see were ships, boats, yachts, destroyers, landing craft, donkeys, rowing boats, locals trying to sell us anything one more time, and this wharf was swarming with military personnel. I remember a lot of French and British soldiers."

Once we were all in place, I took responsibility for the touring duties informally. On Gallipoli, I left it to Tasman and Ismail, but here, I had some local knowledge and of course, my limited language ability. Our two days here were to see us visit the military cemeteries, the hospital sites, and a bath at Therma. I wondered who would be running George's Café now and couldn't wait to find out. I also had to find Maroula's family to give them some gifts from Melbourne and to say that she was doing well with Niko.

Meeting Maroula's daughters, their husbands and children was a treat. Thankfully, they all lived within a short donkey ride of Portianou, and I had a message from Γιαγιά to each of them individually. George was still alive, but the running of his café was now in the safe hands of Maroula's oldest son Panayioti and his family. Walking with our group into the plateia at Portianou was like walking into a place where time had stood still. The only differences were the two old men who used to sit outside the front door of the café had been replaced by George and a friend of his, Stavros. George was forgetting a lot, and his memory wasn't as sharp as I remembered it, but for some reason, he remembered my name and spoke to me as if I had only been away for a few days, not 25 years. He looked old, but content with life. Panayioti prepared a meal for our group, and we sat at tables under the large mulberry tree eating whatever was put in front of us, and drank whatever was on offer. One of the wives asked to see the menu, but I laughed.

"There is no such thing as a menu here, Maude" I told her. "The locals are the only guests, and the food is well known to them. We'll eat whatever is in season, and I bet you'll still love it."

Sure enough, she quickly forgot about choosing from a menu. One thing I will say about Greeks; they have a wonderful ability to conjure a tasty meal out of seemingly thin air for family and friends. We were made to feel most welcome, and when some of the locals saw that a big group was in town, it wasn't long before the café was full. Panayioti had to send out for more helpers in the kitchen and serving tables. It wasn't long before our group was well fuelled by bread, wine, tomatoes, cucumbers, white cheese, oregano, olives, dried figs, fried fish, dolmades, grapes and watermelon. Not a lot of meat, but the barbequed sheep's heart and liver seemed to go down very well.

During the afternoon feast in the town square of Portianou, which was after we had visited the military cemetery, I informed the group that I had a special surprise. Normally, I would take a donkey to the thermal bath house, but with Panayioti's help, we had arranged to have an old WW2 army vehicle drive us. After WW2, some of the German vehicles survived the demolition and destruction orders, and a farmer was now using this old truck as a type of bus service between villages when needed. Apparently, Niko and one of the German soldiers living at Maroula's house had managed to hide this vehicle by dismantling it under the guise of needing a massive mechanical overhaul. They hid parts in different locations, and when an officer came with orders to destroy any usable machinery, the beast of a vehicle appeared to be in ruins naturally, so the vehicle evaded destruction.

Once the Germans departed the island, Niko gathered all the parts together, re-built it and named it the 'Beast'. He had spent a few years as its chief mechanic, and I wanted to show him a photograph that the old Beast was still operating.

The normal track to Therma from Portianou was around Mt Elias, a fairly direct route. Using the Beast was an experience in itself. Knowing the history of the vehicle, and given that we were a group of army veterans, it was a bumpy, riotously funny circuitous journey. I wished Maroula could have been with us. At Therma, we took many photographs, and I made sure I had some photos taken of the Beast for Niko.

While the remainder of our visit to Limnos was mainly predictable, the farmer wanted to take us into Kastro for a visit on the morning of our last day. Of all my times on Limnos, I had never visited this village, and I was as excited as the others were. Climbing the ancient castle was a treat, and the views of the island from its crumbling fortified walls were stunning. Instead of taking the old army vehicle on a return trip to Portianou, we had loaded our luggage from the hotel at Moudros onto our boat. It motored around the bay to pick us up at Kastro for the concluding sea leg to Athens. Our final meal was in a portside café, where we could watch local fishermen arrive with boats full of their heaving daily catch.

After completing our meal, I vowed to return one day in the future with Maroula to sit at the same café, watch the fishermen repair nets, drink coffee, and eat olives, watermelon and freshly baked bread.

CHAPTER 29

FOOTBALL AND WRESTLING

(1956)

I had been living in Melbourne now for over a year. In that time, I learned many things about the people who live here. Men and some women love all things about sport, especially this game played on a field of grass and mud in the shape of an oval. Our house was walking distance from the place where this game was played, and it seemed that every second Saturday afternoon from April to the end of August, thousands of people would take a tram, train or walk like us to this oval to watch a game of '*fooball*'.

Niko and some of his work friends had been to some of the games to watch our suburb Carlton play at the place that was called 'Princes Park'. It was to be the last game for the year at this place, and Niko asked me if I wanted to see it, so I said 'yes'.

It was mid-August, and apparently Carlton were going to play a team called Footscray at Princes Park. I had only heard people talking about the game of '*fooball*', and when I saw it for this first time, it started to make sense. Not the rules, because I don't think I will ever be able to understand them, but the sheer number of people who attended this particular game. Over 45,000 people were packed into the oval tighter that a herd of sheep in a pen just before milking time. Every instance a Carlton player went near the oval shaped leather ball, they would scream. Sometimes, they cheered, sometimes they booed, especially to a player for the Footscray team called *'Teddy'* and most of the time, they managed to direct all their anxiety and rage towards a man dressed in a white shirt, white short pants and long black socks and boots who had a whistle. I loved how the crowd would all yell together the word *'ball'*, followed by a pause and then scream *'yes'*. We had no idea what this all meant, but by the end of the game, we were yelling along with them. It was a lot of fun. Walking home together after the game with thousands of people made us feel like we were part of a wider community. Although I didn't understand the rules of the game, it was a most entertaining way to spend an afternoon. Niko and I were very happy, even though our suburb Carlton had lost the game. I didn't know what this young man meant when he said to me while we were walking home *"better luck next year missus"*. I think he assumed I knew what he said, but I did not understand anything.

Niko's Greek and Italian friends loved Carlton, and for them, it was a way of being accepted as an Australian. If you liked *'fooball'*, drank a beer and smoked a cigarette, then you were an Australian male. I didn't drink beer, hated smoking anything, and after one game, didn't like *'fooball'* much either, but loved being in the crowd. I did learn that the word was not *'fooball'*. It did have a letter 't' in it, and the correct name is football. When my ears could understand some more English, I often heard of the game of *'foody'*. I was thoroughly confused, but apparently football is also *'fooball'* and also *'foody'*!

What was clear to me was how much Australians love sport. Being 1956, it was the year that the entire sporting world descended on Melbourne for the Olympic Games. As a proud Greek woman, I told anyone who wanted to listen that we Greeks invented the

Olympic Games, but no one really took any notice of me. Not only that, but the Limnians invented the Pentathlon, an event of five disciplines which included jumping, discus, javelin, racing and wrestling, and was first recorded in the Olympic program in 708 BC. I tried to tell my new Australian friends this piece of historical trivia, but no one really cared.

After the football finished in Melbourne in mid-September, the whole city seemed to prepare for the Olympic Games. New venues had been constructed all over the city and many Limnian men here in Melbourne gained employment at some of these venues as part of the construction crews. Some of our men were lucky enough to obtain tickets to wrestling events held at the Exhibition Building in Carlton, which fortunately was just the event they wanted to see. Greece had two competitors in wrestling, so we hoped to see them compete.

I managed to obtain two tickets from a friend of Niko's, who wanted me to go to the wrestling. I contacted Angus to see if he wanted to see some Olympic Wrestling. Luckily, he said yes, and on the day of the event, he drove to Melbourne early to be with us. Walking to the Exhibition Building on the morning of November 28, 1956, was a group of 10 Greeks and one Aussie. I was the only female, and Angus was now becoming one of us too. I think because he spoke Greek, our young men liked him, and treated him differently. I mean this in a good way, because Angus could talk to any Greek man about milking sheep, goats, growing olives and making wine. Come to think of it, they loved him. Like me being an older woman, Angus was an older man and reminded many of the young men of their fathers who were back in Greece.

Niko purchased an official program for a shilling, and although I couldn't read much English at the time, I was designated as the one to hold this important document for the day. Before we entered the building to take our seats, we noticed Greek athletes warming up outside the big building on the lawn area. Some of the men went over to the athletes and their coaches and struck up conversations. I also noticed some other teams outside, and particularly noted the Turkish and Bulgarian teams doing warm up exercises nearby. As I still spoke some Turkish, I wandered over to where they were stretching and walked up to one of their officials. Angus was looking for the Australian competitors, and we lost sight of him for a few minutes.

I struck up a conversation with Yusef, one of the Turkish team officials, a man in his early 40s, and told him I was a Greek citizen living in Melbourne but knew some Turkish. He spoke with me for a short while but wanted to return to the team as they were preparing to enter the venue. I mentioned that I was from Limnos, and fondly remembered my Turkish friends before the 1912 departure from the island. Yusef suddenly became interested and said he once lived on the Greek island of Tenedos, which was now in Turkish hands, and he remembered his Greek friends who were also forced to leave.

"Do you speak any Greek Yusef?" I asked him in Turkish.

"No, not really. I did learn some when I was young, but I have forgotten most of it."

"I have a friend somewhere here today who is an Australian man and he visited Tenedos while fighting in WW1 in 1915, and again in 1919. In fact, he was in Gallipoli and Chanak only a year ago."

"One of our senior trainers also fought in that war, and he speaks very highly of the courage and dignity of the Australian soldier."

"My friend would love to meet him. I can translate for them both. Wait here for one minute while I go and find him."

Yusef quickly left to locate the old trainer. I could see Angus walking in my direction and when he came closer, I asked him if he would like to talk to an old enemy from the Great War. Suddenly coming to life, Angus said "that would be wonderful."

Like most men of his age, Angus needed eyeglasses in order to make out people's faces and to read, but in his haste and excitement to travel to Melbourne, he inadvertently left them at home. Walking together in the direction of the Turkish wrestling team, I could see Yusef coming our way, and with him was the old man he told me about. Suddenly, looking in our direction, the old trainer with Yusef stopped walking, and just looked at us.

"Maroula? Is that you?"

Yusef was stunned because the old man was speaking flawless Greek.

Could it be? No, it couldn't.

"Is that you Mustafa?"

"Mustafa. I know a Mustafa" said Angus.

Yusef was totally confused.

I walked towards one of my oldest and dearest friends and we embraced like long, lost siblings.

"Mustafa. Do you remember Angus, the Australian who speaks Greek?"

Speaking Greek, Mustafa replied that he most certainly did.

I stepped back from Mustafa and allowed him look directly at Angus. The two old men gave each other an embrace that showed to me the respect and friendship they had, and it was still alive all these years later. I was in tears. Two of the most important people in my life were here, with me!

It was Yusef who broke the ice, with his broken Greek.

"Mustafa. We must now go in."

There were so many questions each of us three had for the others that no-one quite knew where to start. Mustafa attempted to speak first and said that he had to go inside the wrestling venue as the first Turkish Olympic representative was about to compete in his opening bout.

Angus suggested that we all meet here at the end of the day's competition. Mustafa agreed, and left with Yusef to go inside. Angus and I walked behind them, and I could hear what they were saying.

"That lady was a good friend of my sister and I in Limnos before we were forced to leave in 1912. And that man with her tried to kill me and I tried to kill him three years later, and I am so glad we did not succeed."

"What do you mean that he tried to kill you?"

"We both fought in WW1, and he was my enemy, but we met on the battlefield as friends. I'll tell you later, but that man changed my life. And I have no idea why the two of them are here, or why I am here. Allah works in mysterious ways."

I had completely forgotten Niko and the rest of our Greek contingent. Niko saw us talking to the Turkish officials and seemed very confused.

"OK mum, what is going on here. How come you know that Turkish man."

I quickly gave him the abbreviated version of how I knew Mustafa. He had known about the Turkish people on Limnos but had not really met any of them. He had heard Haralambous and I talking about the Turks many times, and he had heard me mention Mustafa and his family.

"I remember you telling me this many years ago Mum. So that is Mustafa. But Angus. How come you know him?"

"Niko. Where do I start? Like your mother, I'll give a simple version. I met him by chance during the big war, and strange as it seems now, we became friends. At the end of the war, I met him again, and secured him some work, helping build cemeteries on the Gallipoli Peninsula. I know where he lived in Pesperago and have been to his family home. I have not seen him for over 26 years, but still consider him a friend."

EPILOGUE

My grandfather died on July 10, 1958. That date is on his gravestone and it is a date I never really understood. I was born on January 10, 1959, so we never met in person. I hope he knew that I was on the way, as mum would have been three months pregnant with me when he died.

As a boy, I had no reason to ask dad how his father died. For as long as I knew my father, I had never asked him about the death of his parents. One of those questions you don't think about at the time, but after your parents are gone, wish you had.

My grandfather's typed pages ended after that day in November 1956. I am guessing he intended to type more, but that was not to be. While he may not have put his fingers to a typewriter keyboard, he did leave copious handwritten notes.

After the Olympic games in 1956, Grandpa Angus visited Maroula on a number of occasions. Sometimes he took the train, but mostly, he drove his much-loved Ford Zephyr Six. I know about these visits to Melbourne because he had handwritten notes in the fourth folder mentioning his trips from October 1956 right up to June 1958.

During the Olympic games of '56, after being in the presence of Maroula and Mustafa, Angus had an idea. He wanted to write his memoirs and asked them both to write some stories of their own, going all the way back to 1912 right up to the present day to add to his. They both agreed to help, and apparently, had their contributions finished within 12 months. Mustafa being a language teacher, was now fluent in many languages, and had a successful teaching career, as well as his Greco Roman wrestling coaching and mentor roles for Turkish athletes. He was a learned man and found it easy to write his chapters. Maroula was not as fluent with her written Greek, but nonetheless, fluent enough to write her stories with the help of her son Niko.

I doubt if Angus and Mustafa ever saw each other again in person, but for the next 19 or so months after the Olympic Games, wrote many letters to each other. These letters from Mustafa were also in the box where I discovered the four bound folders.

In early July 1958, my grandfather visited a jeweller shop in Ballarat and purchased a piece of jewellery for £100. The faded handwritten cash receipt did not say what the item was, and there was no indication in his notes who the intended recipient of the jewellery was to be. One hundred pounds in those days was a considerable amount of money, so the item in question must have been important to him.

Grandpa Angus' notes seemed to end on or about July 6 in 1958. An entry on that day was the last one dated. Another item I found in my father's box of old-time goodies were many newspaper cuttings, from after the war, right up to when my grandfather died. Those cuttings were not in a scrapbook, but simply kept loose. I found mum and dad's newspaper engagement and wedding announcements, stories of his sporting achievements and in fact, many eclectic and varied themes. One small cutting, perhaps the smallest one in the box was dated July 12, 1958. It was blunt.

Death notice:
'Angus Herbert Harrison, died as a result of a single-car accident in Ballan on July 10th, 1958 at 9.00 pm. Angus was a

member of the RSL Club of Ballarat, and fought at Gallipoli, France, and the Western Front in WW1. Lest we Forget.'

Why was Angus driving at that time of night in Ballan, a town 45 minutes away from Ballarat on the Melbourne Highway. There were no other hints in relation to the accident in any of the clippings and cuttings in my father's things.

Rita said something to me when I discovered this death notice that I will never forget. Maybe he was coming back from Melbourne, visiting Maroula, and maybe he had given her a ring or something like that. I thought the idea had credibility, so we began to search for a logical answer.

All we had was an address in Carlton where Maroula was living in 1958 with Niko and family. We also had a surname — Maroula Gerontaras. Rita used her connections with the Limnian community and found someone with that surname, still living in Carlton. We wrote a letter to a Spiros Gerontaras asking if he was related to a Maroula Gerontaras, who migrated to Australia in 1953 with her son, daughter-in-law and one child. After two weeks, we received a reply from Spiro, and he said that Maroula was his *Γιαγιά*. We were excited to say the least, and luckily, Spiro included his email address and mobile phone number, saying that we were welcome to contact him at any stage. Contacting Spiro immediately, we arranged to meet at a café in Carlton at an agreed time in one week.

Meeting Spiro, I couldn't help but feel I had met him before. Rita said the same thing. As it turned out, his wife was also from Limnian background, and he often visited the island, and stayed in her family house in the village of Varos. We agreed that we must have bumped into each other a number of times over the years without knowing who the other was. Spiro said that he also spent a month every second year in Limnos and was looking forward to retiring soon when he and his wife could take off for the entirety of the Australian winter!

We asked him about his grandmother, and if he could tell us anything of her life in Carlton. Before he started, we mentioned that we had a few chapters of a book we were about to publish in which Maroula had contributed. He was amazed at the thought of his grandmother writing anything, as she was such a good talker, and very forthright with her opinions.

"I remember Γιαγιά well. As a little boy, she was simply the funny old lady in her bedroom at our house, but as I grew older, and began to understand her a lot more, I would sit for hours at a time listening to her stories."

"Perhaps the main memory I have of her was that she didn't waste anything. She washed and re-used 'glad wrap' until it no longer had any cling left. Our socks would be so full of little bits of repair, there was hardly any original material left. She hated us leaving food on our plates. We had to finish every morsel. If it wasn't finished, it was never thrown out — just refrigerated for the next day."

"She had stories every day for the grandchildren. I must have heard each story a hundred times, but we never grew tired of them. I find myself using her expressions, her special sayings, and I even have sung songs to my own children that came from her."

"I remember her smell — thyme. She just loved thyme. I only really appreciated that after my first trip to Limnos as a young boy. I could smell θυμάρι all over the island, and every time I smell thyme, it reminds me of her. It didn't matter to Γιαγιά how she felt. All she cared about was how we were and making us happy. I can't even remember her taking medication or going to the doctors!"

"Our favourite place to go with her as little kids were the Exhibition Gardens in Carlton. It wasn't far from home, and I can remember walking around those gardens, stopping at each and every tree, and playing on the grass. We treated it as our own big back yard."

"I don't know why, but every time we walked by this one

particular tree in the gardens at the Exhibition building, she had to stop, look up at its branches and smile. The tree was almost identical to many others in the gardens, but it had two distinct main branches growing out of the trunk. She wouldn't say a word, just stop, stare and smile. The last time she walked there with me, we stopped as usual at the tree, and this time, she said something like '*my boys*'. I didn't know what she meant, and I didn't ask."

Spiro told us that she lived until she was 95 years old, passing away quietly and quickly in 1990. His father and mother were also deceased, but he had heard many stories about their lives in Limnos. But his next story stopped us in our tracks.

"Angus — Γιαγιά had only one regret in her life."

"What was that Spiro?" asked Rita. "Was it that she never went back to Greece?"

"No. She did go back with mum and dad many times. I was there with her a few times, and loved walking around the village she was born in. We have so many relatives there."

"Yes, I know the village. But where is Pesperago? I could never find it. It must have been a small village."

"That is because the village was flattened by an earthquake, and when it started to be re-built, it was renamed Paleo Pedino."

Rita and I must have looked each other with the same stupid expression.

"Did I say something wrong?" asked Spiro.

"No. It is a long story, but quite simply, we have a house in Paleo Pedino. It never occurred to me that Pesperago was the same village. How about that."

"Her regret was that she could have married the love of her life but couldn't because the man died. He even gave her an engagement ring."

"Spiro. Would this have happened around the middle of 1958 by any chance?"

"Yes. How did you know?"

"She was engaged to my Grandfather. His name was Angus, and that is who I am named after."

If we weren't crying by then, the tears in Spiro's eyes set us off. We hugged and cried buckets. As it happened, Grandpa Angus had gone to Melbourne to ask Maroula to marry him on July 10, 1958. She said 'yes'. He gave her a ring. He left to come home, and halfway back, drove into a tree in Ballan and died instantly. Spiro had heard of this story from Maroula when he was old enough to understand.

"She would tell me of this wonderful Australian man she took on a donkey ride to Therma a hundred years ago. She told me many stories of her life, of my Grandfather, my parents, and the reasons they left Limnos to come here to Australia. But she was always beaming when talking about your Grandfather, Angus."

"How did she find out about the car accident?"

"In the car that night, your Grandfather had a piece of paper in his wallet with our telephone number on. My father told me that a telephone call from the Ballan police came the next day, asking if we knew the driver of a Black Zephyr. We found out about the accident almost immediately. Given my father's work with cars at the time, asked the police later on how the accident happened, and he was told that the brakes failed. Your Grandfather would have had no chance."

We talked for hours, ordering lunch and a few glasses of wine. Spiro told us much more about Maroula and her first husband Haralambous.

"Did she ever mention how he had died?"

"No. I don't think so. Only that he had passed away before the war, leaving Γιαγιά alone with the kids and farm to contend with. We used to laugh at her stories of making clothes and shoes for herself and her children. As little kids, we would insensitively laugh at this, but later on, I realised how poor she must have been."

Rita added her own stories about her family during the war

years, and how poor, but strangely happy they were. Spiro's wife Lifota joined us, and more wine and μεζές followed. Then the Limnian game of 'are we related' started in earnest. And what do you know? Rita and Spiro are related — about third cousins or something like that, but they are family. In Limnian circles, that is close enough to be considered family. In my Aussie culture, I would say that I don't know any of my third cousins and would never consider them family if we ever met.

We departed for home feeling that we knew Grandpa Angus a whole lot better, but for us, we began to understand more of Maroula and her life in Australia. Rita had discovered unknown members of her extended family, and I had a new and invigorated sense of deeply personal connected history between the ANZACs and the Limnians.

On our trips to Limnos in the past, we would sleep at our house in Paleo Pedino, and spend the whole day traveling to other villages, to different beaches, different tourist places, shopping in the main town, and eating at restaurants all over the island. I don't think we ever cooked an evening meal at home until this year. In the past we always had two children with us, so we felt obliged to entertain them with a variety of things to do. We used to spend our entire days with people just like us. I can't ever remember going for a simple walk in our village and talking to local people.

After the 100 years of ANZAC commemorations were concluded in 2015, Rita and I travelled to Greece alone a year later, and for the first time, for the entirety of the northern hemisphere summer. We met up with Spiro and Lifota on Limnos, and they introduced us to extended family members, and once again, Rita played the 'are we related' game.

Rita proudly sat for hours outside our front door, speaking to anyone who would walk past. One day, a very old woman, who we knew lived alone in a nearby village, was driven by her daughter to the village water well, next to the plateia. We happened to be there at the same time filling up our drinking water containers, and Rita and the old lady started talking.

The old lady was having difficulty with her vision, but her mind was a sharp as ever.

"Who are you?" she asked.

"I'm Rita Kontouris. I am Spiro and Maria's daughter. I was born just over there in that house 58 years ago. My parents and I left for Australia a year later, and my Australian husband and I have moved back to the family home for summer each year."

"I remember your parents well. Are they with you?"

"Sadly no, Aunty. They died a few years ago now."

"Sorry to hear that. I remember this house as a little girl."

"Do you remember anything about this house Aunty?"

"My Γιαγιά Eleni used to live next door, but I can't remember anyone living in your house. But I do remember one day before the war, I was visiting Γιαγιά, and was playing around here. Two people from Portianou walked past us and went inside the old house. My Γιαγιά knew them."

"Can you remember what they were doing in the house?"

"No. Not really, but I remember them coming out carrying a small colourful box. I don't know if they took that box in with them, but I certainly remember them coming out with it. We both waved goodbye to them, and I asked Γιαγιά who they were."

"Do you remember what she said Aunty?"

"Yes, I can. She said that the lady was Maroula, and the man was the son of the Turkish people who used to own the house."

Author's Note:

The events in this book are a mixture of pure fiction, punctuated with historical markers of activities that did happen. Angus, Mustafa and Maroula were born from my imagination and life experiences, yet people just like them could very well have existed at this time. The inspiration for this book came from our ancestors, both Australian and Greek, and it was their life circumstances that formed the basis of this story.

My paternal grandfather joined the AIF and was a Gallipoli veteran in the 8th Battalion 4th Reinforcements. Although he may have visited Limnos on his way to and from Gallipoli, there is no actual record of him doing so. He was injured after only eight days of fighting and was repatriated home to Ballarat. My wife's family are from Limnos and many of the stories and events in this novel come from firsthand knowledge and accounts.

The story commences with the life of Angus on his family farm outside of Ballarat. He is a sheep farmer, with a flock of sheep used primarily for milking, not wool. This is a complete fabrication as there is no evidence that this breed of sheep was in Australia at that time. But they most definitely are here in 2021.

Many soldiers in the AIF were mono-lingual, with perhaps a small percentage speaking a second or even third language. I found no evidence of an Australian soldier speaking Greek, so Angus' language skills would have been unique. Growing up with multi-lingual parents from England was the basis of the story, and springboard for many exploits with Angus. Someone like Angus' mother would not have been permitted to enrol in University at Cambridge and achieve a degree, but women did take some classes at the discretion of the professors. Women did not graduate from Cambridge until the 1940s.

We are introduced to Angus as a soldier in the 8th Battalion, 4th Reinforcements. Some of the men my Grandfather went to war with are mentioned from time to time in this book. The first part of the book is set against the backdrop of utter despair during WW1, in places like Limnos, Gallipoli, France, the Western Front and finally in London after the Armistice signing. Like a Forrest Gump figure, Angus finds himself an active participant in important historical events. During his time as a soldier, he finds a strange kind of love in the form of Maroula, a girl from the village of Portianou, Limnos. Not knowing at the time, this was to be possibly the most important person in his life.

Many of the events incorporating members of the 8th Battalion came from Ron Austin's book, 'Cobbers in Khaki' and the actual AIF war diaries of the 8th Battalion. Reading the war diaries was a real treat, as they were handwritten at the time, and contain some fascinating insights. These diaries are a treasure trove of information for historians. Ron's book has excerpts of many letters sent home from soldiers at strategic moments in the history of the 8th Battalion.

The character of Tasman Millington was real, and to this day, it is hard to believe his story had not been made into a mini-series, or at least a full-length motion picture. I can't be certain if he ever made it to Limnos to help in the evacuation of Jewish people, but he most certainly did assist in the removal to safety of many Jewish Greek people from Crete, right under the Germans noses, while he was living in Turkey. Millington spent time on Limnos in 1915 suffering from dysentery, but soon had to be sent to Malta as his condition deteriorated. For more information on this amazing Australian, find a copy of John Samuel's book, 'Millington's Mission'. You won't be disappointed.

The hospitals and rest camps on Limnos are well documented, and so too are many of the events Angus participated in at Gallipoli, such as the burial armistice in May 1915, and the informal burial armistice of November that year where he met Mustafa for the first time.

However, the character of Mustafa was a myth in real life, but he also could have existed. Turkish people were forced to leave Limnos in 1912 after that island became part of the Greek nation. Turkish people had been living on the island since around 1473, and there is no reason why a character like Mustafa could not have existed. My father-in-law was from the village of Tsimandria, and he often used many Turkish words in his daily language. The influences both ways of Turkish and Greek culture are quite obvious, and very much alive in spoken Limnian Greek today with older people.

On May 24th 1915 at Gallipoli, a burial armistice did take place so that the Allies and Turks could retrieve and bury their dead. Greeting cards, cigarettes and souvenirs were exchanged. During the burial armistice, there are stories and documented accounts of Australian soldiers speaking to Turkish soldiers in French. In this book, I talk about one such event where a package with French writing was tossed from the Turkish trenches to the Aussies.

There are no official reports of a further burial armistice occurring in November and December, but that does not mean that informally, this did not happen. There is evidence that an unofficial burial did take place in November 1915. It has been called a random and non-regulation act of kindness in some reports. The only documented language spoken by both Allied and Turkish soldiers was French, but there is no reason why Angus and Mustafa could not have been able to use another language to converse.

Charles Bean's Australian Historical Mission in 1919 was a major undertaking. My imagination was to put Angus in the Mission as a valuable member due to his knowledge of Gallipoli and Limnos. Captain Bean's nickname of 'Captain carrot' or 'skipper' was real, and a number of the people did call him by those names. The Mission visited Limnos for a few days, and there is extant evidence of Lambert's paintings, and Wilkins' photographs from that time. Both these members of the Mission had the first name of George, and they both have some sheep farming in their background. However, Wilkins preferred to be called Hubert, but I changed that to make life easier for me. Hubert Wilkins deserves a greater place in Australia's history, and was a truly remarkable man in his own right. Lambert's paintings have stood the test of time, and he was truly a great artist. I would hope that one day, some of Lambert's original water colour paintings created on Limnos would grace the walls of a gallery or museum in Moudros.

Visits to Gallipoli by Australians immediately after WW1 were not encouraged, but over time, throughout the 1920s, a number of people did make the journey. While these trips were not well known, the New Zealand grandmother did actually visit, and it was well documented in newspapers at the time. John Samuel's book on 'Millington's Mission' talks about such visits from Australians over the early years, but these were extremely rare events. There is no known visit of a group from Ballarat visiting Gallipoli and Limnos, but I had to get Angus back somehow! I have a brief snippet of fact which resulted in Russel Crowe's motion picture from 2014, *The Water Diviner*. While the movie is largely fiction, one Australian man did find himself at Gallipoli looking for the grave of his son.

During the years 1941 to 1944, the German armed forces occupied the island of Limnos, and were situated in many villages. My mother-in-law's family had their home in Karpasi occupied for three years by a German officer and seven of his men. This was a common occurrence in many villages. A number of the Germans who found themselves in the position of occupiers of houses were sympathetic to the local people, and over time, developed friendships with them. My mother-in-law's older brother actually went to work for the Germans making bricks and was paid. My mother-in-law also worked for the Germans instead of attending school — until her mother discovered that she had German money!

Parts of Maroula's story come from my own Greek mother-in-law's life and family. For example, having the Germans occupy houses in WW2 was a reality on Limnos. Having a senior German officer give away a young woman about to be married actually happened to a member of my Greek family. Many German soldiers did switch sides and joined the Greek resistance. Wolfgang Abendroth was one of these German soldiers who joined the Greek Resistance and wrote of his experiences on Limnos some years later.

Turkey competed in the 1956 Olympic games in Melbourne and won gold medals at wrestling. The sport of wrestling is perhaps the one Olympic sport where their success speaks for itself. It is quite possible that a former National Wrestling champion like Mustafa could have accompanied the team to Melbourne in 1956 in the capacity as coach and mentor to younger athletes. The venue of the Olympic wrestling was the Melbourne Exhibition Buildings, so anyone living in Carlton could easily walk to the venue and potentially see Olympians warming up outside on the grass. I say this with some trepidation because there were also official warm-up areas inside the venue.

The number of migrants travelling from Limnos to Melbourne in the 1950s is well known, and the Limnian Community of Victoria (Ifestos) was in existence. My own parents-in-law were such people. Day trips to places such as Queenscliff, Mornington, Williamstown and Geelong were arranged, and families packed colourful metallic Eskies with all kinds of food sensations to take on the trains or buses. So, it is quite possible that a day trip via a country train ride to the Ballarat gardens could have happened for the Melbourne Limnian community in the 1950s.

Inspiration for the name of this story 'George's Café' came from a famous photo taken by A. W. Savage in 1915, where you can see a mixture of soldiers, nurses and locals enjoying a coffee outside a Portianou café. With my wife's paternal family coming from this area of Limnos, it seemed like a logical place for people to meet regularly, enjoy coffee and cakes, and it is situated close to where many of the book's stories are set.

The village of Pesperago was re-named Paleo Pedino some-time after an earthquake flattened the village. I remember being driven through the village in the winter of 1983 and having the taxi driver say quite proudly that it was an abandoned village due to an earthquake. In 2021, Paleo Pedino has had many homes lovingly restored using the traditional stone construction method by people wanting a quiet lifestyle in an authentic Limnian village. It is highly unlikely that any Turkish people lived in this village in 1912 or before, but that does not mean that no Turkish families ever lived there between 1470 and 1912.

Finally, I would like to sincerely thank my two eagle-eyed review-ers Jim Sillitoe and Despina Whitefield, who read and re-read my manuscript. Your advice, subtle suggestions and assistance was greatly appreciated and I could not have got this far without your help. Any mistakes found in this book are mine alone.

Selected Bibliography.

There were many references used for this book. Here is a selection of the best of them.

Wolfgang Abendroth (1979) *How Wolfgang Abendroth came to Greece as "999" and fought there with partisans against the Nazi occupiers.* Source — http://www.barth-engelbart.de/?p=29092

Melissa Afentoulis (2018). *Migration from Limnos to Australia: Re-discovering Identity, Belonging and 'Home'*, PhD Thesis, University of Melbourne.

Ron Austin (1997). *Cobbers in Khaki. The History of the 8th Battalion 1914 — 1918*, Slouch Hat Publications.

Charles Bean (1948). *Gallipoli Mission.* 1st Edition, Australian War Memorial, Canberra, Halstead Press.

Kenneth Best (2011). *War Diaries.* A Chaplain at Gallipoli, Simon & Schuster.

Richard Bryant (Unknown). Red Cross Hospital. King Edward Hall, Lindfield, Lindfield History Project Group, http://www2.westsussex.gov.uk/learning-resources/LR/lindfield_red_cross_hospital63a6.pdf?docid=f569d93e-4926-43ad-9d5a-86e5bd5c9a17&version=-1

Paul Byrnes (2019). *The Lost Boys, The untold stories of the under-age Anzac soldiers who fought in the First World War*, Affirm Press.

Les Carlyon (2001). *Gallipoli*, Macmillan.

Les Carlyon (2006). *The Great War*, Macmillan.

Jim Claven (2017). *Remembering the liberation of Lemnos — 1944*, Neos Kosmos, 25 November, 2017 pp 22-3.

Jim Claven (2017). *The day the Germans marched on Lemnos*, Neos Kosmos, 4 November, 2017, pp 20-1.

Ross Coulthart (2014). *Charles Bean*, Harper Collins.

Paul Daley and Michael Bowers (2011). *Armageddon. Two men on an ANZAC Trail*, The Miegunyah Press.

George Frederick Davis (2010). *Anzac Day meanings and memories: New Zealand, Australian and Turkish perspectives on a day of commemoration in the twentieth century*, Doctoral Thesis, University of Otago.

Lena Divani (1994). The Russian Refugees in Greece: A first attempt to register, Athens Law School

Edward J. Erickson (2008). *The History of World War 1. Gallipoli & the Middle East 1914 — 1918*, Amber Books.

Kathryn Gauci (2017). *The Carpet Weaver of Uşak*, Ebony Publishing.

Janda Gooding (2009). *Gallipoli Revisited. In the footsteps of Charles Bean and the Australian Historical Mission*, Hardie Grant Books.

Charles Yale Harrison (2003). *Generals Die in Bed*, Penguin Books.

Roger Hawthorn and Tony Whitefield (2015). *A Lemnos Odyssey. From Jason and the Argonauts to the ANZACs at Gallipoli — The story of the Greek Island of Lemnos*, Australian Scholarly Publishing.

Hedley Howe (1965). *ANZAC. Sparks from an old Controversy*, Australian Army Journal, No. 191, Apr, 1965.

Garrie Hutchinson (1997). *An Australian Odyssey from Giza to Gallipoli*, Sceptre.

Ken Inglis (2015). *Letters from a Pilgrimage: Ken Inglis' despatches from the Anzac tour of Greece and Turkey, April — May 1965*, Inside Story.

Natalya Lapaeva (2011). *Russian Emigration on the Balkans: The "Limnos Episode"*, 1st International Conference on Foreign Language Teaching and Applied Linguistics, May 5 — 7, 2011, Sarajevo pp. 980 -986.

John Masefield (1916). *Gallipoli*, The MacMillan Company.

Norman G. McNicol (1936). *The Thirty-Seventh*. History of the Thirty-Seventh Battalion A.I.F, Modern Printing Company, Melbourne.

Official Report (1958). *The Official Report of the Organising Committee for the Games of the XVI Olympiad Melbourne 1956*, http://www.vrwc.org.au/tim-archive/articles/1956%20Olympics%20-%20Official%20LOC%20Report.pdf

Tolga Ornek and Feza Toker (2006). *Gallipoli. The Front-Line Experience*, Currency Press.

Peter Rees (2014). *ANZAC Girls. The Extraordinary Story of our World War 1 Nurses*, Allen & Unwin.

Richard Reid (2010). *Australians in World War 1, Gallipoli*, Department of Veterans Affairs, Canberra.

Paul Robinson (1999). *The White Russian Army in Exile, 1920 — 1941*, D.Philosophy Thesis, St Antony's College.

Russian Cossack video — https://www.youtube.com/watch?v=2PNe71wtxiA

Julia Smart (2016). *"A sacred duty": locating and creating Australian graves in the aftermath of the First World War*, AWM Summer Scholars, 2016. https://www.awm.gov.au/sites/default/files/julia_smart.pdf

Matthew Smith (2010). *The Relationship Between Australians and the Overseas Graves of the First World War*, Masters Thesis, QUT.

Aristides Tsotroudis (2015). *The Gallipoli Campaign. Lemnos and ANZACS*, Self Published.

Alan Tucker (2013). *Gallipoli. My Australian Story*, Scholastic Press.

War Diaries (1914 — 1919). AWM 4 Australian Imperial Force unit war diaries 1914-1918 War, Infantry, 8th Battalion. https://www.awm.gov.au/collection/C1339156